DEATH

AND

DAMNATION

Edited by Staley Krause and Stewart Wieck

WHITE WOLF
FICTION

DEATH AND DAMNATION
A White Wolf, Inc. Publication

Edited by Staley Krause with Stewart Wieck, Liz Tornabene, Alan Binenstock, Kim Shropshire and Robert Hatch.
Art Direction by Richard Thomas
Interior art by Larry MacDougall
Initial caps by John Cobb
Cover Design by Michelle Prahler

For information write: White Wolf Publishers, 4598 Stonegate Industrial Boulevard, Stone Mountain, GA 30038.

Disclaimer: The characters and events described in this book are fictional. Any resemblance between the characters and any persons, living or dead, is purely coincidental.

The mention of or reference to any companies or products in these pages is not a challenge to the trademarks or copyrights concerned.

Because of the mature themes presented within, reader discretion is advised.

TABLE OF CONTENTS

PRODIGAL SON

Don Bassingthwaite

an swallowed, took a last deep, nervous breath, and knocked on the office door marked 304B in the offices of the Catholic diocese of San Francisco. "Come in!" called a voice from inside.

Dan swallowed again before opening the door.

"Father Matthews?" he asked nervously.

"Yes." The young priest behind the desk in the office rose and extended his hand in greeting. "And you are...?"

"Dan Barr." Dan stepped inside. He closed the door behind him, then walked across the room to shake Father Matthew's hand. The office was very small, so there wasn't actually that much to cross. Dan wasn't sure whether that was good or bad. If the office had been big, he might have had a little more time to think about what he was going to say to the priest. On the other hand, that would have been another few moments of worry. "Umm... Father Roberts from Holy Rosary parish suggested that I come talk to you?"

Father Matthews gave him a sober, penetrating glance, his dark eyes gleaming upon his thin, pale face. "Yes. Father Roberts called me to say that you might be coming. Please sit down." He waited until Dan had seated himself in one of the threadbare chairs in front of his desk before returning to his own chair. "So," he asked frankly, "what brings a police officer to speak with an exorcist?"

Dan felt his cheeks redden. "What gave me away, the haircut or the posture?" he stammered, knowing that he was still trying to put off mentioning his reasons for coming to the diocese. He rubbed his hand through his short, ginger-colored hair.

"Actually, Father Roberts happened to mention your profession." Father Matthews smiled kindly. "But I didn't mean to imply that being a police officer had anything to do with your coming here—I'm sorry. It's just that relatively few people of any sort come to consult me on my specialty." He leaned forward and met Dan's gaze. "It's nothing to be ashamed of, Lieutenant Barr."

The carefully rehearsed story that Dan had prepared   fell apart as soon as he opened his mouth. All he could manage to blurt out at first was, "Something is trying to kill my son!" He could feel his heart jumping around wildly in his chest, pumping adrenaline through his system. Less than a week ago, Dan had been involved in a raid on a drug gang. That raid had exploded into gunfire leaving one cop dead. Somehow, facing bullets didn't seem any less frightening than the prospect of trying to tell his story to the priest. He's going to think I'm nuts, Dan thought to himself, he's going to laugh at me. He waited for the priest to reply, to question his judgment, but Father Matthews just nodded, encouraging him to continue.

And suddenly the words just came spilling out of Dan's mouth. It had started two years ago on Hallowe'en. Hallowe'en was his son Josh's birthday — two years ago, he had turned fourteen. Josh had fallen out of a tree. The fall had broken his arm badly, but the doctor said it could just as easily have broken his neck. Last year, again around Hallowe'en, a runaway car had almost crushed him and an accident in the chemistry lab at school had almost poisoned him. This year, something had gone wrong with the furnace in the house on the Friday before Hallowe'en. Dan had come home from late night duty to a house full of carbon monoxide. Fortunately, Josh had stayed out past his curfew that night. On the night of Hallowe'en itself, Josh had been bobbing for apples at his sixteenth birthday party...

"You see, we always bob for apples on Josh's birthday," Dan explained brokenly. "It might sound sort of old-fashioned, but Maggie — that's my late wife — decided that that was what we should do since the boys were born on Hallowe'en. When Maggie and Jeremy died in a car accident — Jeremy was my other son, Josh's twin — I made sure that Josh and I kept the tradition up, so we do it every year no matter..." He stopped and took a deep breath, shaking his head. "I'm sorry. I'm rambling now."

"It's all right. This sort of thing can be hard to put into words." Father Matthews opened a drawer in his desk and pulled out a glass and a small bottle of whisky. He poured a shot into the glass, then put the bottle away. Dan took the glass gratefully. "The church wouldn't necessarily approve of my keeping liquor in the desk," the priest commented, "but the people who come to see me seem to appreciate it."

"I do. Thank you." Dan drank the whisky in a single swallow. He took another deep breath. "Three nights ago," he repeated, "Josh was bobbing for apples. A lamp fell into the tub." He held up his hands before Father Matthews could say anything. "He's all right. He'd just moved away from the tub when the lamp fell. His girlfriend wasn't so lucky. She's in the hospital with severe burns."

"I'm sorry."

"Josh is blaming himself," Dan said awkwardly.

Father Matthews was silent for several moments before he spoke again. "You'll forgive me, Lieutenant Barr, but I'm obliged to point out that all of those things could have been accidents."

Dan nodded. "I know. That's what I thought for a long time, too." He sipped at the last dribble of whisky in the glass, but shook his head as the priest reached for the bottle again. "Then Josh sat me down and told me something on Saturday morning after the furnace had been fixed." He looked up at Father Matthews. "He's known all along. He was just too afraid to tell anyone. He knows what has been doing this to him."

"And what is it?"

Dan laughed, as much to convince himself that he wasn't crazy as to convince Father Matthews of the same. "This sounds like the plot from a bad movie, but Josh says it's his imaginary friend from childhood. He doesn't like being left alone now that Josh is older. Josh said he was the one causing his accidents." Before he could stop it, Dan's laughter suddenly turned into helpless, frustrated tears. "I didn't believe him, Father! I made an appointment for him to see a counselor on the next Monday. I thought there was something wrong with him!"

The priest had taken the whisky out of the drawer and poured a second glass before Dan could stop him. Father Matthews pressed it on him. "What changed your mind?"

"At Josh's party I saw a kid I didn't know. He was the one who pushed the lamp into the tub. I tried to grab him, but my hands..."

Dan gulped the whisky. It burned in the back of his throat, reminding him of the smells that had filled the air as the lamp sank into the tub: ozone, seared flesh, and hot metal. Josh's girlfriend had screamed. So had several other people. Dan hadn't. After his years on the police force, his reflexes had simply taken over before he even had time to realize exactly what was happening. He remembered reaching out to grab the strange kid, his big hands descending like hammers... only to pass right through the kid. Right through him. Then Dan had realized that the strange child's face was a haze. He couldn't see it clearly, even though he was staring right into it. And the kid was dressed just like Josh.

"He was gone before I could do anything else. He didn't vanish or run — he was just gone. But that's the way Josh described his imaginary friend. No face and always dressed just like him." Dan wiped at the tears on his face. "Father, I'm pretty much a lapsed Catholic. I haven't been to church in years, but I was raised R.C., and I do believe in God." He looked up. "And I love my son. Father Roberts must have thought I was nuts when I asked him if he could perform an exorcism. When he told me about you..."

Father Matthews nodded, sparing him the necessity of any further explanation. Dan was grateful for that. "I'll see what I can do," the priest said.

■

Dan and Josh Barr lived in a comfortable, middle class home just south of San Francisco's Haight-Ashbury district. Dan was waiting by the door when Father Matthews pulled into the driveway at exactly four o'clock that afternoon. He went out to meet him. "Did you have any trouble finding the place? There are enough winding streets around here that it can be tricky."

"No." Father Matthews reached back into his car and pulled out a small black bag. "No trouble at all." He looked toward the house. "Is Josh here yet?"

"Yes. I left a message at the school for him to come straight home tonight. He's in the backyard. Do you want to see him?"

"Maybe I should." Father Matthews shifted the black bag between his hands. "Just to see if there's anything else he can tell me about his... friend. Tell me, has he ever given this friend a name?"

Dan grimaced and led the way through a tall, wooden gate between the house and the garage, then around to the backyard. "He calls him 'Buddy'." He paused to point through the open door of the garage. A twisted and flattened frame of blue-painted metal sat near the garage's far end. "That's the bike Josh was riding last year when he almost got run over."

The priest nodded, then gestured toward a bed of plants with yellow flowers at the side of the house. "I noticed those along the front as well.

Fennel, Lieutenant Barr?"

"Yes. Josh planted them all around the house — he has the green thumb in the family."

"Interesting." Father Matthews knelt, crushed a leaf between his fingers, and inhaled the fragrance. "Not your typical bedding plant. Fennel is supposed to keep away wraiths and ghosts — when did Josh plant these beds?"

"About two years ago." Dan clenched his teeth. "Right after he got the cast off his arm, even though it was the middle of December. He was trying to protect himself? Why didn't it work?"

Father Matthews climbed to his feet. "Fennel has to be specially prepared to be truly useful." He narrowed his eyes, still staring at the plants. "I doubt if he knows that." He looked up. "Time is wasting, Lieutenant Barr. Lead on."

Josh Barr was sitting in a lawn chair on a little stone patio behind the house, reading a comic book. He stood as his father and the priest approached. Although he was only sixteen, Josh had a build that promised that he would be just as big as his father when he finally stopped growing. Like his father, he also had ginger-colored hair. His eyes, though, were completely different, clear, pale blue to his father's muddy hazel. "Josh," said Dan, "this is Father

Matthews."

"Hello, Father."

"Hello, Josh." Father Matthews looked him over carefully. "You have your father's hair."

"And his mother's eyes," Dan replied with quiet pride. "You should have seen him and his brother together. They were the most beautiful babies...Josh, Father Matthews is here to perform the exorcism you suggested."

The priest's eyes rose and he turned to consider Josh again. "An exorcism was your idea?"

The boy flushed. "Yeah. I... well, I kind of know more about this sort of thing than Dad does."

"I noticed the fennel."

"I read a lot."

"You must. Not many people know about fennel's power." Father Matthews fell silent for a moment, weighing his words. Dan stepped behind his son and put his hands on his shoulders. Whatever the priest had to say, he wasn't sure that he wanted to hear it. "Josh," asked Father Matthews at last, "when did Buddy first appear?"

Josh shrugged. "I don't know." He hesitated. "I guess he's always been around. But he wasn't mean 'til I turned about twelve."

"Twelve?" Dan spat in surprise, "He's been doing this to you since you were twelve? Josh, you could have told me!"

"Buddy wasn't hurting me then!" Josh set his comic book down. "He just started getting nasty. I think it was because I was getting older. I wanted real friends."

"So you realize that he's a spirit of some sort? A ghost? A... wraith?" inquired the priest. Josh nodded. "Has anyone else been able to see him?"

"Not until Dad did last Hallowe'en. I'm actually glad that Dad did." A look of exhaustion came over Josh's face. "I think... I think he's getting stronger."

Dan's grip on his son's shoulders tightened protectively, almost convulsively. "You could have told me any time, Josh. You didn't have to wait so long."

"Would you have believed me?"

"I..." Dan clenched his teeth, biting back his words. No, he admitted to himself, he probably wouldn't have believed it.

Fortunately, Father Matthews was there, and Dan didn't have to say anything else. The priest jumped deftly into the gap of Dan's silence, asking Josh, "Was Buddy ever able to move things around before you turned twelve? When you were little, did he appear at other times besides Hallowe'en?"

"He played with me all the time — and, yes, he could move things a little bit. But only on Hallowe'en."

"On your birthday?"

"Yes." Josh glanced away. "Is that all? Can we just do the exorcism now and get rid of this thing?"

Dan looked from Josh to the priest. Father Matthews sighed quietly. He met Dan's gaze. "Yes," he said, almost a little sadly, "We can."

■

Father Matthews had Dan take Josh into the house through the back door while he went around to the front. It was, he told them, most proper for the exorcist to enter through the main door of the haunted building. Dan's palms were sweating by the time the priest knocked slowly three times. The doorknob felt cold against his skin as he turned it.

"Enter," he said as the priest had instructed him, "Be welcome."

"Bless this house," intoned Father Matthews. He had removed his jacket, revealing a simple but obviously ancient crucifix around his neck. In his hands he held a smoking silver censer.

The heavy gray vapors that poured from the vessel sank immediately to the ground. Father Matthews swung the censer ahead of him as he crossed the threshold and entered the Barr home. "Bless this house and all who live in it." His voice was soft, yet firm, confident, and commanding.

Dan stepped in behind the priest as he paced solemnly around the room, praying quietly. When Father Matthews had finished his circuit of the room, he moved on to the next, repeating his blessing before entering the new room. The ribbons of incense almost seemed to snag on the furniture that Father Matthews passed, clinging as if they were nearly solid. The odor made Dan want to sneeze, but he struggled against the urge. He didn't want to disturb the atmosphere of sanctity that the priest was creating. The smoke lent an otherworldly quality to the house. Dan felt almost as though he could reach out through the lingering smoke and touch the other side of the afterlife...

The house wasn't large, but Father Matthews' slow, careful steps meant that his progress through the rooms of the first and second floors took quite some time. He insisted on entering every nook and cranny of the house, extending the gray ribbons of incense into closets and corners. Finally, though, it was done. All that remained was the basement, where Josh was waiting and where here Buddy had last appeared.

Father Matthews spared Dan a glance as they stood at the head of the stairs. "You know," he said hoarsely, "there is the possibility that this might not work."

"It can't hurt, can it?"

"No. No, it can't."

Dan nodded. Once again, he felt as though he were walking into a gunfight. "Then let's do it."

"Bless this house," Father Matthews proclaimed firmly. He swung the censer out into the air above the stairs. The heavy smoke sank down to twine about his right foot as he stepped onto the first step. "Bless this house and all who live in it. Bless them in the name of the Father, the Son, and the Holy Ghost!"

Josh was standing in the center of the recreation room that filled the basement, just as Father Matthews had asked him to. Dan smiled at his son as he followed the chanting priest down the stairs and into the room. Josh smiled back, a little nervously, and gave him a thumbs-up sign. Father Matthews frowned sternly at him.

Instead of making a single circuit around the room as he had elsewhere in the house, the priest traced three circles around Dan's son. Each circle was a bit smaller, and by the time he had completed the third, Father Matthews was standing almost directly in front of Josh. Dan stood slightly behind the priest while the smoky incense gathered like a pool of fog around their feet. When Father Matthews set the censer down, it disappeared in the smoke. The priest took hold of his crucifix with one hand and made the sign of the cross with the other. "Bless this house," he said a final time, "and bless all of those who belong in it."

Dan didn't miss the change in Father Matthews' words, but he didn't think of them much. They didn't seem important. Josh, though, blinked in surprise. "Dad..." he began.

"Hush," his father ordered. The priest had begun to chant in Latin now.

"But, Dad..."

"Quiet!" Dan hissed, glaring at his son. Josh seemed agitated, his eyes darting left and right as though he expected his imaginary friend to appear from the shadows and smoke. The thought suddenly struck Dan that perhaps Josh was right to be worried. If Buddy had been so violent in his attempts to harm Josh, surely he would resist the exorcism just as violently.

What was that creaking he could hear over the

sound of the priest's chanting? Were those footsteps that he heard or just products of his imagination? Dan thought of his service pistol, upstairs in his bedroom. He wished that he had it in his hands now, even though the bullets would probably be no good against the spirit.

Father Matthews' voice rose to a crescendo, and he reached out with his right hand to lay his fingers on Josh's forehead. "In the name of the Father," he shouted, his words in English once more, "let that which does not belong here depart! In the name of the Son..."

"No!"

Josh pulled back suddenly, away from the priest's blessing hand. His eyes were hard and his mouth twisted. "Josh!" Dan yelled, "Hold still!" He moved around Father Matthews, ready to hold Josh himself if he had to.

"No!" Josh kept backing away, heading for the stairs. "Don't you see, Dad?" He pointed accusingly at the priest. "I don't know what he's trying to pull, but we can't trust him. That's not an exorcism ceremony!"

Dan glanced at Father Matthews. The priest was still speaking, though more quietly and rapidly. Dan looked at him questioningly, but he only shook his head as he whispered, "In the name of the Holy Ghost..."

"Josh, what do you mean it's not an exorcism?"

"I mean it's not an exorcism!" Josh had one foot on the stairs out of the basement. "I know the words to exorcisms and those aren't them."

"Maybe if you let him finish..."

"No!" Fright washed over Josh's face. "Dad, if you love me, you'll make him stop!" He turned and began to run up the stairs. "Please! Make him stop!"

The exorcism could be repeated, Dan thought. Surely it could. Maybe it would be best if he stopped the ceremony now and let Father Matthews talk to Josh. Dan half-turned toward the priest, but something in Father Matthews' face made him look back toward the stairs just as Josh reached the top.

Outside, the sun was just beginning to set, and the warm, red light that came streaming in through the upstairs windows contrasted starkly with the artificial light in the basement. The figure that stepped into the doorway at the head of stairs, confronting Josh, was little more than a shadow upon the brightness. The dim light washing up the stairs from the basement showed Dan that the figure was dressed in the same clothes as Josh. He couldn't see its face but recongnized a familiar, dull, gleam as the light fell against a metal object in the figure's hand.

Buddy was holding Dan's own service pistol.

Josh started, almost falling backwards in surprise and horror. The figure fired once, at point blank range. Father Matthews fell silent.

Dan was rushing up the stairs before Josh had begun to fall from the impact, maybe even before the bullet had left his son's body in a spray of blood. He might have even been shouting something. He wasn't sure. His only thoughts were of Josh.

Buddy stood frozen, the gun in his hand smoking slightly taking a step forward he looked intently into Josh's face. Josh turned his head away desperately. The movement cost him his precarious balance and this time he fell over backwards.

Dan caught Josh and Buddy vanished. Dan's pistol fell to the floor and clattered down the steps, disappearing into the smoke streaming over the basement floor. Dan tried to ease Josh down as well, but his position on the stairs was awkward. He had to settle for propping his son against his shoulder, struggling to keep his own balance against the weight. He could see and feel the blood running from Josh's chest and back. It seemed to be everywhere.

Then Father Matthews was squeezing past him and pulling open Josh's shirt. "Just below the heart," he said, examining the wound quickly. "Very serious, but he has some time." He reached up to take some of Josh's weight off Dan. "Let's get him somewhere and lay him down."

Dan shrugged off the priest's help angrily. "You said the exorcism couldn't hurt him!" He shifted his arms around Josh and, with a grunt, managed to lift him up by himself. He carried his son back down the stairs, cradling him like a child. There was an old couch in the recreation room. Dan laid his son down. Josh's eyes were squeezed tightly shut and he gasped in pain. Dan glared at Father Matthews. "You said the exorcism couldn't hurt him!"

"Lieutenant Barr..." The priest put his hand on Dan's shoulder. Dan pushed him away.

"Phone 911, damn it! Just phone 911!" he screamed. "You killed him!"

"No! Listen to me — there's something you have to know!" Father Matthews face was urgent. "I can't exorcise that wraith!"

"Dad." Josh's voice was a whisper. His eyes fluttered open. Pale eyes like Maggie's. His strong body trembled. "Don't trust him. Do whatever you have to, but please... keep him away. Keep him and Buddy away!" He shrieked suddenly, focusing on something Dan couldn't see. "He's coming back, Dad! He's coming back to take me away!"

There was terror in his son's eyes. Terror and pain. Dan felt helpless. If Father Matthews could be believed, the thing that was threatening his son could not be cast out by the priest's faith. And he could do nothing to it. Nothing! His hands had passed right through it before! It was a ghostly wraith. He couldn't even touch it!

But maybe...

Josh wanted him to do whatever he had to. For Josh, for his son, he would do whatever it took. If a living man couldn't fight Buddy, perhaps another wraith could. He kissed Josh tenderly on the forehead, then spat at Father Matthews, "When you get around to making that phone call, tell them to send two ambulances!"

Dan pushed himself away from the couch and groped in the smoke at the base of the stairs. His hands found his pistol almost immediately. Father Matthews must have figured out what he was thinking because he leaped at him, grabbing for the gun. Dan held him off easily as he put the muzzle of the pistol to his own forehead. Hoping that his love for Josh would anchor his spirit in this world, he pulled the trigger.

■

First, there was horror and then panic. He was dead! Dead! Dan pushed past the panic, past the visions of his life that tried to tempt him into pausing for a moment, past the urges that came over him to visit the places that had once been special to him. There was only one thing that was special to him now. Josh. His desire to protect Josh drove him forward. He didn't dare stop. He didn't know how long he would have here before he moved on. He just hoped it would be long enough for him to take care of the evil that haunted his son.

He was still in the basement of the house. Everything looked blurred and watery, as though he were peering through a wet veil. Father Matthews was desperately dialing the telephone. For a moment, Dan felt bad. How was the priest going to explain the situation to the emergency crews and the police? His heart went hard, though, when he glanced down at his own body lying in front of him. Father Matthew's failure had led him to this. Why should he feel sorry for Father Matthews when he was the one who had lost his life?

There was a hazy form of a person crouched on the floor beside Josh, its head close to his. Buddy. The wraith seemed so absorbed in whatever he was doing that he hadn't yet realized what Dan had done. "Get away from him!" Dan shouted.

Josh's imaginary friend looked up and although Dan still couldn't see his face clearly, he saw the surprise that passed over it. "Jesus!" gasped Buddy in a voice that seemed somehow familiar, "What are you doing here?"

"Protecting my son!"

Dan surged forward, but the other wraith was faster. He jumped back before Dan could grab him. "Don't do this!"

"I have to!"

"You don't understand!" Dan thought Buddy was crying. Impossible. "I can't fight you!"

"Well, you're going to have to."

"No!" Buddy dodged around him. "Father Matthews!" he yelled, "Help!"

The priest looked up suddenly, his eyes flicking between Buddy and Dan. "I'm sorry!" he said quickly, one hand covering the mouthpiece of the telephone, "I can't help! Not until the sun goes down!"

He could see them! But that meant... Father Matthews had been able to see Buddy all along! Dan's spectral face curled into a snarl. "You're helping him? You bastard!" Dan lashed out. His fist went right past the priest, as if he were punching a cloud of mist. How he could have missed the priest, Dan did not know.

Father Matthews flinched all the same."
Please, Lieutenant Barr, if you would let me
explain..."

"Damn you!" Dan turned his back on the
priest, returning his attention to Buddy. The
wraith was standing by the foot of the stairs, as
if trying to decide whether to flee or to try and
go back to Josh. Dan didn't let him make that
decision. He charged toward him. Buddy fled up
and out of the basement. Dan followed. The
wraith ran through the house, toward the front
door. Dan kept following him, right on his heels.
The wraith plunged through the door — right
through, not bothering to open it. Dan hesitated
for only a moment before following him. He
could feel the wood of the door sliding through
him, an eerie, rough feeling like skin on
sandpaper. Then he was on the other side of the
door.

The sight that greeted him froze him for a
moment.

It was very late in the afternoon now. The sun
was settling down below the horizon. The
shadows were lengthening, creating deep velvety
pools of darkness that seemed to call to him,
offering comfort. But there was no comfort to
be found here. Everywhere Dan looked, all that

he saw was the shadow of death.

The grass on his lawn was a burned brown color, even though he knew that earlier that day it had been healthy and green. Father Matthews' car was rusting in the driveway. The twilight sky was yellow and bruised with pollution. Dan could see no birds, even though he could hear them distinctly. His neighbor, old Jack Dean, was out trimming a sparse hedge with shears that squealed for want of oil. Jack's age lay heavy upon him, but somehow Dan could tell that he would be alive for many years to come. His little granddaughter was playing on the lawn behind him. Her left eye glowed an angry red. Unlike her grandfather, she would die soon. Dan shook his head. How did he know that? He couldn't understand it. Was there really so much death in the world? He put it out of his head. He had other things to worry about now.

Buddy was nowhere in sight. Dan stepped slowly down from the porch of the house. The vicious wraith had to be nearby. He hadn't had time to escape. "Think!" Dan muttered to himself, "You're a cop. You've chased bad guys before."

There hadn't been time for the wraith to run anywhere. Dan had come through the door on his heels. He couldn't have run away. There was nowhere for him to hide out here. He couldn't have had time even to get around the corner of the house. Dan frowned. What if he was hiding inside of something? He was a ghost and intangible. It was possible. The priest's car? The ground itself? He hoped not. No, the wraith would have had to hide quickly. Almost instantly. As if he had stepped through the door and then vanished...

Dan turned suddenly, leaping through the porch stairs and down underneath the porch itself. There was the rough, sandpaper sensation of moving through wood again, and a very brief moment of disorientation in the darkness before he realized that he could see fairly well. Dan found himself facing, as he had hoped he might, a very startled Buddy. He gave the other wraith a merciless grin and reached for him. Buddy scrambled out through the porch, but this time Dan was right behind him. "You stay the fuck away from my son!"

"I can't!" Buddy turned to look at him. The last rays of the sun played across his blurred face. "I can't! Please — you have to let me see him!"

"Forget it!"

"There's nothing you can do to me."

"Wanna bet?" Dan's fist shot out in a solid punch, one that should have sent Buddy reeling.

Instead, his hand went right past him, just as it had gone past Father Matthews. Shocked, Dan threw another punch, and another. None of his blows connected. He felt as though he was a drunk in some kind of daze. Buddy just looked miserable. "Please," he pleaded, "let me see him! I could just ignore you if I wanted to."

Dan clenched his teeth, continuing to flail away at the other wraith and trying desperately to hold back the tears of frustration that threatened to overwhelm him. He had killed himself for Josh, and there was still nothing he could do to stop Buddy! Was he completely helpless? "Stay away from him!" he growled, knowing that his threats were empty, "Or so help me..."

Dan felt a sudden light touch on his shoulder. He turned his head to see Father Matthews standing behind him. There was something strange about the priest, a deathlessness. Even though he stood in the middle of a world of death, life clung to him. He wasn't a wraith, but he didn't seem fully alive either. "Let him go, Lieutenant Barr."

"You'd like that, wouldn't you!" Dan snapped angrily.

Father Matthews shook his head. "You don't understand." He reached out, his fingers brushing Dan's face. "Let me show you."

"No!" Buddy stiffened and stepped back.

"I'm sorry, but he has to know, and he can't do that unless he can see for himself." Father Matthews' hand curled around something covering Dan's face and tugged on it. There was a wet, tearing sound as a soaking mass fell from Dan's face and to the ground. Dan could see clearly again. "Welcome to the Shadowlands, Lieutenant Barr."

Dan didn't feel any different, but Buddy was looking at him with fear in his eyes. He looked like he might try to run again. Dan's hand shot out and grabbed at the front of the wraith's shirt. This time, Dan connected. Smiling grimly, Barr lifted him up into the air. Buddy cried out and began to struggle.

Father Matthews laid his hand on Dan's arm, pushing down. "I didn't remove your caul so you could threaten him, Lieutenant Barr. Please. Let him go."

"Why should I? Why should I believe you? You helped him kill Josh."

"No." The priest looked up at Buddy. The wraith nodded slowly. Father Matthews looked back to Dan. "Take off his mask."

"What?"

"He's wearing a mask, lieutenant. Take it off."

Dan reached up with his free hand and felt at Buddy's face. There was something covering it. Not wet, like the thing that Father Matthews had pulled off of his face, but dry and strangely textured. Dan flicked the mask aside.

The face underneath was the face of his son.

For a moment, Dan was too stunned to speak. Josh... or Buddy... or whoever he was... just sagged in his grip. "Let me go, Dad," he said quietly, "Please? I have to go back in and see him."

"But what..." Dan squeezed his eyes shut. "I don't understand." Almost reluctantly, Dan let his arm sink under the gentle pressure the priest was exerting. He opened his grasp and let the wraith with Josh's face go free.

Father Matthews nodded at Buddy. "I think he's still conscious. You should be able to talk to him. The ambulance is on its way."

"Thank you, Father."

Dan watched the wraith run into the house. "What... Is that Josh?"

"No." Father Matthews ushered him back inside and down into the basement. Buddy was crouched by the couch again, his head once more close to Josh's. Dan could see now that they were talking. Father Matthews had laid his coat over Dan's body.

Dan felt as if he were seeing double. There seemed to be duplicates of everyone present: Josh on the sofa and Josh the wraith, Dan the wraith and Dan the corpse. There was even a second Father Matthews seated comfortably in an armchair, his eyes closed and his chest rising and falling as if he were asleep.

"How...?" asked Dan in confusion. He understood his own situation, but how could there be two Joshes and two Father Matthews? "How is this... oh, God!"

Father Matthews helped him into a chair. Dan couldn't feel the upholstery beneath him, but it supported him. "Sit, lieutenant."

"Tell me what's going on!" Dan pointed at the two Joshes. The living one, lying on the sofa, shuddered suddenly and coughed up blood. The dead one, the wraith, put his arm around him tenderly. "Who is that? Who is Buddy?"

"I think you know."

Two Joshes. Dressed identically, both well built and good-looking, alike down to their father's ginger hair and their mother's pale blue eyes. *You should have seen him and his brother together*, Dan had told Father Matthews, *they were the most beautiful babies*. He gasped. "Jeremy?"

The wraith glanced up and smiled sadly, but

shook his head.

"That's Josh," whispered Father Matthews.

His own son. The wraith was his own son. No wonder he hadn't wanted to fight Dan. A horrible thought sprang into Dan's mind. "My God. You mean... after the accident...?" The death of Maggie and one of the twins had shaken him badly. Everything had been so confusing. He could have made a mistake. "It was Josh that died with Maggie? I raised Jeremy as Josh and Josh wanted revenge or something?"

"No. Jeremy died."

"But then how...? You said that wraith is Josh!" Dan's head ached. His heart ached, too, and he could feel tears beginning to run from his eyes. He stood and walked over to look down on his sons. Both looked back up at him. He pointed at the wraith. "Josh?" he asked quietly. The wraith nodded. Dan pointed at the wounded boy on the sofa. "Jeremy?"

"He can't hear you, Dad," Josh replied. "He can only see me. We've always been able to see and hear each other." Josh put his mouth close to his brother's ear. "Jer? Dad's here. He says hello."

Jeremy smiled weakly. "Hi, Dad. Please... don't be mad at me."

"Why would I be, Jeremy?"

"I wouldn't let Josh back in. I kept him out."

Dan sat down heavily on the end of the sofa. His ghostly body didn't make a dent in the cushions. "I don't understand." He looked from one son to the other. Both looked like normal sixteen year-olds — except that one was dead and the other was dying. "Jeremy died when he was a baby!"

"Babies have desires, Lieutenant Barr," Father Matthews explained. "Very simple desires, but often very strong ones. Jeremy wanted to be with his brother. So they were. Jeremy grew up along with Josh."

Josh reached out and took his father's hands in one of his. "We can switch back and forth, Dad. On our birthday. It's not much fun being dead all the time, so every year we'd switch. I would have our body for a year while Jer was a wraith, then he'd have the body and I'd be a wraith."

Dan gazed up at Father Matthews, silently begging him to make sense of his child's words. The priest nodded and said simply, "They're twins. Born on Hallowe'en, when the barriers between the worlds of the living and the dead are at their weakest. You've heard that the bond between twins is strong?" Father Matthews settled himself on the arm of the couch beside

Dan. "The bond between Josh and Jeremy was stronger than death."

Dan turned to Josh. "Why were you trying to kill each other then?"

"We weren't... I mean, I wasn't." Josh let go of his father's hands. "When we were little, we could switch easily. We were always playmates. 'Buddy' was our name for the one of us who was dead. I think that when we were really young, we could switch anytime, not just on Hallowe'en. Then, when we were around twelve, it started getting hard to make the switch." He wiped tears from his face. "We discovered that it was easier if our body was unconscious or dying. It was pretty scary, but we wanted to do it. Then Jeremy got afraid."

Dan looked up. "Afraid of what?"

"Afraid that some day we wouldn't be able to make the switch at all. So he stopped talking to me and refused to make the switch three years ago. I started making the accidents happen to bring him closer to me so I could make him listen." Josh hugged his brother close. "We're always going to be able to switch, pal."

"I'm sorry, Josh," Jeremy murmured.

"So am I, Jer." Josh glanced at Dan. "I've gotten more powerful over the last three years. At first I could only make the switch on

Hallowe'en, so that's when I caused the accidents. Then I figured out how to make the switch closer to Hallowe'en —the day before or the day after. When Jer finally told you about 'Buddy' this year, I knew I was close and that I might be able to get someone to help me."

"So he contacted me." Father Matthews stood again and stepped beside his sleeping body. "I'm what is called a Benandanti, Lieutenant Barr. I can see wraiths, and after sunset I can send my soul out of my body to walk among them. I try to help them in their dealings with the living. Josh came to me and told me of his problems. We took a gamble that if he did something really extreme and showed himself to you, you might try to have an exorcism performed." He spread his hands. "One of Josh's wraith friends influenced Father Roberts to make sure that he told you to come to me."

"But why the exorcism?" Dan reached out to touch his dying son. It was as if his hand was numb. He couldn't feel Jeremy at all. "Why did you have to kill him?"

Father Matthews cleared his throat. "Jeremy was right when he told you that the ceremony wasn't an exorcism. I know ways of weakening the barrier between death and life — special incense, whispered prayers. I was trying to make it easier for Josh and Jeremy to switch, so far away from the Hallowe'en season. If Jeremy hadn't tried to break away, nothing would have happened."

"I panicked, Dad," Josh said softly. There was grief in his voice. "I got your gun and stopped him so we could talk. But he's not going to die. I missed his heart deliberately. I'm actually a very good shot." Suddenly his voice broke. "I would never have killed him, I would never have hurt him, but this time he had to be right on the edge of death." He looked at his father with tear-filled eyes. "He's going to live though, Dad. We're both going to be fine."

"So..." Dan felt his heart sink suddenly. He knew that what Josh said was true. Just as he had somehow known that Jack Dean would live while his granddaughter would soon die, he knew that Jeremy would recover. The only specter of death that touched Jeremy was his brother. "So, he was never in real danger? I didn't have to..."

"No," supplied Father Matthews quietly, "You didn't have to kill yourself. I tried to tell you."

Dan felt numb. He got up from the sofa and walked over to peer out of one of the little windows that let light into the basement. He could still see Jack Dean's granddaughter outside next door, the red light of death glowing in her left eye. He slammed his fist against the wall suddenly. " That's it? It was all for nothing?"

His anger — at himself, at Josh, at Jeremy, at Father Matthews — was like acid eating away at his insides. He had killed himself to protect his son from a threat that had turned out to be no threat at all. "I did it for nothing!"

"I wouldn't say that." Father Matthews joined him. "You saw both of your sons again."

"Great consolation that is!" Dan bit his tongue. "No. I'm sorry, Josh..."

"It's okay, Dad. I know what dying is like." Josh put his arm around Jeremy. "We both do." He hesitated, then added. "Things don't have to change much. San Francisco is full of people like us. It's not like being alive, but it could be worse."

Father Matthews nodded. "He's right. You've been given a second chance of sorts, Lieutenant Barr."

Dan squeezed his eyes shut and took a deep breath. His anger was bitter, but he could see the truth in the priest's words. How much had really changed for him? He was dead — but he felt as though he were still alive. He had lost his career as a police officer, his house, everything he had worked for — but he still had

Josh and he had Jeremy back again, too. He opened his eyes again. "Father, can you give us a moment alone?"

"Of course." Outside, there was the sound of sirens as ambulances pulled up in front of the house. Father Matthews glanced toward the stairs. "I'll have to let them into the house. I'm afraid you won't have long." He stepped toward his body, then walked right into it, his soul merging with his physical form. Watching the priest's body jerk into sudden waking was eerie. Father Matthews rose, nodded toward the wraiths, and left the basement.

Dan turned to Josh. Josh smiled back at him. "It's going to be hard for you, Dad. You're going to have a lot to learn."

"But I'll have you boys. It's going to be harder for you to live on your own."

"We'll be able to handle it. We've survived death already, haven't we?"

There was the sound of voices from upstairs as Father Matthews opened the door to let the emergency crews into the house. Josh looked down at Jeremy. His brother's face was drawn tight against the pain. "I'm going to have to make the switch now, Dad. I'm sorry I can't stay."

"It's all right." Dan forced himself to say the words, even though he didn't want to let either of his sons go. "At least I'll still be able to stay with you, even if you won't be able to see me."

"Jer can talk to me for you." Josh closed his eyes. The transfer of souls was seamless, as if nothing had happened. When the wraith-twin opened his eyes, Dan knew that the switch had taken place. He opened his arms and Jeremy rushed to him, just as the ambulance attendants came down the basement stairs. One of the attendants gasped in shock at the sight of Dan's body on the floor and of Josh, wounded but smiling, on the couch. Dan didn't hear him, though. He was hugging Jeremy fiercely. For a moment, he could almost forget that both of them were dead.

CROSSINGS

Nigel D. Findley

 read somewhere that the first step toward overcoming a fear is to face it, to admit it.

Okay. I admit it. I'm scared. Scared shitless.

Something's going on here, I don't know what it is, and it's really messing with my mind.

It's cold out here, brutally cold. It's one of those nights when you can feel the dampness in the air, feel it right down into the marrow of your bones. It settles in there like an ache, like arthritis. Like grief that's been in your soul so long you don't remember what you're grieving about. All that's left is the sadness.

That's what it's like on the street tonight.

There's no wind out here. None at all, which is a wonder. The air is still and dead down in the city. Not the faintest breeze to stir my hair or brush like ghost-fingers across my cheek. I look up at the moon — full, swollen, just now rising above the lighted ziggurats of the financial district. Clouds are scudding across its face — *racing* across. There's wind up there. Down here it's unnaturally still. Probably a result of the fog.

Heavy fog. Not around me where I'm standing at the moment. There are traces of mist, like threads or strands of hair, low to the ground, a foot or two above the sidewalk. They're moving slowly, drifting aimlessly. How, when there's no breeze to move them? A good question. But then, my mind's *full* of questions, most of them much more important.

For a moment, I push all my questions, all my fears, all my thoughts, from my mind. For an instant, I am void of analysis, pure experience. It's comforting. But it doesn't last. The thoughts and the fears flood back in, like water from a breached dam. I'm engulfed by them.

I turn to look west.

I guess that I'm standing somewhere in the Nob Hill region. Somewhere around Van Ness and California Street, I think, although for some reason it's hard to be sure. The streetlights are on, here on this residential street. They cast bright light in a small radius about themselves, but somehow the light doesn't seem to shine as far as it normally would. I'm standing right at a street corner, I can see the signs on the green-painted post, but the light just isn't bright enough to read the street names.

Nob Hill somewhere, that's a start. When I turn west, I'm looking out over Lafayette Park, and toward the Presidio. On another night, from here I might be able to see the lights on top of the Golden Gate support pillars. But tonight the fog is much too thick, piled up like a wall of impenetrable darkness. The Presidio, the Golden Gate, and Sausalito — they're all invisible under the weight of that fog.

I shiver. Not from the cold, I'm getting used to that.

What in the name of God has happened to me?

What am I doing out here on the street? No coat, no jacket. Just slacks and a shirt. And my tiny cellular flip-phone, a familiar weight in my shirt pocket. Dressed just the same as I was in my home office, upstairs in my condo on Buchanan, down toward the Marina.

I don't know how I got here, a couple of miles away from home. I don't remember going downstairs and getting in the Jaguar, driving across town to Nob Hill. I check my pants pockets — no car keys. No house keys either, and no money. Nothing but the cell phone.

What's the last thing I can remember? I was upstairs in my office, I know that. Working through the numbers one last time on the Hayward shopping mall deal. Commercial real estate's been going crazy in the Bay Area since the earthquakes — the San Francisco tremblor a few years back and the big one down south in LA. Big risks, but big pay-offs too. If you've got the market savvy — and a pair of big brass ones — you can make a killing in a skittish market. Take the Hayward mall. I picked up the package from a developer whose bag shrank when interest rates started shifting. It's a good package: good property with all the right zoning waivers and exceptions in place. Sure, there's a chance that it's going to go tits-up... but there are ways of minimizing the downside. A slick player with the balls to stay the course can turn it into a winner. Just my kind of deal.

The radio was tuned to KFOG, volume turned low. Some mid-sixties psychedelic tune, the drums synchronized with the headache that had started throbbing in my temples. The numbers on the computer screen started to blur. Time to take a break. The time tick on the radio said it was nine in the evening. I could hear Juli moving around downstairs. She knows not to disturb me when I'm chewing through a deal. And then...

No. My mind balks at the next memory. It shies away, like a skittish horse.

I hear my pulse pounding in my ears, a strangely dull thudding. Distant, somehow. I concentrate on my breathing — keeping it slow and deep the way the doctors told me. Just in time. The thin, tinny ringing in my ears is just starting. But the flood of oxygen into my blood drives it back.

It's not fair. It's just not fucking fair. I'm 35 — thirty-fucking-five years old. Young. Too young for this shit. My father pushed himself as hard as I push myself — harder, maybe. He didn't have to slow down until he had his first heart attack at 55. If the world was fair, I'd have another 20 years of hard charging before I had to back off on the throttle.

Yeah, I know. Whoever said the world was fair? I had the first "episode" five years ago. In the shower, of all places. The tinny buzzing in my ears. Then the flickering stars around the periphery of my visual field. And then everything went to hell. The left side of my

body just *died*, that's what it felt like. My left
arm just hanging like a slab of meat as I tried
to prop myself up against the shower wall. Then
my left leg started to give out, and I just folded
up in the shampoo suds around the floor drain.
There was nobody to call to, nobody to help me.
(This was before Juli.)

I really thought I was dying. A stroke, a heart
attack, a brain fucking aneurysm. There I was,
trying to drag myself out of the shower stall —
tearing off my skin against the metal door sill,
even though I couldn't feel it — trying to haul
myself to the phone in the bedroom. And all
the time, all I could think about was my
obituary, how it would read in the *Chronicle* the
next day. "John Cross dead at 30. Local real
estate *wunderkind* found dead in his shower..."

So I didn't die, of course. After maybe ten
minutes — it felt much longer — the feeling
and control started coming back, and the
flickering lights went away. It wasn't a stroke
— at least, that's what all the high-powered,
high-priced neurologists told me. An acute
stress reaction, they called it. Something like a
migraine, where the blood vessels in the brain
start to squeeze themselves off, or some
goddamn thing. There was no lasting effect —
apart from the fear that it would happen again,

but even that faded with time.

The specialists all nodded their heads sagely and told me I had to back off. Slow down. Take it easy. There's something in my makeup that makes me acutely sensitive to stress, that's what they said. If I keep pushing the way I'd been pushing, I'm going to be sucking shower scum again, or worse. That's what the guy I went to for a second opinion said too, *and* the third.

So I backed off.

Well, I *did*. I closed up my business. Cross & Associates folded its tents, and all the young up-and-comers I'd groomed and trained went out on their own. I had enough salted away that I could be really selective about the projects I took on — at least, for the next few years. Okay, granted, some of those projects took a lot of time and effort, like the Hayward mall — lots of skull-sweat and late nights, lots of coffee-fueled indigestion and bouts of insomnia. But I did slow down. I *did*. I married Juli, didn't I, and tried to get myself a real life?

I look around at the quiet residential street. Not just quiet, *deserted*. Which is strange. Judging by the position of the moon, it can't be much later than nine o'clock. (Which means I somehow crossed a couple of miles in a few minutes without a car or money... But I force that thought aside again.) Shouldn't there be people on the street on a Halloween night...?

What's happened to me?

I can't avoid the memory any more, I can't deny it. I think I know what's happened, and I have to face it.

I was working the Hayward numbers. The whiskey-voiced KFOG DJ was announcing that it was nine o'clock. Juli was doing something downstairs. The numbers on the computer screen started to swim. I rubbed the back of my neck to relieve the tension.

That's when the pain hit. A brutal, lancing pain like an icepick driven into my skull directly behind my right ear. Shocking, crystalline, all-encompassing. In an instant, my vision tunneled down to blood-red nothingness.

And then I found myself on Nob Hill without a coat. No memory of how I got here, just a jolting transition, like a badly edited movie. No headache, just the distant pounding of my pulse in my ears. And a sense of... of what? Of *absence* — that's the best way I can describe it — of something missing in my head. As though there's something missing in there — the lost memory, but something more — that I can't access.

I think I know what it is. I'm terrified to think

about it, but I've got to deal with it some time.

Stroke. Even thinking the word — not saying it out loud, but hearing it ringing in my mind — is enough to make me nauseous. My bowels feel like they're full of ice-water, and my stomach clenches like a fist.

I've had a stroke. What else could it be? Those asshole neurologists, telling me "don't worry, it's only a migraine" — they were wrong all along. My "episode" of five years ago was a minor stroke, one I recovered from, quickly and fully.

I did some reading on strokes five years ago while I was waiting for the test results, a kind of "know your enemy" reflex. I know about small blood clots blocking a major blood vessel that delivers oxygen to the brain. Without oxygen, the affected part of the brain dies — *suffocates*, basically — and the functions it normally performs are lost. Memory, language, motor control, whatever. If the part that is cut off is important — the part that keeps your heart beating, for example — you're dead. Otherwise, you can sometimes come back — maybe not all the way, but part of the way at least — as other sections of the brain learn to take over for the dead part, a kind of cerebral "cross-training." I can imagine part of my brain

— part of my *mind* — stifling, smothering, *dying* as the blood supply is cut off. There's dead tissue inside my head. It's *that* thought that makes me feel like retching.

When it hit me, I must have gotten up from my desk, gone downstairs — without Juli seeing me — and out into the night. Wandering aimlessly, maybe under the influence of the dying parts of my mind.

A stroke. It has to be. What *else* could it be? What else could explain the disorientation, the memory loss, the fact I can't read the street signs? Why else would I have hallucinations...?

Hallucinations — that's the only word for them. They're not excessive, flamboyant things. No dancing pink elephants, no melting streets, no ghosts of my dead father telling me I'm a self-absorbed fuck-up. No, they're more subtle than that, and that very subtlety makes them even more unsettling.

See, I know this neighborhood. Not this specific street, maybe, but I know this region of Nob Hill. Hell, my aunt and uncle used to live here back in the late '60s and early '70s. I lived with them for almost a year while mother and father were going through one of their bad spells. The buildings in this part of the city, they're old. Some of them date back to the beginning of this century. But they've all be renovated — "gentrified," that's the word that some of my colleagues would use. Hundreds of millions of dollars have been poured into these buildings over the last thirty years. (I used to joke about wishing that Cross & Associates had been around at the time to get some of that business...) The upshot is that Nob Hill is one of the most expensive places to live in San Francisco. Neighborhood councils have made it next to a felony to let your building get run-down and crappy-looking.

So that means the cracks I see in the facades of the buildings around me... the boarded-up windows... the sagging, collapsed eaves... They've got to be hallucinations. Haven't they?

I'm suddenly a lot colder.

■

It happens in an instant too short to measure, or even sense. Another jump-cut in the film that is my experience. In mid-shiver, it happens. One instant of time and I'm in Nob Hill, alone on a street surrounded by buildings that — impossibly — have been left to decay for twenty years. The very next moment I'm on a busy street. Typical Saturday night crowds on the sidewalk, cars on the street.

Instinctively, I lunge out of the way of the pedestrian traffic. I flatten myself in the boarded-up doorway of a failed porno palace as I struggle to get my heart rate back under control.

Again... Jesus God, it happened again... Another chunk of time *gone*, experiences and memories excised from my life as if cut out with the sharpest of scalpels, no trace remaining. My heart's pounding in my chest... no, not so much pounding, as fluttering. Like some panicked bird in a cage. I'm breathing in short, shallow pants, my mouth gaping open. I'm shaking so hard my vision's blurring, like I'm having some kind of seizure. Shivering. But again it's not from the cold. There's the faintest ringing in my ears, a high-pitched metallic note like the buzz from a swarm synthetic mosquitos.

I clench my mouth shut so hard that the pain shoots through the muscles of my jaw. Biting back on the scream that wants to escape me. For a moment, I have the feeling — no, the *absolute certainty* — that if I open my mouth I'll start howling with panic and never stop. Fear twists in my chest like a live being, something trying to claw and tear its way out like a monster...

No! I close my eyes and I force myself to breathe deeply, slowly. It's one of the hardest things I've ever done.

But it works. I can feel the panic recede. I'm still scared shitless, but there's a very real difference. This is scared that I can deal with.

I realize my arms are crossed over my chest, each hand gripping the opposite shoulder. Hugging myself like an abandoned child. I force my arms down until my hands are at my sides.

I look around. I'm on a main road, a boulevard with a median down the middle. It takes me a moment to recognize it: Lombard Street, near Van Ness, highway 101 heading west to the Presidio then north over the Golden Gate. I'm maybe a mile and a half from where I'd been what seems like a couple of seconds ago. The shivering threatens to start again, but I keep it under control.

How long has it actually been? Instinctively I glance at my left wrist, but I'm not wearing my Rolex. I *always* wear it, it's almost as much of a personal trademark as my flip-phone. I know I had it on while I was working the Hayward numbers. Normally I'd worry about where I lost it — Christ, it cost me three grand, after all — but at the moment it just doesn't seem to matter. I turn to the east and look at the moon, trying to judge how much time has passed by how far it's climbed into the sky. Impossible. I'm at a different elevation, and the moon's barely rising behind Russian Hill. For all I can judge, it could be seconds or hours since I last looked at it. I suppose I could stop one of the pedestrians and ask him the time, but that wouldn't help much. I don't know what time it was when I was on Nob Hill. But maybe I should ask anyway...

I look at the people passing by. Really look at them for the first time, seeing them as they are, as people, not as moving objects about to run me down.

They're just people, just the typical Saturday night crowd out on the town. But... but there's something different about them. It's the way they look, partially. But it's more than their appearance, it's the feeling they give me.

They're pale and drawn, all of them. Drained of life, the skin of their faces is white as paper.

Okay, I've seen people who look like that, who hasn't? The Generation Xers — or whatever today's term for them is — the kids who try to look dead, like vampires. Bleached skin, eye-liner to make their eyes look sunken, all that crap. But most of the people passing by me aren't of the right generation. They're my age or older, not Xers at all. And, like I say, it's not just the way they *look*, it's the way they *feel*. It's the eyes, I think, something scary about their eyes. Something... I know it doesn't make sense, but it keys into that sense of *absence* in my own head. It's like I'm drawn to their eyes because I'm looking for something in them that I've lost. And it scares the piss out of me for some reason.

My gaze is drawn to a small man, heading east toward Van Ness. Short but kind of stocky, my age or a couple of years younger. His hair's cut so short it's almost like suede over his bullet-shaped skull. His stride seems to crackle with energy. But it's his eyes that fix my attention.

Or rather, *one* eye. It's red. Not bloodshot. Solid, unrelieved red, like smooth and glistening partially-clotted blood.

I recoil from the sight, and it's all I can do not to gag. By the time I've got myself back under control, the suede-headed man's passed on out of sight. I stare after him anyway, panic churning in my stomach.

No matter how vibrant, how energetic the man looked... I know that death is close to him. I *know* it, I don't know how. The knowledge is far below the level of rational thought, which just makes it all that much more convincing, somehow. *Death is with that man*, in some sense that I don't — *can't* — understand.

I have to get home. Home, then to a hospital. I realize I'm hugging myself again, and this time I feel something digging into my chest. My phone, of course, in my shirt pocket. Somehow I'd forgotten it.

The rush of relief as I pull the phone out and flip it open is so strong it almost unlocks my knees. Its familiar, reassuring weight and solidity seems to recharge my soul. My fingers tremble slightly as I punch the keys. Juli. Yes, Juli will come and pick me up. I can almost feel myself sinking into the warm upholstery of her Saab as she drives me to the UC Medical Center. I raise the phone to my ear.

It's dead. Totally dead. No dial tone, no beeps as I dial the number, no ringing. Not even the faint hiss of atmospherics over the carrier. Dead, no doubt about it. The alphanumeric display is blank, the LEDs cold and inert. Slowly, dully, I snap it closed and return it to my pocket.

I'm on my own, but I still need help. It's uncomfortable to admit — I've never been good at asking for help — but I have to face it. I look back at the passers-by, trying to pick out... pick out what ? Someone who's not threatening, someone I can approach? Christ, what a stupid idea. Normally I can talk to anyone about anything, and fuck what they think of me.

There's someone. A woman — tall, slender. Curly blonde hair, wearing a jade-green raincoat that looks expensive. For some reason I can't even guess how old she is. She moves as though she's young, maybe my own age. But when I look at her eyes, I feel as though she could be a hundred years old. She's walking alone, strolling idly, a faint smile on her face. A people-watcher, the way I used to be when I was younger. I step out in front of her.

"Excuse me, but could I talk to you for a moment?" That's what I want to say — *try* to say — but I can't force the words out. I open my mouth, but my voice catches in my throat. I can't make a sound.

I'm standing right in front of her, looking into her face, her eyes. Normal human reaction would be for her to look me in the face, to make eye contact.

She doesn't. She doesn't look at me at all, she looks *through* me. She blinks, and hesitates in her stride. The faint smile vanishes from her face — *drains* away, leaving a disturbed, almost frightened expression. I take a step toward her, and in the same instant she turns aside. Steps around me and hurries across the street through a gap in the traffic. Leaving me standing bereft, watching her go.

I shut my mouth, and again I feel shooting pains in my jaw muscles as I grind my teeth together. She didn't see me... No, that doesn't make sense. She reacted to my presence. But that reaction was strange, abnormal.

I stand there, looking around. People are passing by me, their eyes averted... almost the same way I refuse to make eye contact with a panhandler on Market Street, the way I give them the old "neutral scan." Their faces and their eyes don't acknowledge my presence, my existence. Yet I'm still surrounded by a kind of bubble of empty space, an arm's-length or so of it. My gaze is drawn to a teenage couple strolling arm-in-arm, right toward me. At the last moment, in the instant before they'd enter my "dead space," I see something change in their eyes. The girl's face goes pale — paler than it already is — and together they step aside, to pass me by. Again, there's no eye contact, none at all.

It scares me, terribly. What's happening? Do I look so hideous, so threatening, that everybody is giving me the neutral scan? In my mind's eye,

I flash on a horrible image of myself, half my face hanging dead, paralyzed by the stroke. Instinctively, I step back into the haven of my doorway.

The shivering starts again. I close my eyes, concentrate on my breathing.

And as soon as my eyes are closed, I notice something I wasn't aware of before. Sounds. Cars are passing by on Lombard Street, many with stereos blasting. The sidewalks are full of people, many of them talking. Yet somehow everything's quiet. Muffled, flat. I can make out the sounds, but they're somehow distant, remote. Similar to the way things sound in a thick fog, or after a heavy snowfall. Yet there's no snow, and only thin, writhing snakes of fog. It's as if my ears are plugged with cotton wool. I feel isolated from the world, removed. It's a paranoiac sensation. My eyes snap open. I feel them staring, wide. The stroke again? It's affected my hearing, maybe robbed me of the power of speech...

■

And again, I'm suddenly somewhere else. A distant whimper of fear sounds in my ears. It takes me a moment to realize it's my own voice.

Again the panic twists and thrashes like a live thing in my chest. I take a half-step back. A wall is against my back, hard and cold. I sink down into a crouch, my back to the wall.

The panic grows into what feels like a *void*, *a gaping* void inside me. I'm hollow. My soul has been hollowed out. A cold wind seems to whistle, echoing, in the core of my being. I feel like I'm on a crumbling precipice, over an infinite drop, yet that drop isn't part of the world around me, it's *within* me. I'm falling, falling into the hole that's inside me. The street, the buildings spin wildly.

No!! Something flares within me — maybe anger, maybe fear, maybe both or neither. Somehow I recoil from that internal void.

I'm crouching on the sidewalk, my back against a building, shaking like I'm consumed with fever. My breath hisses through my teeth, a broken, staccato sibilance.

Somehow I force the fear, the panic down. Brutally I suppress them, struggling to turn off my emotions the way I learned so many years ago. I slow down my breathing, inhaling until my lungs strain, then letting the air out in a steady, slow hiss. Control. I'm in control again. I look around me.

Again, I know this place. Memories flood back. Old memories, the recollection of how I came to be here. I recognize the Grace Cathedral. Its illuminated rose window and the gilded bronze doors at the east entrance are unmistakable. Nob Hill again. Again, I've traveled almost a mile in what seems like no time at all. There's Taylor Street, and over there is Sacramento Street. With an effort, I force myself to stand up. I'm still hugging myself, but this time I can't force my arms to my sides.

Almost against my will, my eyes are drawn to the gilded doors, to the reliefs on them. Ghiberti's "Gates of Paradise," perfect copies of the originals in Florence. They're familiar, those doors, this church, even though it's been a long time since I last saw them.

When was the last time? Last year, my father's funeral, it had to be. Mother and I walked through those doors, arm in arm — the perfect picture of grieving widow and dutiful son, even though we hadn't spoken in the preceding three years. Those doors were at my back, reflecting the morning light, as we accepted the condolences of my father's colleagues.

Solemn, well-meaning... and as phoney as a whore's embrace. The movers and shakers of the financial world, all doing their duty to the memory of a man most of them hated. I remember looking around for my father's friends — friends, not acquaintances, not business contacts, not colleagues or competitors. There weren't any.

And I remember thinking about my *own* funeral. (Morbid thoughts, of course.) It would take place here at Grace, the seat of the Episcopal Church in San Francisco. Irrelevant that I'm not a church-goer, and about as religious as a barracuda — the same was true of my father. Still, there are certain niceties that must be observed.

My funeral would be a major event within the business community. It would be well-attended, of course: my squash partners, my business associates. All the scions of the corporate world, the ones who respected me and envied me. One of my old colleagues — possibly Michael Drummond — would deliver the eulogy, his rich voice rolling through the soaring Gothic structure...

But would anyone cry? Would anyone shed a single tear for me, or feel that the world was somehow diminished by my passing? Oh, Juli would weep prettily for her audience and accept the condolences of people who really care no more than she does. And then everyone would go on with their own lives, unaffected. I remember the momentary sense of emptiness that the image brought with it. Now the emptiness is back, doubled, and somehow this time I can't suppress it.

Where is my father now? The thought comes out of left field. I hesitate, as though the question really matters.

Is there a heaven, like I used to hear about in Sunday school? And is that where my father is, icily sailing through the afterlife, surrounded by the same impenetrable armor of arrogance and aloofness that protected him on Earth? The same armor I learned to wear? Would my father even let *God* draw close to him?

I cover my face with my hands. The precipice, the void — they're there again, threatening to swallow me.

Why do I fight them? Why don't I just let go? The void — maybe it's death. Maybe more of my brain tissue is dying, withering more of my psyche, of who I am. Wouldn't I rather just let go, fall into the oblivion, than cling to a life that might leave me a vegetable...?

But I *can't* let go, I *can't* give up the fight. I never could, it's not in my nature to give up, to surrender myself to *anything* not of my own making. The panic is less this time. No, not really less — just somehow more distant. Overlaid by something calm. Acceptance? No, acceptance isn't in my nature either. It's a sense of imminence — of *immanence*. Of understanding just beyond my grasp.

No. I force it away, the understanding and the panic both. I lower my hands from my face.

I know this place, too. Van Ness Avenue again. I'm outside the bar called Cpl. Henry Africa. I remember my first visit here, ten years ago, maybe more. I'd read somewhere that Henry Africa used to be a gathering-place for mercenaries and would-be soldiers-of-fortune. I'd imagined some harsh, austere place, trophies and memorabilia of combat on the walls, frequented by iron-faced men with the eyes of those who've stared down death itself. I remember being disappointed, then amused, as I'd walked in the door. Maybe it had once been a watering-hole for mercenaries, but times change. Now it was just another of the hundreds of fern-draped yuppie bars that dot the city.

In the lights of the passing cars, the gilt window glints. The gold paint is faded, much more weathered than I remember it. It's all I can do to trace out the inscription — *Vive la mort, vive la guerre, vive la légion étrangère.* "Long live death, long live war, long live the Foreign Legion"... Long live death. When I first saw it, I was jarred by the incongruity of that statement. Now, somehow, it doesn't seem so strange.

It was at Henry Africa that I first met Juli. Glamorous, blonde Juli, one of the thousands of would-be actresses, starlet wannabes, you can find in any big city. Flashing wit and unstudied sensuality overlying a tottering self-esteem.

I was looking for a wife. It was after my first "episode," my first stroke. The doctors had told me to slow down, to settle myself down, and I was taking them at their word. I'd always played as hard as I'd worked — pretty fucking hard — and I'd come to admit that it made sense to back off there, too. It was time to settle down, time to give up on the pursuits and the conquests and the one-night-stands — the play-acting and the recriminations. I'd always been successful with women. It was just a matter of applying the same skills I'd learned from my father, the same skills I used in business.

I've always been good at reading people, at sensing what they want, what they need, what they expect... sometimes better than they could themselves. It's easy, anyone can do it... or they could, if they didn't let emotions cloud their vision. When you're trying to close — a deal or a seduction, it doesn't matter — all you do is figure out what kind of person your prospect wants you to be, and then you feed it back to them. For the duration of the process, you become that person. Simple and almost infallible.

A lot of work, though. And if you're doing it in your social life as well as your business life, it means you're always wearing a mask. I figured it was time to arrange it so at least one person didn't require that kind of effort from me. A wife.

There were other benefits, of course, other than avoiding effort. Most of the men I did business with — particularly the older ones, the ones my father's age — had families, had wives who doubled as social coordinators, caterers, and decorative hostesses. I didn't, of course, and I knew that in their eyes that sometimes made me suspect, as though the fact that I wasn't following the same life-path they'd selected cast some kind of doubt on the wisdom of their decision. Sometimes I thought they saw it as some kind of a provocation for questioning me and my business practices...

It was an obstacle and I was experienced in the art of overcoming obstacles.

Let's face it, it was a business relationship I was looking for, a *quid pro quo* arrangement. In return for being a hostess, an accessory to my career — and sharing my bed — I allow her, Juli, the life which she'd like to become accustomed. A good deal all round, a true win-win. After spending some time with Juli, I decided she'd fit the bill perfectly. She was certainly decorative, she was a good hostess, and she was good in bed. What more could I hope for?

It took me awhile to arrange, just as I'd expected it would. As usual, I'd got her into bed the first night... and, according to Julie, that meant we were "going out." (That's the way most women seem to view things, at least.) Eventually I broached the subject and made my proposal.

She didn't accept it at once, but then I hadn't really expected her to. She cried, and she flung on her clothes and stormed out of my condo. I stuck with my program, though, the plan I'd already laid out in my mind. The next day, and the next, and the day after that, I had bouquets of flowers delivered to her office and her home.

Finally, after five days, the knock came on my door, and Juli was part of my life. She seemed sad — I don't quite understand why — but the deal was in place. We were married at Grace Cathedral, under the approving eyes of the part of the business community that counts.

Everything worked out just as well as I'd expected it would. At dinner parties, balls and galas, Juli wielded her scintillating wit and charmed everyone she met. It made me happy to see — I've always appreciated skill, and Juli turned out to be a better actress than I'd given her credit for. She was the life of every party... but, now that I think about it, that was the only time I saw her flashing wit. When we were alone, she was always there, always attentive — physically present, *physically* attentive, at least. Yet emotionally she seemed withdrawn, quiet. Her body was there, but her spirit, her emotions, were somewhere else. As though she were sad.

Sad? Why would she be sad? The lifestyle she was enjoying was better than anything she could have imagined. I never made unreasonable demands of her, in or out of the bedroom. The only constraint I put on her behavior was *discretion.* I'd have understood and accepted it — hell, I guess I *expected* it — if she'd had affairs outside the marriage...

But she never did, did she? I realize now I'd never thought much about that. I'd just been quietly reassured that she wasn't going to do something unwise, something that was going to destroy what I'd so carefully constructed.

Love? It had never even entered my mind. I cared about her, I suppose. I felt protective of her — that was part of the deal, after all — and it gave me satisfaction when she smiled over a birthday or Christmas gift. But love... that was something else again, wasn't it? Love had no place in this kind of deal.

Did it?

■

I almost expected that one. I felt some kind of strange, internal *shift* — a sudden emptiness in the heart. A sweet and bitter pain in the middle of my chest. What could that be, other than some warning that my damaged brain was about to begin another fugue? Well, what?

Panic is there again, but strangely it seems... one step removed, if that makes any sense. Almost as if I'm *observing* fear upon the face of a stranger. To my utmost surprise, that sensation seems familiar...

It takes me a second to place it. I remember the last time I blew out my knee playing squash. (I'd never really liked the game, but I'd trained myself to be the best. So much business gets done in the squash clubs.) The Medical Center surgeons had pulled out the errant flap of cartilage, and I was tranked to the eyeballs on Demerol. I can still remember the sensation. I knew I was lying on the bed, but somehow I wasn't really there. Whatever it was that was *me* — in contrast to the slab of meat that is the human body — was hovering somewhere up near the ceiling, looking down at myself. I knew the "I" on the bed was hurting, hurting like hell, but it was like looking at someone else in pain. I could empathize with the "me" on the bed, but I couldn't really *feel* the pain. *That*'s what it's like with the panic, except on an emotional rather than a physical level.

The full moon, still streaked with clouds and fog, has risen clear of the buildings atop Russian Hill. By its light, I can see where I am.

Where I expected to be, in some sense. (Where did *that* thought come from...?)

I'm on Buchanan Street, a couple of blocks above the Marina. Outside my townhouse. Juli's silver Saab is parked by the curb. The garage door is shut, and I know my green Jag V12 is inside. Lights shine warmly from the upstairs windows — from my office, with its view over the Bay, and from Juli's bedroom. The light by the front door is burned out — Juli *still* hasn't got an electrician to fix it — but by the nearby street lamp I can see the building.

Faded, dilapidated. Could we really have neglected the upkeep that badly? Could I really have been so distracted that I never noticed it before...? The stucco is cracked, long zigzag lines skirt the sides of the structure, discolored as if by mildew or mold. Like the buildings I saw on Nob Hill. A chill hits me again, but this time I feel it in my heart, not my bones. Why is it that, wherever I look, I see corruption, decay... even where I know there shouldn't be ...?

Light glints dully off the brass doorknocker, the eagle's head. One of the few things that Juli had selected for the place. I remember how hard she'd had to fight before I'd let her put it up.

The eagle seems to be looking at me, with its empty eyes. It draws me. I want to go inside...

Of course I want to go inside. It's my home. I've been wandering the streets of the goddamn city for hours. Something's seriously wrong with me. Of course I want to go inside...

Yet the prospect terrifies me. And I don't know why.

Imminence. Immanence.
I take a step forward.

■

The upper hallway. I'm inside, without
knowing how. I don't remember opening the
door. How could I have opened it? I don't have
a key.

I know it's warm in here. Juli always keeps it
warm, no matter how much I complain about
the utility bills. But the warmth doesn't reach
me, doesn't penetrate me. It's as if I'm
insulated... as if the emotional armor I chose to
wear is shielding me from the warmth, the way
it's always shielded me from pain.

I look down at the expensive burgundy carpet.
I never liked burgundy, but it was the
fashionable color when I had the place
decorated. To my right down the hallway is Juli's
room, the study she's turned into her craft room.
To my left is my office. The door stands open,
but from this angle I can't see in.

I want to turn to my right. More than
anything else in the world — more than
anything I've ever wanted — I want to walk
down the hall to Juli's room. I want to step in
the door. I want to see her look up from her

latest project — needlepoint, or whatever she's doing now — and I want to see her smile. I want to gaze into her eyes — they look green sometimes, sometimes brown and sometimes blue, depending on the light — and I want to see warmth there. I want her to come to me. Desperately, I want to feel her arms around me, I want to hear her voice telling me it's all right...

But it's left that I turn. It's the office that draws me, even more strongly than the sightless eagle. There's something I need to see there, something I need to know. What was it Oedipus said? "I'm on the brink of terrible knowing... but I must know." Something like that.

I reach out to push the door wider, at the last moment I stop what I suddenly know to be a futile gesture.

I see what I knew I'd see, what I somehow knew I'd be facing all along. Juli is on her knees, face buried in her hands, hair like a waterfall of gold pouring to the floor. And on the floor before her...

My body. Face contorted, blue about the lips. Eyes open, staring, pupils dilated. Blood pooled under one ear.

Juli's weeping. Alone, with no audience at all, she's crying her guts out. Great wracking, wrenching sobs. With no one there to see, or to impress with her devotion. Alone.

And the realization drives me to my knees.

Two realizations, the second even more terrible than the first. She loved me. Juli loved me. She *always* loved me — so much that she'd put up with anything to be with me. Deep down inside, I realized that I had always *known*. Why else would I have gone so far out of my way to push her away, to keep her out, to keep her from getting close enough to hurt me?

She needed me...

And I needed her, too. In my own way, I *needed* her, I just didn't know it. I can feel the emptiness in my soul that she used to fill. I can see her in front of me, but now we're separated by a gulf greater than the one I worked to create all my life. She's separated from me and now I realize what I've lost. When it's too late to do anything about it. When it's too late to tell her that *she* was what I needed — not another deal, or another car, or another million. When it is too late to reach out.

Only now, now that my life is over, do I realize how incomplete I was... and only now do I know how to fill the emptiness that has forever howled within me.

The precipice and the pit, they're back. Reality fractures around me. An abyss yawns inside me, in the center of my being, an abyss filled with the howling and gibbering of countless lost souls. As I fall over the edge, the last thing I see is a flash of gold in Juli's hair.

END

ROOTBOUND

R. S. Martin

 wake up with the ground grinding against itself like teeth. Earthquake. All around, my house is shivering loose from itself. Has this happened before? I don't remember.

It's dark in here and it's dark outside, so it's night. What time is it? This is one of those times when a clock would come in handy, but they always stop. Call it three in the morning for want of working clocks. A good time for teeth to grind. A cityful of broken bones screeching like yellow chalk when they touch, making sure they hit all each other's sore spots. The ground's not supposed to do that. It's supposed to lie there, buried underfoot, and carry its burdens in peace.

While the firm ground gnashes its teeth and snarls on all sides, I start to panic, hoping that the world didn't change while I slept. So I pull on my eyes and look out the cracks in the window glass. My hair falls in my eyes almost at once, force of habit, and I brush it back again. I don't know what color it is or what I look like, so I don't ask. I forget.

Outside my window there's Richmond, same as it ever was. Rows of close-trimmed yards, unassuming houses reflecting each other across long, undistinguished streets. Richmond. My neighborhood of square houses embroidered with personal touches that distract us in the suburbs from the numbness of the days. Land of garden furniture and quaint wicker arches, where lawns are taken seriously. If ever a neighborhood were to put off grinding the teeth in its foundations until three in the morning, to keep the neighbors from hearing, it would be Richmond. I can respect that philosophy.

Always a relief when your neighborhood doesn't die in your sleep. It's happened. You lay your body down to rest a little piece, and when you wake up, they've bulldozed your house and you're in a parking lot. Every time I fall asleep, I'm always a little afraid it'll happen to me. I'll wake up, and it'll be the year 2525 or something. Everything and all the people will be gone, and that will be that.

The ground keeps straining against the foundations of the house. One by one the splinters of the broken windows fall from their frames, making sounds like sighing. Upstairs, something heavy falls to the floor, and the roots of the house creak in sympathy. A crash like that is about as close to coffee as I get these days. I am awake.

There's a fog up tonight, but between the streetlamps' haze and the thick moonlight, the trees along the street look like autumn. Hard to tell, though. With a few of them bare of leaves and the rest of them gold and black, it's hard to tell. Could be the tail end of winter, just before budding starts. Could be October. Call it October.

Out of the broken corner of the window, the beacon at Saint Ignatius' shimmies at me through the fog. Such a tease. I already have a girl.

Girl. Angel. I'm in love with a statue, you know, a wooden statue of an angel. I know full well what "statue" means. Inanimate person-shaped object. Mute, immobile, insensate for all

I know. Doll. Around here, though, you take
love where you find it.

I keep her upstairs. Where I just heard
something heavy fall. I drop my eyes to the floor
and I'm up the stairs and in the Angel's room
now and she's in bad shape.

The earthquake must have knocked her off
her pedestal. Instead of smiling down at me, she
grimaces up from the floor, almost snapped in
half, with dry leaves and dust pouring out from
all these new cracks in her. In her willowy figure.
She always was slim. There's a branching
fracture in her left side, just under... just under
her heart.

I really don't want to see any more, but I've
seen worse. It may be my job to see worse, but I
still feel sick to see you like this, Angel. What's
this, a dull spot on the wall behind you, like a
bruise made of sawdust? Did you hit yourself
against the wall? Why are your wings just
hanging there, all crumpled? They've shaken
loose. Why are you holding your arm like that?
It looks like it's broken. Is there something
wrong with your face? Don't tell me. It can wait.

My poor wooden angel. The earthquake's
shaken her all loose from herself. I know all
about that.

I'm not going to let her suffer any longer than

she has to.

It hurts to see her like this, unanchored. I try to lever her back to her place on her pedestal, make her comfortable. but she's heavy. I'd forgotten how heavy she is. Every few minutes her head and shoulders bounce a bit against the wall when the ground reminds us to take it seriously. I remember, I remember how that feels.

Push. Pull. Sick. Shove. Swear. Plead. Pull, don't cry. There are splinters where her hair was.

This isn't working. I've got to get focused here. I'm in San Francisco. California. My name is Andrew. Andrew Patrick Malone. I go to the University of San Francisco. Dick Nixon is president. There's a war on. Focus.

Hold her hands. My hands hold her. She lurches, half-doll, half-dancer, and I pull her upright again. As I pull, her wedged, twisted, bent parts scrape against the wall, spilling the dust of her insides everywhere. But she's upright.

I made her myself, a long time ago. There's birch bark in her, and brown, papery leaves for her wingfeathers. I found a smashed chair in the garage and made the pieces into a skeleton for her. Slats for her ribcage, chair-legs for her delicate forearm bones, and the seat for her hips. Then I worked outward, tying everything together with roots twined and knotted together.

Roots are what bind her together, binding everything to make a single Angel.

I feel a little lightheaded. Something's changed. Roots. Roots are beautiful things. The tragedy's that they're almost always buried, down in the earth where no one can see them. The smallest, palest flowers, blooming upside down in the dark, whispering to each other with no one else to hear. In my Angel, like everything else here in the shadows, everything works upside down, and for once the roots walk around out in the open, above ground. That's the secret. Here, it's the flowers that work to bind the roots in place.

The aftershocks are finally winding down. The ground loses interest in saying whatever it had to say and trails off, mumbling to itself more and more quietly until the night is silent again.

I hate earthquakes. Either they wake you up at three in the morning or they kill you before your eyes are open. I'm always afraid I won't be able to tell which is which before it's too late: whether I'm awake or dead, whether it's the first day of the world or the last.

Outside my windows, morning's breaking and the sky cuts itself on the pieces. Dawn turns the sky red in streaks like gashes and they bleed for awhile, but then the white sun finally rises through the fog and the clouds go white again. Gradually, the room goes gray. It settles into the routine of morning like the colorless dust on floors and walls. Dust trying to settle in an empty, wooden room.

Someone used to like to say I always "took the weather too personally." I wonder if I should remember who it was. Whether I take the morning too personally or not, the light helps me evaluate the damage, which is the important thing. The house really doesn't matter, but there doesn't seem to be anything wrong that wasn't wrong before. The plaster's still cracked, the pipes are still rusting, the window's still broken. If anything, the earthquake only managed to shake the dust off things. It's a tough old house.

The important thing is always the Angel. Her wings need new weaving before I lace them back into her shoulders, but first I need to mend that hole in her side. Experimentally, I trace the jagged, splintery edges of the crack and gently kiss her dust off my fingers. My poor, shaken Angel. It won't hurt long.

What if I can't fix this? For courage, I look down into the perfect curves of her face, to draw balance from her, but instead, I draw only dust. I can hardly recognize her. The fall shifted something in her cheek. Now when she smiles at me, her roots unwoven and exposed, I feel weaker. Weaker and so very tired. Please don't look at me like that.

There's also something wrong with her eyes. I made them out of heartwood, the palest, tenderest treasure of the vegetable kingdom. This morning, they're infected with something red, accusing, and feverish. Instead of looking softly at me, they glare. It's not my fault. Does her left look darker? Bloodshot as dawn. I wonder what it means for an angel's eyes to go all red in earthquake weather. Something in the air? The delicate fibers in the heartwood chips seem dried out, like fruits left out in the air for too long. Red in heartwood. A bad sign, whatever it is, and it needs to be fixed.

It reminds me of how Ceille looked, how red and tired-looking her eyes got when we had the argument and didn't look back. They looked like golden islands in a watery red sea. The first continents must have looked like that, when everything was earthquakes and Atlantis swam on the magma ocean and rain fell for a hundred thousand years. I remember thinking, "This must be what real life is like: red and bottomless, brimming over, dilating, afraid to blink."

Ceille. Celatia. That was her name. She always used to tease me about taking the weather too personally, getting too nervous when it was just the world.

Now it's my Angel who's crying. It's not my fault. I'd do the crying for her if I could take the time, but there's too much to do and it's not my fault. I didn't mean to say the wrong thing, Ceille. It just got to where I couldn't keep quiet any more.

I wish I'd told you sooner.

This Angel of mine. She may be made of wood, but even broken like this, she's the only angel I have. That means something.

Whatever happened to Ceille, I wonder. I don't think I ever saw her again, after the gold continents of her eyes got red. I went off to school and woke up every day and made my face and voice work. She wrote me for a few months, but I could never bring myself to open the letters. Finally, I had the accident, and the mail stopped coming.

Sometimes, around this time of the evening, the wooden angel reminds me of her.

And I begin to work.

The first part's covering the gaps in her side. As gently as I can, I unroll her bark skin from the wound's edges and unlatch her rib cage. It slides easily on its hinge; when I first made her, I made sure that I'd be able to adjust her heartstrings whenever I needed to. Ceille taught me that much. Then the work begins, and one by one I knot each of her roots and twigs back into place in the weave of her body. The tremor and the fall knocked whole tissues of her loose and distorted what was left. This will take awhile, but it distracts me from how hurt she is.

It's a complicated trade, making things, making people, but it's what we Pardoners do. Every one of her now-frayed threads needs to be laced by hand, woven back into the fabric of my Angel, coerced to follow the pattern on its own. Most of these roots and things in here have been dead for a long time, and they've gotten dry and stiff. The dry parts don't go out of their way to help you, especially if they're old bits of the weave that have come loose in an earthquake. They need to be coaxed, one by one, gently bent back and ever so slowly re-knotted about one another in the corset of her small Angel's body.

Pardoners. Pardon me. When I was younger, I was always apologizing. I took responsibility for everything. Taking the weather personally. It got to be a habit, then a responsibility by itself, even when, really, I wasn't sorry at all. Ceille always used to poke me when I did that. What did she say? "There's a difference between truth and manners," was that it? It doesn't matter. I work for Manners, for the pale ghosts up in the Presidio, and not for not truth.

As the day goes on, the wind picks up outside, and the sky never recovers from being cold and white. Funny, these ghosts of absent weather. When you sit still for a bit and listen closely, the wind blows up off the ocean, and no matter how hard it shakes the houses and old, jagged trees it can't blow the fog away. The sky has faultlines, too, and every so often it stumbles up there on the tightrope: ghosts of absent weather.

Finally, her insides are all back in place and I tie the laces of her ribcage tight. Not even scars remain to embarrass her. I owe her that much at least. I crumple up some newspaper headlines I've been saving and fill her empty corners with them, assassinations and wedding attempts. No time for hugs; the most I can manage is to trail my fingers across the memory of her wound. Arm comes next.

She was wrong, that girl Ceille. It's the weather that takes me personally. As I wind the vegetable tendons in her graceful, pianist forearm, I can hear this dry ocean wind pour down the streets in gusts, shearing what's left of the seeing, hearing leaves of the elm trees. All around me out there wooden giants are going blind, and the isolation of winter's starting again. Unless they sleep with their roots twined, every one of them is alone now. I'd almost feel sorry for them.

I caught one in the air once. A falling leaf. I just put out my hand and it fell right into my fingers. I'd never caught a leaf on the fall before. I felt so proud, turning it over in my fingers to look at it and marvel.

And it was all diseased. Infested. There was some kind of fungus in its side that had made it grow a patch of little, tiny centipede legs. A leaf with legs, or hair, or tentacles. That was the leaf that I managed to catch in the air, before it even hit the ground.

I braid the tender, new-sprouted roots of her open wrist as carefully as I can, holding every tendril of her flesh between my fingers as if it were something living, and I look at her face. Her veins, her nerves, the tendons of a cheek muscle to let her smile and sob. When I first made her, I had to weave every thread of angel separately. I worked without rest breaks. I worked without slowing. When I got too exhausted to touch her any more with my hands, I held her roots between my teeth and nudged them into place with my face, kissing her to perfection.

Other people in my age cohort were always making visits to see their families, their loved ones, anything they'd left behind. I had my wooden angel for all of that. I wove her out of the wooden thoughts of plants, and the others struggled and despaired, and now they are all gone and only I remain. But I am a Master Pardoner, and I have perfected my trade. Everything a Pardoner can teach you is woven in my angel's hair.

The wind's picking up. You can always tell when the weak joints in the houses begin to rock, slowly and gently, and underneath your brain you think you're at sea. Strong weather tends to follow earthquakes, which makes sense when you think about it. It's like this new science, ecology: everything's connected, and when you unbalance one piece of it, the others wobble too. I like to think of it as some kind of circus act, tightropes again. Once the seismic plates lose their balance, the tightrope swings wildly, disturbing the other acrobats. At the bottom of the world, everything's roots are connected. For better balancing.

I was going to be a writer, you know. In the style of Professor Tolkien at Oxford, and David Lindsay and Mervyn Peake, I was going to make worlds. She was going to be an actress. I never had anything perfect enough to publish before the accident. The Presidio crowd must be hating this weather, though. Especially Brannan; he's always going around saying, "When the wind blows, Cradle will rock." I can see him now, huddled in a packing crate with his money, trying to take it with him just in case. Not the best kind of boss I can think of, but there are worse.

The nice thing about work is that it gives you something to do with your time. Every now and then, they send someone down from the Presidio with a work order: "This manacle seems to be fraying; this thrall's chains need to be let out a bit so it can sleep; could you work this line of thralls into the new buttresses for the Citadel; think about techniques for getting Beacons." Brannan thinks he needs to move his money into a smaller, tighter box. The Spaniard doesn't trust his harbingers any more so he sends a pre-recorded Oratorio, burning cold and whispery. He wants some pikes.

They all like my chains best, of course. I learned manacles when I was building my angel out of gathered roots. If you want the deepest secret of manacle-molding, it's there: gather the heartstrings of your thrall and put them in his mouth, and let your thrall chain himself for you.

Chains have to work out from the inmost if they're going to work at all. They've got to start near the face. I chain all the new acquisitions.

I'm touching up the delicate roots of her face now. Re-weaving a face is one of the hardest tricks of the trade, harder even than names. There are thousands of roots in any expression, and every single one has to speak with its own voice if you don't want to end up with just another death mask. Anyone can craft a still life. Anyone can map someone's scars and memories. What I do is make dead things that seem to move, to breathe when you're not paying attention.

It takes complete concentration over a period of several days to put a decent face on anything. I tend to charge extra for custom work: "brave" faces, "strong" faces. It's not that I mind the extra effort, but it's distracting, and the request usually goes against the grain of the material.

I love her face. It's my best work, only the best raw ingredients. She reminds me of Ceille. That's ingredients enough.

After awhile the day starts again, but the wind never stops. If anything, it's getting worse. Behind the familiar white of the sky, the clouds look like sore, black bruises forming. Looks like a storm coming soon. All the leaves have fallen.

I'm buried deep in her face, with roots knotted around both hands, vegetable rings on all my fingers. Every contour in her face matters. The way it used to get a little lopsided when she laughed late at night. The way her chin jutted when she talked about her parents. Her forehead. Every fiber is the most important thing in the world. You need absolute precision to fix a face, and complete concentration. You have to be able to close your eyes and rebuild it from memory. Faces are complicated, mysterious things. When I'm doing one, I don't notice the weather. I don't apologize. You can't afford it on facework.

I'm buried deep in her jawline, where everything comes together. Jaw, neck, earlobe. Hairline and the roots of her teeth. Suddenly, a noise. I turn slightly without realizing it and pull something loose from her throat. It sounds like a scream of some kind, but also like a police siren and like the call of large birds, and then it cries again.

Company?

When I pull out to get the door, I'm stuck in her and she won't let go. Her jaw's snarled around my fingers. I try to disentangle myself, but the roots of her face argue with me, and the siren screams again. Let me go, Angel. I'll be back soon. Please.

Something bangs downstairs, but my hands are stuck. Crazy thing. Before, all I could think about was how beautiful Ceille's face was, but I could never let myself get close enough to touch it. Now here I am, and her cheek won't let go. No matter how hard I try to slip out, she won't let go. Finally I'm reduced to yanking my fingers out of her face, one by one. I'm sorry. I'm sorry. I try not to look, but I know she's watching me with those red eyes. Masses of half-knitted root flesh rip out with my fingers.

Another bang. No time to cry, no time to fix things. I wedge the door open and it's one of Brannan's Greenback messengers, wearing his Crown of Thorns and Brannan's colors. The faded, almost-yellow green the shade of collector's paper dollars, trimmed in much darker green for Emerald Legion; the color of shadows cast by leaves in sunlight. He looks like he's in a hurry. Young. The house moans with the wind, but somehow he manages to stand tall. The weather doesn't affect him, but he's letting it into my house.

He touches a finger to the point of his Crown of Thorns in salute, and I tug at the Pardoners' banded chain on my arm in return, my fingers still a mass of knotted roots. I look like I'm sprouting. I wonder what they want in the Presidio now. Surgical tools? Bayonets?

He glances at me and into the house and gets a little skittish. All the Presidio errand boys do that. There seems to be something invisible on the walls that only he can see, and he develops a kind of tic, always darting his head about. Nod, jerk his head to check behind him, as if he's heard something. Smile, glance down in horror to check out his feet. Wasteful use of one's time. And energy. The harbingers always remind me of magpies.

He starts with the usual preamble and steals another minute of my working time. I wish he'd hurry up. He's stilted, pretentious, and even a bit arrogant around the mouth, but not in any way of which he's self-conscious. Of course.

Shoddy face-work. It looks like he did it himself. I could fix that around the mouth. All it needs is to pull his lip back a bit on this side, give him a little humility.

"Brannan the Shopkeeper, LXIVth Hegemon of the Legion of Thorns, Thane of the Inflators, Greenback Despot and True Founder of the Dominion of San Francisco, sends this message to Malone, Master in the Guild of Pardons. In Charon, all."

In what must have become a sleepwalker

habit, he pulls the black leather collar of his uniform open and shows me the brands on his throat. I've seen it before and nod, go ahead. He gives his message. Apparently a party of old-time Temperance wrackers managed to escape from the Winchester House up in San Jose and got caught trying to hook up with Lo Ma Cameron's people near Chinatown. Needless to say, "Greenback" Brannan wants only the best manacles to graft onto his new "investments." The best for his money.

None of this matters to me. Brannan and the others get their toys, and they leave me alone. But now, I've got an angel's face drying in my fingers, and the errand boy goes on, listing the members of the Winchester group, their marks, visible signs of childbearing on one of the females, and I catch myself noticing that none of this matters to me. Is this a bad thing? I think it used to bother me when things like this didn't matter. He seems to be winding down so I force myself to pay attention. "...Terms of payment satisfactory. I can't ask you to labor on the Sabbath of course, so you can start measuring for the bridles tomorrow night, or as it suits you. Yrs, Samuel Brannan, Hegemon so on, so forth. Message ends."

Sabbath? I look for my voice, trying to

remember where I'd last heard it, how it worked. For a moment or two I experiment with what sounds like wheezing. Finally, I come close enough to make myself heard, and I ask him. "Sabbath? A holiday soon, I take it. We won the war?"

He pauses for the smallest moment and reaches up to tip his Crown of Thorns to a slightly different and probably more comfortable angle. Finding his off-duty face, I imagine. His posture shifts slightly and he nods again, a little taller, a bit relaxed. "Halloween! Not even Brannan can ask you to work on Halloween, and he knows that."

"Oh yes," I say.

His mouth twitches. "You do remember that it's tonight, don't you? The big one. Halloween."

I try to remember what comes next in conversations like this. "Halloween. Um. October. Trick and treat. I'm sure you're excited."

He nods, and you'd almost think there was more to him than the uniform, winged shoes, ears that hear and mouth that talks. I say "Well, hurry up. Message receipt acknowledged. Close to sundown. Get going." He's gone before I finish.

Halloween. I'm back in the Angel's room, through my darkened windows watching the boy flicker as he darts back up to the citadel. I catch myself hoping I'm his last duty of the day so he can get to whatever it is he wants to do.

He's probably going to spend the night tracking down the "mystery" of his death. Stupid to wear your heart on your uniform like that, but that's the way those guys are, so confident that the world is holding its breath just because they died without knowing why.

I miss Ceille. I wonder what she's doing.

It's getting dark out again. Halloween, mm?

When we were younger, we had this game where we'd call up all the radio stations and dedicate songs to each other. Any song. It got to where we'd have to make up fake voices to trick the DJs, or bribe them, or whatever it took.

I still remember the phone numbers. Funny. I push my voice in the direction of next door, where my phone is. Push. Tip the table, knock the earpiece off. Turn the dial, one number at a time. I don't even notice how hard this is. The other end rings. Someone, a woman, says "KOTO Request Line."

I push my voice over the telephone. "Could I make a dedication? The Fairports, 'Meet on the Ledge'? From Andrew to Ceille?"

She asks "Could you turn your radio down, please? We're getting a lot of feedback and I can't hear you."

I push harder to make myself heard. "Could you play 'Meet on the Ledge?' By the Fairport Convention."

My voice is starting to get heavy, and I have to sit down, very slowly to keep the connection. She comes back. "No, we don't have it. It's either too new or stolen or something. Got an alternate?"

Push. It's heavy, and I can't make it very loud. "Also by them, "Who Knows Where the Time Goes"?"

She says, "Also by them? Sorry, but they said we don't have anything by the 'Fairport Convention' down here. To tell the truth, I don't think I've ever heard of them. Must be too obscure or too new for the station."

Pause. "Hello? Must be a bad connection. Hang up and try again."

The phone clicks and I drop my connection too. I'm too tired to dial again.

It's still very dark in here with my Angel. I look at her for a second or two before I remember what I'm looking at. She doesn't return the favor, but stares at the ceiling with her dried-blood heartwood eyes. Angel, angel.

Have you forgotten me, Celatia? I know, it happens to me when I just wake up, too. It's me, though. Andrew. Every day in school I wrote you letters, and you wrote me back. Do you remember now?

It's me, Angel. We talked a lot about being perfect. About living life as a work of art, with every breath counting, every move of your head a gesture for the finished product. You wanted everything you did to be perfect. Whenever anyone wanted you to compromise, you'd do something extreme instead. I just wanted to be perfect, and that meant never doing anything too extreme.

We talked. About mind games, about life, about trust and about truth. We promised each other we'd never lie to each other. You showed me your scars and I showed you mine.

Ceille? Something's gone wrong with your eyes.

I need to go back downstairs to get some fresh materials from the backyard. To replace what got wasted when the idiot from Thorn interrupted me. The nice thing about work is that it makes you forget that time is going by.

It's spooky out here now. The moon's out, glimmering in the fog. Is it still Halloween? I've lost track again. The weather's gotten past the point of a thunderstorm. It's heavy, like a cut that's been put off for too long and which has festered. Too much up in the air even to fall as rain, so we have wind without movement, fog without rain. Up above, the moon gives light but no heat.

I go to one of the overgrown flowerbeds and start digging, down through the dry husks, black and cloudy amber in the moonlight. Down through the piles of brown, blind leaves. Down between the jagged stumps of rotten poppies until I get to the depth of the soft, dark mud, where the roots are.

Odd how I don't dig up any bones. You see, this entire neighborhood used to be the big cemetery district. Blocks and blocks of boneyard, from the park to the other side of that hill over there where St. Ignatius' is, but they had to move the corpses to build houses for the living. I don't know what they did with the tombstones. Pardoners got hold of enough of them to build the seawall back in the '30s, but I don't know what happened to the others. I hear you can still read the names on that sea wall, if you know where to look at low tide.

In this neighborhood, you get used to digging up bones in your yard. Generations of hereditary gardening has mined out most of the deposits by now, but you always wonder if today will be the day you find someone's finger in your roses. Some people dig and they get treasure. Here, you dig up bones.

No bones this time, only roots. Nothing in my hole but the white, twisted roots of the dead flowers. Dad was right when he said there's nothing worse than a tree that's gotten its roots knotted, growing inward, slowly strangling itself. They grow underground, like a cannibal forest, all these vegetable worms crawling over each other with no room to stretch out, no time to stop and think. Feeding frenzy over not enough dust.

The dogwood trees that Dad brought in from back east look dead, so I bet they're rootbound too. It's hard to tell in autumn, of course, but I wouldn't be surprised if this whole yard wasn't a huge, petrified thicket of suffocated roots just under the surface. I bet they tried to get under the house, hitting their heads in vegetable blind slow-motion against the concrete foundations until they ran out of strength. Under the house.

It's almost funny, walking on roots. Every step I take, I'm walking on tightropes. A hundred, a million tightropes, all tangled back on themselves like a maze, without ever knowing when I took that first step out on the wire.

Without knowing where the other end is, if there is one. Tightropes wound around skulls and tectonic fissures, and none of us can sleep at night. You either keep moving or you fall.

One of the last notes I ever wrote to Ceille had a tightrope in it. Maybe it was the last one. I don't remember that much, but I remember this one. I used to work on them for hours, writing and then re-writing to leave just enough hints but not enough to get myself in trouble. It was a balancing act, and I guess I was too careful up there, didn't take enough risks. She should have figured it out. I made enough hints.

But because of all the re-writing I remember what I said, more or less, about tightropes.

It is possible, Ceille, to lead one's life with perfect circumspection. They tell you that nobody's perfect, that everyone makes mistakes. That's bogus. Every single tightrope walker now living is perfect. Balance is the secret. Being perfect means having total balance, being able to remain perfectly still. There are a lot of tightrope walkers out there in a lot of carnivals; if anyone ever tells you that everyone makes mistakes, point to the tightrope walkers, suspended alone between heaven and earth. The tightrope walkers. Happiness doesn't matter. It's a distraction. The wire cuts your feet up there, and your feet bleed, but it has to be tight if you're going to balance.

There. Behold my only surviving work. Andrew P. Malone, R.I.P., survived by a pretentious fragment on tightropes, now probably also lost.

I remember the way your head would tilt when you were struck by something completely tangential to what people were actually trying to say. It was... it was as if someone invisible were talking to you, and you were trying very hard to listen, the way that dogs and cats listen. Looking at you listening, I always wondered what had struck you that was so terribly important that you would freeze like a forest animal. I wanted to touch your cheek then, every time. I remember the way you held a pencil, the way you ducked your chin when you'd swallow.

All the windows are still broken in the garage. I did that, right before my accident, broke them one by one. Funny how my hands never hurt.

I wish I'd told you sooner, Ceille. I wish I'd had the guts or the sense or the confidence to have told you sooner and then gotten on with it from there.

I wish my life had somehow been allowed to

have more dialogue in it.

It's begun to rain.

It starts like it always does, with one drop falling for its own reasons, preparing the way, cooling the air as it falls. Then another drop falls, and another soon after, and then the sky loses control of itself. Before you know what's happening, drops are falling in sheets of water, running together in falling streams, and the clouds collapse into a vertical river falling to earth as they forget more and more of their balance.

Rain smells different now. Before the accident, it smelled fresher, more like lightning in the air. Now it smells like old newspapers in the gutter, or like inland, shut-in oceans, rain from the Dead Sea, whole lakes clotted with the white corpses of fish. I bring a hand up to cover my nose, but that only makes the rot worse, and the rain fills my eyes faster than I can blink it away. I'm running apart in the rain, like wax. There's a shape in the second-story window of the house and it looks at me with red eyes.

Rain-channels cut deep into the lawn, tracing strange calligraphy around flowerbeds and between blades of grass. Wherever they go, the channels unbury the roots of plants. In their tangles, the roots are their own maze, with the giants under the dogwood trees and the eyelashes of the dead poppies all together in knots. The roots are growing in secret, underground, a inverted garden of white flowers, a sea-anemone garden swaying underwater.

The storm and the thunder run together with the raindrops into a drone. Ohhh, says the voice behind the thunder. Looooow. Naaaay. Oh. Lo. Ne, and again. Does that sound familiar somehow? Is that you, Angel? No, it's someone else. Was it one of the voices buried deep in the earthquake, one of the teeth that ground? I don't remember. I don't remember. I wasn't paying attention.

It is easy, it is easy, someone says. I am fascinated by these trenches opening up like canyons, like the map of a battle or the human hand, forcing solid ground apart like wet paper. I feel like I'm on the only bit of firm land left in the world. I sway a little, almost falling.

It is easy, it is easy. I take a step onto the tightrope garden. Roots and rivulets. Step, then another. Balance.

Oh low ne.

There are other people here, men and women and children with olive skin and long dark hair, just standing still, dressed in loincloths, all of them crying. Some of them have seashells in their hair, and their alphabet is knots. Ohhhh, low nay. Oh. Lonely. Oh lo ne.

Everything is blooming upside down. I can't see straight with eyes full of rain. I forgot the important things like eyelashes. I stagger a little, it's thrown my balance off. The mud is slippery and I have to go slow to keep from falling.

There's something just ahead. The dogwoods are bursting into rootbound bloom.

Here I am, and you are walking very slowly against the gray sky, the yellow haze. She is going away again.

On the other end of the strand between the rising water she is there. Ceille, I missed you. How've you been? She smiles. The smile I remember best. I've been well, Ceille. I've been dead, but otherwise no complaints. She nods.

We're in a scene now, the ghost of her and I. Both of us have our lines perfectly. It's like we've been doing this dialogue every night for years. We're old pros.

"Ceille, I was wondering if we could maybe get married," I say, reading from the script in my head. I wanted to write.

She tilts her head and looks sad. As if it comes as any surprise, but she was always an actress. "Andrew?" she says.

I nod sadly, going over the lines one more

time. "I mean," I say, quoting myself, "we could wait until after school, but I think it would be nice. We could wait, or maybe even just get an apartment or something somewhere for awhile."

She flashes a small smile. There's a nervous giggle in her voice that makes me want to break something. "Andrew, this is a joke, right? We haven't even really dated or anything."

"But...." I say. "I don't know any couples closer than we are. None of them really talk. We're great together, and I love you."

The smallest pause in the rain. The ghost twitch of a smile. "I love you too, Andrew, but just not like that. I never knew you were interested.

"You're my favorite person in the world, but I just never thought about you that way. Romantically."

"Why?" I say, losing interest in keeping up my part. I just want to leave.

"You can't explain these things, Andrew. I just never did. Maybe if you'd made some sign, given me some kind of hint, I would have had some time to think about this. It wouldn't be so much of a surprise." She looks somehow different from what I remember. Not nearly as fragile, but nicer somehow. More solid?

"I can change. C'mon. Just give me a hint.

What have I been doing wrong?"

"Nothing, Andrew. You're fine, I'm sure. I just... oh, Andrew, don't be sad. It'd kill me if you were sad over this."

I think of reasons, then. She doesn't want to talk about them. I say some other things. She walks away, back into the rainstorm. She writes, but I never read the letters. And then I'm dead.

This time, I change the scene. When she turns away, I follow.

It's hard in the rain to keep track of her and keep my footing both. I wish she'd turn around and notice me. Between the roots and the mud trying to make me stumble I'm not making much ground. None of the tightropes in the lawn leads to where I need to go. Tracing their dead ends and knots wears me out, and I can barely see her in the rain now.

There's something in my way. Is it her? It looks like her. It has her eyes and her hair the color of cinnamon, and her height and her wrists and her neck. I'm so grateful she noticed I was following her.

I start to apologize for what I said when I notice that it has wings, and it isn't her. I'm too tired to go around the angel, so I stop. I can't go around. I might trip on a bone. I might get tangled in roots. I'd fall off my wire. But she's in my way and I can't see Ceille any more.

"Pardon me," I say to my angel, hoping she will move so I can catch up with Ceille.

The angel doesn't say anything.

"Move over," I say. "I have to catch her."

The angel doesn't move. I shouldn't be surprised. When did she ever move, what did she ever say?

"Please get out of the way," I say, almost sobbing. Every word takes an entire breath. I can't see where Ceille's gone. Talking to the statue only kills valuable time that I need. I need it so much to meet up with her one last time.

I'm tired.

I scream at the angel. "You're just a doll! Get out of the way!" I try to push past it, but the rain makes me lose my balance and we both fall together in the mud. I dart my head up to try and see Ceille, but it's too late. The statue lies there, unblinking, with red wooden eyes in the rainstorm.

I call, but I've lost sight of her. "I miss you," I yell. "I love you." No one answers. She's gone. All the people are gone. After awhile, my voice breaks and I start to cry and it goes on for a long time with the rain.

After awhile I notice that I'm still here, face-down in the mud. The storm has tapered off into a sort of warm drizzle. The thunder has stopped talking. I am alone again in the yard.

No allegories, no angels, wooden or otherwise. This is what is true. I am in my backyard, in San Francisco, after the rain. The grass has gone wild over the years, and the dogwood tree I used to play in when I was small has gone to thorns and knotted, mazy branches. In the moonlight, the grass is silvery black against the fence, and the last of the dogwood flowers are fragile, ghost-white, caught in the thorns. My father planted the dogwoods and he made that fence. Here, behind it, the yard is tangled and overgrown with weeds, rootbound and dry, but it is alive. And I am here, dry and dead, but I can still move, and maybe move to somewhere better.

There is a woman with the improbable, searing name of Celatia Thompson, and she was a girl who breathed and who was wonderful. There was a statue made of dry tinder and many, many gathered roots, and it cast a shadow that resembled the woman and blocked the sight of her until she was gone.

It's too late. Again.

It would be easy to die here, to breathe mud and run downstream with it. It would be easy to linger and dry out here with my roots exposed, turning red and dusty. But on the other hand, it's just as easy to drink the rain. I stand up and step off the tightrope and I'm on solid ground.

Time goes by. It's day, now night again, with a million small stars blinking in space and no one but a few specialists knows their names. From time to time one of them loses its balance, sparks, goes out. Time goes on. I'm not going to chain the Winchester ghosts for Brannan. Or anyone else. No more chains, not for awhile, if ever. Starting now, I resign all my commissions. When I turn back from the sky, I see my Angel staring up at me from her place. She can stay there. I don't think I'll go back to working on her, at least for awhile.

SHACKLES

Richard Lee Byers

hen I came out of my daze — that's what it felt like — everything was ugly. The air stank of rot. The rasp of feeble lungs scraped my ears. All the shriveled bodies in the hospital beds were as dry and still as mummies. All but the nearest one, that is. Maggots wriggled in the pockets of slime on its sunken chest and withering cheeks.

Kind of scary, definitely disgusting. And I didn't like it. But in another way, I felt high. It was a rush just to stand up, to know that I could think and talk and move, even though I didn't understand why that should be.

I was afraid and happy at the same time. Later

I would figure out that death is always like that. It splits you into two pieces that never agree on anything. Sometimes one even tries to kill the other.

"Joey!" a man's voice called. "Joey Castelo!" I jerked around.

And I saw a scrawny guy in a filthy brown trenchcoat edging toward me. He had a badly sewn gray leather bag in his hand. I noticed eye holes and realized it was a mask. Somewhere on his body, metal clicked. I backpedaled.

It made me ashamed of myself. I must have had ninety pounds on him. I was a heavyweight boxer, for Christ's sake. But, as hard as he was trying to look friendly, I saw a hunger in his eyes. The same sick eagerness I'd seen in some of the fight fans when they thought somebody was really going to get the crap beaten out of him, or in junkies scoring a fix. At that moment, when I didn't understand anything that was happening, that desperate greed spooked me. I was sure he didn't have good intentions.

"It's okay," he said. "I'm your friend." I bolted through a doorway and down a hall. He yelled, "Stop!" His feet pounded after me.

The air still stank like rotten meat, but now I noticed an antiseptic smell too. A wheelchair and an IV rack gleamed in the fluorescent light and cardboard Halloween decorations, pumpkins, black cats, witches, ghosts, and skulls, hung on the wall.

That rattled me too. It wasn't Halloween, it was the middle of April, wasn't it? And the decorations didn't look cheerful and cartoony. Or rather, they did, but with an underlying strength and cruelty. Especially the ghosts and skulls. I almost expected them to bulge off the walls and come to life.

A voice spoke to me: They bother you because *of what they mean.* Even as I looked around, I realized I hadn't *heard* anything. The words were in my head, but not part of my thoughts. Like the voices crazy people hear.

No time to think about it, not with the rat in the coat chasing me. Somehow I knew I didn't want to think about it anyway. I ran on.

Who was that, asked the voice, *feeding the worms? Don't lie to yourself. You know.*

And suddenly, I did. The face on the pillow had been thin. Old. *Dead.* But it had been *mine.* And that meant I was dead too.

A black whirlwind screamed around me. I lost my balance and fell to one knee. The miniature tornado didn't rattle the venetian blinds hanging over the window at the end of the hall, or blow the decorations away. But the scrawny man had to fight his way through it. Leaning into the wind, coat and long, greasy hair flapping, he reached for me.

Just before he could touch me, the linoleum opened under me, and the whirlwind sucked me down into the floor. I tried to grab the edge of the hole, but only managed to cut my hands. The scrawny man screamed.

Then everything was roaring, spinning darkness. It felt like the storm was real but inside my head at the same time. Blasting away memories.

To this day, I don't know what I forgot. How could I? But I do know that the memories were a part of who I was. I can still feel the holes they left when they ripped away.

I tried to hold on to them, but I didn't know how. I guessed this was real death. The cyclone would strip me down to nothing.

Then the darkness brightened, and the shrieking died. I thumped down on a huge couch that smelled like somebody's dog. Cigarette burns dotted the cushions and arms.

I looked around. Everything was too big. The rat trap by the hold in the baseboard. The portable TV with the coat hanger wrapped around the antenna. My mom, sitting at the kitchen table with her checkbook and a stack of bills. Looking like she wanted to cry, she was separating the Final Notices from the others.

And then I got it. Things weren't too big. I was little again, a kid in the Tenderloin.

Once again, I felt too many things, emotions that didn't go together. I was grateful just to get out of the whirlwind with some of my mind left. I loved Mom so much that, horrible as death had been so far, I almost felt I'd gone to heaven, just because we were together. But it broke my heart to see her look as sad and tired as she always had in life. I hated the apartment, always shabby, with faded paper peeling off the walls, chipped porcelain in the sinks, torn screens in the windows, no matter how hard she tried to make it nice. Hated the hollow ache in my gut.

I tried to tell myself I was seeing the past. That all this was over. But everything felt as real as it ever had.

I started to cry myself, and then, without warning, the storm came back and blasted the room to pieces. I screamed, "Mom!" And stretched out my hand as the wind tumbled her away.

This time I only fell, flew, whatever, for a second, and I landed on my feet. The stink of sweaty socks, the musty smell of Franklin's Gym, filled my nose. People babbled. Bob Franklin's squeaky voice, a voice like a ten-year-old's even though he was as old and fat as a dinosaur, cut through the drone. "Move! Always move! And keep your left up!"

A punch wobbled at me, and my reflexes kicked in. I blocked, then moved in. My gloves slapped flesh. The other boy, a lanky black kid, covered up and stumbled back. I kept after him until the bell rang.

My friends swarmed through the ropes to pound me on the back, like I was some kind of hero. Even before the judges said anything, it was obvious I'd won.

It was the best moment of my life. I felt like I was growing, as if my body had to get bigger just to hold so much joy. I'd found something I liked, something I was really good at, something that made me feel strong and important. Maybe, if I worked hard, a ticket out of the slums. I could buy the sports car, designer clothes, and all the other luxuries I saw on TV. I could give Mom her own house, and make sure she'd never worry about money again.

My body swelled, growing from child to adult. The room ballooned to seat bigger and bigger crowds. One by one, fighters popped into the ring, and one by one I knocked them down. At the end, the hall turned into Madison Square

Garden and the man facing me was Larry Holmes. When he fell, the fans roared.

As soon as the ref lifted my arm, Emily, sweet, black-haired, laughing Emily, and my wonderful four-year-old Sarah, who looked just like her, jumped out of their seats and scrambled into the ring, just the way the guys had the day it all began.

I stooped to pick Sarah up. Grinning, she opened her arms. Then, as suddenly as bubbles burst, she, Emily, and everyone else vanished. Most of the lights exploded, showering sparks and plunging the arena into an empty blackness. Cheers echoed for another moment, then died away.

I peered around in horror and confusion. Soft laughter whispered through the dark. Squinting, I made out a handful of white faces scattered among the shadowy rows of endless seats.

"Who are you?" I yelled. "Where are my wife and little girl?"

"A beautiful dream," said one of the figures in the seats. Somehow I knew he meant winning the title, getting rich and famous. "But I'm afraid it's time to face reality."

The wind roared and the arena went completely dark. The storm tumbled me through the blackness, then threw me down on my back on a lumpy mattress.

My face, chest, and stomach throbbed. I pried my gummy eyes open. The left one, anyway. The right had swollen shut. The water stain on the bedroom ceiling was diarrhea brown in the pale sunlight seeping through the curtains.

I rolled over toward the night stand where I kept a pint of bourbon, my industrial-strength pain killers, and the baton. Moving hurt. It wrung a groan out of me.

As I popped the cap off an orange pill bottle, Emily came into the room. "Hi," she said gently. She'd learned to be quiet on days like this, the way she would if I'd had a hangover. "How do you feel?"

I just shrugged. I resented her sympathy. It made me feel guilty. Sometimes I wished she'd scream, What the hell's the matter *with you? Why can't you ever win?*

Actually, I did win, at least as often as I lost. But never the important matches, the ones that could start me up the ladder.

I felt like washing the pills down with a slug or two of booze, but I didn't want to see her wince. So I dry-swallowed them instead. "What time is it?" I asked.

"Just after two," she said.

I stood up. The floor rocked, then steadied.

"I've got to go."

"No! The doctor said you have to rest."

"Did he say he was going to pay for our groceries, too?" I limped to the dresser.

She followed. "I know we need money, but there has to be a better way to get it. What if somebody tries to hurt you?" Since I was a fighter and looked tough, people sometimes hired me as a bodyguard, or sort of a half-assed enforcer. To tag along when they had to meet people or run errands that made them nervous. I had a job like that today.

My guts churned. The pills were hard on an empty stomach. "Don't be stupid. There's nothing to it. All I ever have to do is stick out my chest and frown."

"Even if that's been true so far, it might not always be. And some of your" — her mouth twisted — "clients are criminals."

I pulled a black T-shirt over my head. Took a deep breath, trying to flush the anger out of my system. "Look, we've been through this. I can't work a regular job. I need the time to train."

Her big brown eyes studied me. Weighed me. I could tell she wanted to say something more, but was afraid to. Finally it came out. "You wouldn't have to if you quit."

Now it was my turn to stare at her. "What?"

"I know it's your dream," she said, touching my arm. "For a long time it was mine too, because you wanted it. But you aren't getting anywhere. Just more scarred and desperate every year. Maybe it's time to move on. You're smart, you could go back to school —"

I didn't mean to slap her. It was like my hand shot out by itself. She reeled back and fell across the foot of the bed. I saw the shape of my fingers, printed in white on her cheek.

Someone gasped. I turned. Sarah stood in the doorway, wide-eyed and trembling.

I froze. Her voice brittle, Emily said, "It's all right, sweetheart. Daddy was just... playing. Showing me something Mr. Franklin taught him. Go watch TV or something. Please."

The little girl stared for a moment longer, then fled.

I reached for Emily. "I'm sorry. I —"

She scrambled away from my hand. "Go! I can't be around you right now."

"I didn't mean —"

"Get out!"

The black storm howled, shattering the apartment and spinning me into darkness. When the roar died and the light came back, I was walking through the Castro, past leather shops, antique galleries and restaurants. David, my client, as Em had put it, was beside me. Gay couples strolled, holding hands. I felt more ashamed than I ever had before, but also mad at Emily for provoking me. In my pocket, my fist clenched on the ridged rubber grip of the baton.

I'd bought the club not long after I stumbled into the goon business. If I had to hit anybody I didn't want to use my bare fists, for fear of messing them up. The steel sections telescoped into the handle, making it easy and inconspicuous to carry, and they snapped out if I flicked my wrist.

When I first got the thing it was just a tool, but over the last year or so it had grown into something more. I carried it everywhere, liked to play with it, tapping it against my palm, or sliding the sections in and out. It soothed me. Made me feel good, the way that thinking about boxing used to.

This afternoon, I wished I'd get a chance to use it. Take out my frustrations. That made me even more ashamed.

David was a beach-boy type with a peroxided crewcut and teeth so white they could make you snowblind. He pointed at a bar with smoked windows. "That's the place," he said.

The world skipped and we were inside, sitting

at a corner table, schooners of beer and a platter of vegetables and dip in front of us. Across from us was Pete, David's ex-lover, the guy we'd come to see. Waving his hands, David begged him to stop making threatening phone calls to his new boyfriend.

With his horn-rimmed glasses, goatee, and corduroy jacket with leather elbow patches, Pete looked like an English teacher. The kind that didn't care if you knew how to spell or where to stick the commas as long as you could bullshit about your feelings. He seemed harmless, embarrassed and remorseful — a lot of that going around today. Eventually he even started to cry.

God knew what David had been so scared of. My mind wandered. I wondered how I could ever make things right with Emily and Sarah. And why I could never catch a break. Then David yelped and lurched backward, nearly upsetting his chair. The legs squealed on the hardwood floor.

I looked at Pete. On his feet now, he pointed a little snub-nosed revolver. The barrel glinted in the light of the tiffany lamp.

I'd scooted my seat too close to the table — God, what part of the job hadn't I screwed up? Somehow I jumped up anyway, snapped out the baton, leaned forward, and swung at Pete's shooting arm.

I clipped it, but not hard enough to make him drop the revolver. It exploded, and a dark spot appeared in the middle of David's chest. He sighed and slumped sideways out of his chair. Then the gun swung to cover me.

As I tried to recover my balance, the revolver spat pain into my head. The world turned red, then black. I never heard the second shot.

After that everything was dull aching or numbness, murk and shadows, voices I couldn't understand. I was a vegetable. But even though I couldn't think, certainly couldn't put ideas into words, a part of me still felt trapped inside my ruined brain and withered body. Still mourned the loss of Emily, Sarah, and everything else I loved. If I knew how, I would have died.

A voice said, "And finally, of course, you did die."

Abruptly I had my smarts and muscles again. I was back in the ring at the Garden. I hated the pale figures in the seats for making me relive the bad times, and felt sickeningly grateful to them for bringing the nightmare to an end. I wanted to jump out of the ring, kill them — and drop to my knees, sobbing, begging them not to hurt me anymore.

Mainly, though, I wanted to deny them the satisfaction of seeing how badly they'd shaken me. Pride, maybe, or self-preservation — look weak and the enemy will move in for the kill. So I took a deep breath, tried to make my voice come out strong and steady, and said, "Which one of you guys is Ralph Edwards? And when do I get my prizes?"

"Almost immediately," said one of the pale people. He stood up and sauntered down the aisle. "Provided you make an intelligent decision."

"About what?" I fought the urge to run. I needed to find out what this was all about. Besides, they had me surrounded. There was nowhere to go.

"About loyalty." By now he'd ambled close enough that I could see him pretty well. He was thin, with high cheekbones and a long nose. Maybe in his forties or early fifties. His haircut and manicure would have set a living man back a hundred bucks; his tux, a thousand. But rich and slick as he looked, he reminded me of the awkward, scroungy guy I'd seen before the whirlwind swept me away. He had the same greedy glitter in his sea-green eyes.

Later I came to expect that look in every face I met. That's another big truth you learn about death. It seems every one of us spooks is starving for something.

"We're talking about loyalty to you, right? Who are you?" I said.

I never saw him climb into the ring, but suddenly he was beside me. I flinched back a step. "The people who know how this place works," he said. "The ones who can help you shape your new existence."

"Meaning what?"

"Your life here will mirror your time on earth," he said. Up close, he smelled of cologne. Too much of it, really; the one crack in his classy image. "That's called karma. The question is, will it reflect your dreams or your sorrows? You can spend eternity as a champion fighter with a loving family, or as a vegetable in a nursing home. In one sense, it's up to you. In another, to us."

"Are you saying you're God?" I asked. "Or an angel?"

"This place isn't what you imagine," he said. "It's not what any church taught anybody to expect. I'm one of the people with access to the machinery. That will have to do for now."

"Why? Why won't you give me a straight answer?"

"Because the truth is complicated, and you're

short on time."

A chill oozed up my back. "At least tell me what you really want. What am I supposed to do for you?"

He shrugged. "Maybe nothing. But we want you to promise that if we ever need a favor, you'll do it for us. Oh, and we'd like that baton."

I felt a familiar weight in my bare fingers. I glanced down. Sure enough, my gloves were gone and I was holding the club. My trunks had turned into jeans and a T-shirt too.

My fist tightened. Like I said, I'd gotten attached to the baton, and in the middle of all this weirdness I liked having it all the more, just because it was familiar. "What do you need it for?"

"As a token of allegiance," said the man in the tux. "To seal the bargain. What's the difference? You don't need it anymore. You only acquired it because you were a *losing* fighter. On this side, my friends and I will make sure you win. That is, if we have a deal." He held out his hand.

Once again I didn't have a clue about what to do. The more the thin guy talked, the less I trusted him. He was way too smooth. I even wondered if he were the devil. But on the other hand, I was willing to suck up to Satan if that were what it took to avoid winding up with a bullet hole back in my brain.

I started to give him the baton, and then I got lucky. Skin slid over his left eye. For a second I thought he'd winked. Then I saw that his whole face looked loose and lopsided. He was wearing a mask, one so lifelike that I hadn't recognized it for what it was until it slipped.

There was something awful about that, and it made me distrust him even more. Scared as I was, instinct took over. I snapped the baton out and laid it across his forehead.

He staggered backward. The mask fell into two pieces, giving me a glimpse of the twisted leper face beneath.

The black whirlwind swept me up again. When it set me down I was standing on grass, and the sky overhead was a mass of fat gray clouds. I was standing in a cemetery, a spectator at a sparsely attended burial. Strangely, the flowers on the bronze coffin were already wilted.

I realized this must be my burial, because Emily was standing by the grave. She was wearing a gray suit. The skirt stirred in the fitful breeze. Her eyes and nose were red, and she dabbed at them with a lacy handkerchief. I wanted to call her name, or run to her, but something held me back. Maybe I sensed that she wouldn't hear or see me. Or maybe it was because I'd noticed the way the chunky guy beside her held her hand. Evidently, some time after I'd gotten shot she'd found herself another man.

I'm pretty sure I would have started to cry if a hand hadn't shot at my face. I tried to jerk away, but I was too slow. Grimy fingers grabbed a filmy sheet, a sort of membrane I hadn't realized was there, and ripped it off.

I felt the world shift. Either it was more real than it had been a second before, or I was.

The hand belonged to the rat in the trenchcoat. He had the hood on now. "Figured you'd come here," he chattered. "Figured you would, if you got away from the spectres." He reached inside his coat, brought out a pair of shackles, and reached to snap them on my wrists.

I guessed he thought I was in a daze. He was wrong. I was mad, sad, and glad to have somebody to take it out on. I whipped the baton down on his forearms. The blow cracked. He yelped, dropped the chain, and stumbled back.

I lunged after him and grabbed him by the collar. "Hi," I said. "I need information, so I'm going to ask you some questions. If you don't answer them, I'll beat you until you do."

"No!" he said. "You can't do that! I pulled off your Caul. I'm your Reaper! You're supposed to love and respect me!" He looked like a homeless person, and hearing this I wondered if, like a number of the bag ladies and beggars I'd run into, he wasn't at least a little nuts.

I yanked off his mask, exposing scared beady eyes, a big nose, and a weak, stubbly chin. His breath was rank. "Right," I said sarcastically, "seeing the handcuffs made me feel really devoted. Who are you? What are you?"

"George Montaigne," he said. "Just a wraith — a dead man —like you." He cringed. "No offense. I mean, you know you're dead?"

"Yeah. Who are the spectres?"

"Nasty spirits that Larvae — new wraiths — meet while they relieve their lives. They want to recruit you. Steal things." Trying not to be obvious about it, he squirmed, testing my grip.

I nodded. "I saw them." It made me feel a little better to hear that I hadn't clubbed St. Peter or the devil. "Now for the sixty-four-thousand-dollar question. Why are you following me? Why did you want to chain me up?"

"I've been watching you for a long time," George said. "At first, a lot of people were. But when you didn't die right away, they lost

interest. But not me! Nobody likes me, did you
know that? They all think George is weak and
off his head. But I was smart enough to be
patient! I kept coming back to check on you.
And now I'm the one who's got you!"

I jerked him up on tiptoe, just to plug him
back into reality. "That's not exactly the way it
looks to me. What did you and the other ghosts
want me for?"

"Every soul has value," he said. "But a
heavyweight boxer! A bodyguard! That could
be special. Our Mr. Montaigne could really get
to be somebody, controlling a property like that.
And then wouldn't the rest of them be sorry!"

"You're telling me that dead people don't
spend their time playing harps or burning in
hellfire or haunting houses. You have a" — I
groped for the right word — "society, just like
the living. Only you guys keep slaves."

"We call them thralls." He cringed again.

He didn't have to worry. Now that we'd
talked, he seemed too pitiful for me to enjoy
roughing him up. I shoved him away. "Get out
of here."

"Wait!" he said. "Maybe you and George can
make a different kind of arrangement. You need
somebody to show you the ropes. Otherwise
you'll die the final death! Or wind up with a

worse boss than me!"

"I'll take my chances," I said. Then a rust-spotted sedan with a crumpled fender, a make I didn't recognize, sped through the cemetery gate. It wove up the narrow lane, drifting on and off the grass, then pulled in behind one of the mourners' cars, lurching to a stop just inches short of a collision.

The driver climbed out and stumbled toward the grave. When I saw her face, I gasped.

It was Sarah, all grown up. That meant I'd lain in the nursing home for twenty years. No wonder every Reaper but George had gotten tired of waiting for me to croak.

Much as I adored my daughter, it didn't give me any pleasure to see her. She was drunk, and had on a low-cut shirt that left her slightly pudgy midriff bare. Her nipples poked bumps in the satiny cloth of her top. Her miniskirt scarcely reached the top of her thighs, and God knew how anyone as blitzed as she was could walk in her stiletto heels. Lipstick, rouge and eye shadow plastered her face. Much as I hated the thought, she looked like a whore.

But that didn't matter. The thing that filled me with horror was the ragged gash in her throat. Blood caked her chest. Weirdly, none of the funeral party seemed to notice. Her mother just looked glad to see her, but sad and embarrassed at the same time.

Earlier I'd sensed that I couldn't talk to the living, but I forgot all about that now. I ran to Sarah and gripped her shoulder. She reeked of blood, tobacco, and rum. "Sarah! What happened?" I cried.

It was like I'd grabbed some powerful machine. She tottered on toward the service, dragging me along as if I were weightless, not acknowledging me any more than a bus or a tractor would.

I dashed back to George, who was stowing the manacles back in his coat. "I don't understand," I said. "How can she walk around like that? Why don't the others help her?"

George smirked. "Who are you asking? Surely not young Mr. Montaigne. You've made it abundantly clear that you don't need his guidance."

I lifted the baton. "You said that wraiths can die again. Answer my questions, or I swear I'll kill you."

"All right!" George said. "The reason the quick — the living — can't see the cut is that it hasn't happened yet."

I started to understand. "Just like the flowers on the casket won't really wilt for a while."

George nodded. "Wraiths see death's shadow falling across the Skinlands. Death's clock, ticking away inside life. Sometimes we can even tell when the clock is about to strike."

I felt like I'd taken a hard punch. "You're saying she's going to die."

"Most likely before morning."

"That's my daughter!"

"I know. I remember her from when she used to visit you."

"There must be a way to save her!"

The little man said, "It would be hard." He paused to scratch the inside of his nostril. "But maybe. George has picked up some tricks, more than anybody thinks, even if the snotty guilds won't teach him. So, if we can make a deal —"

"Same deal as before. You help me or else."

To my surprise, he looked me in the eye and said, "No. Hurt me, kill me if you want to. But that won't save sweet Sarah, will it?"

"What do you want?" I asked.

He smiled. "Just let me put the shackles on you. After that, whatever happens, happens."

I told myself that wasn't so bad. Chained or not, I could overpower the little weasel, take the key away from him and free myself.

But I didn't believe it. I'd never believed in the spirit world, either, but that didn't change the fact that this was a different place, one where George understood the rules and I didn't. If he figured the manacles would hold me, he was probably right.

God, how could I even consider selling myself to anyone, let alone this sleazy little head case? The idea made me sick to my stomach. But not as sick as the thought of my daughter dying. "All right. But you don't chain me till afterwards."

I didn't expect him to go for it, but he did. "Deal." We shook hands. His was soft and clammy.

The service ended. People murmured to Emily, hugged her, patted her shoulder. As quickly as she could, she responded and moved on, working her way toward Sarah. I guessed she was afraid the kid would take off before she caught up with her.

But Sarah waited. "Hi, Mom," she said, digging a pack of Kools out of her sequin-studded purse. "Are you holding up okay?"

"Yes," Emily replied. Moving closer, I finally noticed the fine wrinkles at the corners of her eyes, the sprinkle of white in her thick black hair. "I've had a long time to get ready for this. I'm glad you came."

Sarah's mouth twisted. "Even looking like I

do?"

"All that matters is you're here. I hope you remember how much Daddy loved you."

I thought that for a second Sarah's hard expression softened, but I couldn't be sure. "Whatever. It was a long time ago." Blue smoke billowed from the hole in her neck.

"Why don't you come home for a few days," Emily said. "Mark and I would love to have you."

"Yes, do it!" I said. Though I didn't know why Sarah was in danger, it made sense that she'd be safer with her mom.

Emily's new man was standing just behind her. Sarah grinned at him. "Yeah, I'll bet he would. But I've got stuff to do."

"You really are welcome," said Mark. I could tell he meant it, but he had to work to mean it. I wondered if she'd insulted him, ripped him off, or what.

"Well, isn't that special? But come on, it's Halloween. Time to get out and par-ty!" She punched the air and bucked her hips.

"All right," said Mark, "but at least let your mother or me drive you wherever you're going. You're in no condition —"

"Jesus Christ!" said Sarah. "I came to see Daddy get planted, didn't I? Why can't you guys be satisfied with that? Why do you always have to hassle me?" She whirled and marched unsteadily back to her car.

"Go after her!" I said, but everyone just stood and stared. Em sniffled and lifted her hanky.

George grabbed my arm and yanked me off balance. "Come on! It's up to us now! Don't let her get away!"

We ran to the battered white sedan, reaching it just as Sarah opened the door. A Styrofoam cup and several miniature liquor bottles lay strewn across the floor. As she clambered in, George said, "Get on the roof!" Then he flowed into the back seat.

Even though I knew he was a wraith, that we both were, it still shocked me to see him melt through a solid object. For a second I froze, but the roar of the motor jolted me into action. I scrambled onto the car, threw myself down on the roof just as it jerked into motion. After another moment, Sarah slammed the door.

The ride back into the city was hellish. Sarah kept veering left of center. Taking curves too fast. Racing under lights that had already turned red. I was sure we were going to crash. That her head would shoot through the windshield and the broken glass would cut her throat.

I was holding on by my fingertips. Every time the car swerved, sped up or braked, it nearly threw me off. Even so, I pounded on the roof, trying to signal George to make Sarah pull over.

But he didn't, and somehow she avoided an accident. Finally the car rocketed past the sidewalk shills and neon lights of the sex clubs on Broadway, turned down a side street, and stopped in front of a rundown apartment complex.

As soon as George slid through the door, I grabbed him by the arm. "What's the matter with you?" I said. "How could you let her drive like that?"

"Do you think it's easy to reach them?" he asked. "That I can do it over and over, any time I want? Well, I can't. Not even on All Hallows. We won't open a door till we're sure she's in real trouble."

"What if it happens fast? What if you don't have time to react?"

He giggled. "Then I guess you won't have to try on George's chain after all." I stifled the urge to slug him.

Sarah climbed awkwardly out of the car. "Come on," George said. "When she goes in someplace, you have to slip in with her or get left outside. It'll take you days to learn to walk through walls."

We followed her through a wrought-iron

security gate and up an unlit flight of concrete stairs. The click of her high heels echoed. She kept swaying and fumbling at the wall to catch her balance. What if she slips? I thought. What if she tears her neck open on the edge of one of the steps?

She didn't, but I almost fell scrambling to get into her apartment. I wondered, if the door had closed on me, would it have cut me in two?

Her place was even more of a dump than my childhood home, because unlike my mom, she wasn't even trying to keep it clean. The furniture was dusty. Ashtrays overflowed. Dirty glasses, empty beer bottles, pizza boxes, and Chinese take-out cartons littered the floor. The air smelled of garbage.

Sarah turned on the stereo and music blared. At least I guessed it was music. I'd always loved rock, but I'd never heard any like this. I couldn't catch the words or a tune either. It seemed like the band had just tried to make as loud and ugly a noise as possible. It jolted me, reminded me again of just how many years I'd been away.

Sarah wove into the bathroom. George flopped down on the couch. "Might as well get comfortable," he said.

It was good advice, but I was too edgy to take it. I fidgeted and paced. Sarah sat down with a beer, dozed off, and started to snore. Time crawled by. Finally, beyond the smudgy windows, the sun went down.

My fist clenched on the baton. I wanted to break something, but knew I couldn't. Not when the world was more solid than I was.

"What's the problem?" asked George.

"I don't know. I guess I don't like it that whatever's going to try to hurt her is going to come at her out of the dark."

"Hey, that's good. We want it to happen at night, because now it really is All Hallows. It would have been a bitch reaching her before."

Head lolling, Sarah snorted in another breath. "She was such a sweet kid," I said, wondering why I was telling him. I guess it just needed to come out. "You should have seen her at the gym. When she was around, every thug, bouncer, and biker who worked out there turned into Captain Kangaroo. And I was going to give her all the things I never had. This perfect life. Now look at her. Passed out in this shithouse. If she hadn't seen me hit her mom, if I hadn't gone off and died —"

"Did you love her?" George asked.

"I still do."

"Did you do your best for her? Would you have stayed with her?"

"Sure."

"Then don't beat yourself up. What's the point?"

For a moment, I almost liked him. I felt like I'd caught a glimpse of what was left of a nice guy, still hiding inside the shifty, crazy lowlife he'd turned into. Then somebody banged on the door.

Sarah moaned and squirmed. Her bloodshot eyes fluttered open. She muttered a curse, lurched up, and trudged across the room.

Horrified, I realized the caller could stick a knife in her as soon as she opened the door. For all I knew, he was a jealous ex-lover, like David.

Fortunately, he wasn't. He was a she, a tall, light-skinned black woman dressed in a sexy parody of a cop uniform. Except for studded bracelets, her arms and shoulders were bare, and only fishnet stockings covered her shapely legs. A domino mask hung under the bill of her cap.

"You look like shit," she said. "Why aren't you ready?"

"Chill," said Sarah. "It'll only take me a minute. Make yourself a drink."

To my surprise, it did only take her a few minutes to change from a punchy-looking wreck with tangled hair, smeared makeup, and stale, wrinkled clothes to a lively, pretty young woman

— or at least that's what she would have looked like if I could have ignored the phantom wound — in a skintight devil suit. She still had a teenager's energy, and apparently the nap had done her good. She pulled on a headband with a pair of horns attached, picked up her purse and a plastic pitchfork, and then she and her friend went out to paint the town.

For the next few hours they drank and danced their way from one club, one Halloween party, to the next. Eventually they wound up in SoMa. Except for the bars everything was closed, and the landscape looked spooky. Wisps of fog coiled in the empty streets. A full moon floated overhead.

Now and again I saw things I knew the living didn't, sights that were part of my new world. Shimmering, seething cracks and potholes, and shadows that looked too black. A woman on fire, chained ten feet up a telephone pole. The crackle of the flames and the stink of burnt meat made me sick.

But I was too worried about Sarah to think about any of it. It was all I could do just to stay close to her. Often the quick stepped out of my way, but not when the room was so jammed that they didn't have anywhere to go. And I could no more shove through them than I could have pushed through a stone wall.

Without warning, in the middle of a dance, she turned and headed for the front of the bar, twisting and squirming through the crowd. When I tried to follow, two long-haired kids in black started slamming their bodies together. The bigger one clipped me and knocked me down.

Feet stamped all around me, feet that could probably mash me to jelly. Somehow I scrambled up without getting trampled, but by then both Sarah and George had disappeared.

I tried to follow Sarah, aiming for spaces in the crowd that generally closed just as I reached them. As I grew increasingly frantic the room seemed to get hotter, until I felt like I was suffocating. Drunks in costumes lurched against me, bouncing me back and forth like a ping-pong ball.

Then a tiny redhead in a pink ballerina outfit jostled me into a corner. I slammed into the wall, turned, and saw a solid wall of bodies penning me in.

I started to lose it then. Suddenly I was sure that the time had come, Sarah was going to die while I was trapped. I threw myself at the people in the way, cursing them, shoving, lashing out with the baton.

At first it did about as much good as beating on the side of a battleship. But then something happened.

I'd already seen that sometimes the living avoided me without quite knowing why. Now, somehow, frantic as I was, I got more noticeable and scary than before. The people in my way started to look nervous. Then downright panicky. Finally one guy in a Stetson, vest and chaps yelled and threw himself backward, reeling into somebody else's table. Wine and highball glasses crashed to the floor.

I dove through the gap the cowboy had left me. Now other people scrambled aside. They couldn't see what was charging across the room — in a minute they'd probably convince themselves that nothing had been — but they knew they didn't want it touching them.

I found George hanging around the exit. "Where is she?" I said.

"She needed to pee," he said. "There's a line for the ladies' room, so she went into the alley."

"Why aren't you watching her?" God, it wasn't bad enough that he was crazy and wanted to make me a slave. He had to be an idiot too.

"Our Mr. Montaigne is a gentleman," he said. "He'd never spy on a woman at such an intimate moment. A lot of wraiths do, stuck-up bastards who think they're better than I am —"

"Get out there and check on her!"

Inside the hood, his beady eyes blinked. "Well. If you insist." He slid through the wall. When he came back I could see that something had jolted the goofiness out of him. "It's happening," he said.

I spun toward the door, then remembered I couldn't open it. And even if some quick guy opened it for me right away, before it was too late, what was I supposed to do after that?

George threw his arms around me. "Brace yourself," he said. "This is going to hurt."

For a second, nothing happened. Then pain ripped through my body. George and I both dropped to our knees.

I could tell the little guy had done it. Shifted us into the world of the living. The air felt different. Cleaner somehow, even in a crowded, smoky bar. I lifted my head, expecting to see everyone staring, but nobody was. No one had noticed us pop in.

"Go," George wheezed. "I can't —" He started coughing.

I jumped up, tore the door open, and ran out. Except for the scuff of my sneakers and the hiss of my breath, the night was silent.

I dashed around the concrete-block building,

not trying to move quietly, just fast. And apparently Sarah's attackers heard me coming. They were waiting for me.

They looked like teenagers. The big one in the Frankenstein mask pointed a pistol at me and the smaller one with the fluffy multicolored wig and red clown nose waved a knife.

Behind them, her shirt hiked up above her breasts, my daughter sprawled motionless on the asphalt. The bottom of her costume lay several feet away. Its pointed tail looked like a dead snake. Sarah still had the bloody hole in her neck, and by now, for all I knew, it might be real.

"Hey, asshole," said Frankenstein. "What's —"

I threw myself at him. I guess I startled him and made his arm jerk, because the gun banged, but he missed. I clubbed him on the shoulder, then the head. He fell.

As I turned, the clown lunged, his knife flashing at my chest. I threw up my left arm to block. The knife stabbed into my wrist, then slid, drawing a line of pain down to my elbow. I hit the clown three times. He dropped the knife, staggered back, and turned to run. Mad as I was, much as I would have liked to smash his skull in, I let him go. All I really cared about was Sarah.

And as I knelt beside her, the gash in her neck closed and the blood evaporated from her chest. I touched her and she wailed and thrashed away from me.

"It's okay!" I said. "It's all over!"

She turned her head hesitantly, like she was afraid I was one of the rapists playing a cruel joke on her. "Who are you?" she asked.

"Don't tell her," said a voice behind me.

I looked around. It was George, still panting, holding on to the side of a dumpster.

"It's not a good idea," he continued. "Not when you have to go back."

"The hell with that," I said. "Why should we? I saw enough to know it's better here."

"Because we're not alive," said George. Trembling, dazed, Sarah stared at him, then back at me. "Look at your arm."

I didn't want to, but I did. The cut still stung, but it hadn't bled at all.

"I don't care what I am. My kid's messed up. She needs me. And I don't think you're up to the job of dragging me back."

He sighed. "I didn't say I was. But I don't have to be. It's going to happen by itself."

He was right. A moment later I felt the shift. I tried to fight it by sheer willpower, but it didn't work. Going back didn't hurt, I guess because the death side was where I belonged.

Sarah looked about wildly. "Where are you?" she yelled. "Where did you go?"

"I'm still here!" I said. "I'm right beside you!"

She didn't hear. She just fumbled to get her pants on, picked up her purse and stupid toy pitchfork, and staggered around the corner of the building. I wanted to go after her, but something held me back. I guess I knew it wouldn't do either of us any good.

"Cheer up," said George. "You saved her."

"For tonight."

"Don't complain. That's as much as anybody ever accomplishes." He unbuttoned his filthy coat. Inside, the chain rattled. "And now I believe it's time to pay the invaluable Mr. Montaigne for services rendered."

Fear wriggled in my guts. I said, "Right now I'm grateful to you. But if you put those bracelets on me, we're enemies. Do the decent thing, let me off the hook, and we can be friends. Partners, like you talked about before."

It was no good. When he sneered, I could see that the nice-guy part of him had crawled back into its hole. "Oh, great idea! Pass up a sure thing for an IOU! No, I think we'll stick with the original arrangement."

I took a deep breath and held out my arms.

Even today, I don't know why I did it. Maybe because I'd broken too many promises before. I'd told myself I'd be heavyweight champ; Emily and Sarah that I'd give them happy lives; David that I'd protect him; and I hadn't delivered on any of it. Now, in a strange, sick way, I had a chance to do better.

Besides, I heard the nasty voice from the nursing home snarling away inside my head: Hit him! Just hit him and walk away! It doesn't matter what he did for you, or what you promised! You can't let anybody make you a slave! Even though it was echoing my own feelings, I didn't trust it. Maybe I already sensed that it was the part of me that had slapped Emily, the part of me I hated. At any rate, I had a hunch that it wanted to hurt me.

When the second cuff snapped shut, a wave of cold and weakness washed through me. My knees went rubbery. After a second my strength trickled back, but I had a hunch it would drain away again, any time I tried to hurt George or disobey his orders.

"Oh, yes!" he crowed, dancing for joy. "Chains of Stygia! Even the ordinary ones will hold anything, and that one's special. You wouldn't believe how hard it was for even a sharp operator like George to get his hands on it. And now, as soon as you feel up to it, we have places to go and people to see. You have matches to fight and opponents to kill!"

As I trudged after him, I promised myself that someday, somehow, I'd win my freedom back, then find a way to help Sarah straighten out her life. The voice laughed at my intentions. The shackle chain clinked, and the hard cuffs cut into my wrists.

CANCER

Marc Miller

t has been years since I spent a day without pain. Pain is more than the chemical signal of an anguished nerve ending: When processed by the brain, it becomes an emotion, enhanced and flavored by its meaning in a larger sense, as it portends change, disappointment, and death. That emotion has filled my days.

My suffering began four years ago when I noticed, in passing, that a small sore on my wrist would not heal. I made an appointment at the HMO and waited the standard three weeks. Perhaps my initial concerns were a result of having too much time to think — too much time to worry.

Friends and relatives have always claimed that I take things too seriously, that I think too much. Perhaps it was in the course of my normal thought process that I developed the fear that there was more to the abrasion than a bit of discomfort.

Waiting for the appointment compounded my fears. By the day of the appointment, I had half convinced myself that I had only a few months to live. In the weeks before my visit with the doctor, I spent several evenings in the local university library, reading medical textbooks, journals, even a CD-ROM about modern medical miracles. I looked up unhealed sores, the seven warning signs of cancer, even cancer itself.

Dr. Wertz was originally a Canadian, educated in Nova Scotia. He had worked for more than five years in the Canadian medical system before emigrating to the United States. He had been my doctor for more than twenty years. When I first came to San Francisco, a friend at work had recommended him when I was having trouble with my allergies. I kept going back for physicals, check-ups, small things.

Ten years ago, Dr. Wertz had transferred his

personal practice to the HMO. He'd sent me a nice letter detailing his decision and how difficult it was for him to close down the practice he had spent so much of his life building. He felt that he needed more time to be with his family and that the HMO would allow him to do so. He also wrote about the benefits of the HMO, and he invited me to join. I checked with my personnel department, filed some forms, and made the switch.

I liked the familiarity of knowing my own doctor. He was always interested in me, talking about my job, my hobbies, before dealing with whatever minor medical problems I had. A trust factor had developed between us, and I felt good about what he had to say:

"This isn't anything to worry about, John," Dr. Wertz reassured me. "It's a nick like everyone gets in the course of yard work. It's almost healed now."

"Aren't there tests or something you can do to make sure?"

"Of what? Do you think this could be something specific?"

I hesitated. He was the expert, not me. "Cancer?"

He laughed, gently. "It's just a nick, John." His bedside manner was superb; he had said my name twice already. "I'm going to prescribe a vitamin E salve; you can pick it up at the pharmacy downstairs. If you don't see any improvement by the beginning of the month, we'll look at it again."

The salve was free, covered by the HMO plan at the pharmacy.

■

Eventually, the sore healed. Three months later, I had another one. I used what was left of the salve and it cleared up in about a month. A year later, I had yet another. I made an appointment, waited four weeks, and finally saw Dr. Wertz. Again he reassured me, again I asked about cancer, and again he prescribed a salve. Eventually, the sore cleared up.

The sores were more an annoyance than a real problem. Once Dr. Wertz discounted their malignancy, I did as well. Sometimes I wonder why I saw the doctor about the sores at all.

The third time I brought an unhealed sore to Dr. Wertz, he looked over my file and suggested additional tests. Scheduling took several weeks; analyzing the results took several more.

This time, we met in the doctor's office

(rather than in an examination room). His desk was clean and well polished. As I waited, I spent a long time looking at his diplomas, the framed prints, the pictures of his wife and children. I had absorbed myself so completely in the lives of this happy, smiling family that I did not notice Dr. Wertz entering the room. In retrospect, perhaps my mind was not able to handle the anticipation and my body unable to contain the physical manifestations of my fear. I reflected upon the simple and convivial lives of a family I knew little about because I could not handle the pain in my own.

He came in, greeted me, sat down heavily behind his well-polished desk and leaned forward to speak.

"John, I have some serious news for you. Based on our lab tests, our preliminary diagnosis is a malignancy."

"Cancer?" I wanted to protest. That was what I had been afraid of the first time. My fears from those first few weeks came back in a wave. I felt cheated; he was my doctor and he was supposed to take care of me. But I couldn't find the words.

"We may have caught it in time. Let's talk about your options."

He scheduled me for chemotherapy. He

prescribed painkillers. He referred me to a counselor and to group therapy sessions titled "Dealing With Your Illness," and "How To Fight Back."

After I left his office, I realized that Dr. Wertz's usual smile had been absent.

Following months of failed treatments and painful tests, I gradually began to realize that, regardless of the doctor's optimism, I was dying. I would be dead within a year. Nothing would cure me. Nothing would save me. Perhaps the chemotherapy would delay the end for a few months, but no more.

■

My cancer became a constant source of pain and it is pain that heightens the sensibilities and strengthens the thought processes. I often thought about the unresolved parts of my life: my relationships with my parents, with my children. I thought about dying, and of my now never-to-be-accomplished plans for life. Beneath a philosophical exterior, I raged at my body for betraying me.

■

"Do you know how an HMO works?" I was having lunch with a newfound friend, a fellow outpatient in chemotherapy. He explained it to me.

"With most doctors, you pay for the treatment they give you. If you're well, you don't pay anything. It's different with an HMO. You pay so much a month or a year; everyone in the HMO does, whether you use it or not. When you're sick, they're supposed to treat you, no matter what. If you have a broken arm, they set it. If you need a heart transplant, they do it. If you have cancer, they treat it."

"That's what they're doing for me. Treating my cancer." I thought I understood.

"John, you don't understand. They get the same money whether they treat you or not. They charge a thousand people a thousand dollars a year: that gives them a million dollar budget to treat everyone on the plan. Their profit comes from cutting costs. Why do you think it takes four weeks to see a doctor? Why do you think the doctor ignored your symptoms for two years?"

"You mean..."

"Any competent doctor would have caught your cancer the first time he saw it. There are tests; it's just that they cost money. He's under orders not to exceed a certain dollar amount on the first visit. Sure they gave you a vitamin E salve; it cost them next to nothing. They only do the big tests once you become insistent enough."

My frustration and anger found a focus. I had trusted my doctor. I had trusted the hospital. I had never questioned it; I'd just depended on them to take care of me. And they had let me down.

I remembered a news item from Texas: A man walked into a doctor's office in the hospital, shot him dead, and walked out before anyone could react. They never caught him.

For a time I rooted for the victims in medical malpractice suits. I became fascinated with news stories about medical incompetence; I clipped out the newspaper accounts, saving them and filing them away. My compulsive behaviors continued apart from my family and without the knowledge of my friends. Dying in style—with grace—is what they wanted from me, and that is what I would give them.

I thought about heaven. I suppose if death is the final end, then there is nothing to be done about it, but I chose not to waste time pursuing that end. There were days when my death promised to be a release... a passing on to the heaven that we expect. On the other hand, I felt a profound regret that the things I wanted most in this life for myself and my family would never come to be. The gentle end we all expect—old, surrounded by family and children and grandchildren—would not be mine.

■

On the last day of my life, I woke with an intense pain in my gut. It tortured me; I writhed trying to find a position that would reduce or relieve the intensity. Nothing helped. I couldn't think; I couldn't focus. I wanted to scream, to do anything I could to stop the searing pain.

Sometime during that day, my wife called the paramedics. In a swirl of activity, they transported me to the hospital. By the end of the day, I was half-way comfortable in a sterile room with my family by my side and pain-killers pumping through my veins.

And through the red haze of pain and delirium that clouded my mind that day, thoughts came back to me time after time: This shouldn't have happened... I shouldn't be dying... my own doctor has failed me...

When I died that day there was no reluctant acceptance, no resolution, no peaceful escape from the anguish of physical ills. I did not ascend to a distant bright light that held me captured by it's utter peace and tranquil splendor. I simply went in pain and regret...nothing more.

■

Death is a turbulent sea filled with delusions and shadows. I awoke drowning, deep beneath the surface, my limbs turned and twisted by the current. I never thought to breathe, didn't need to. Everywhere, I was bitten by small fish with knife-sharp teeth. I screamed, but no one heard. I drifted fathoms down, tossed by a current of disorientation. From time to time, the current would slow and I saw things.

I found myself standing in a crowd. One person I recognized...my wife with red, dry eyes drained of tears. Some comforted her; still others made polite conversation in the corners of the room. And the faces of relatives and friends drifted, approaching me, expanding themselves as they drew near — distorted images of those I once knew. The colors of their eyes and the tones of their skin blended in winding bands of light and dark, color and shade. I stood before them, squinting in confusion as a man gazeing upon a distant place upon a landscape far before him.

I drifted for just the slightest moment, and found myself standing on a hill between a line of cars and a crowd of people. The sky was clear and cloudless and its dull blaze brightened the scene before me. I could make out faces and landscapes. The distortions of death had lessoned their load.

This was an average day, my funeral day. I was drawn to the crowd. I walked through them, and as I passed through each one, I felt their emotions: Boredom, distraction, intellectual sympathy, mild grief... Deeper emotions closer to graveside: Despair, greed, depression, relief. As I stepped through to the grave itself, my casket began its six-foot journey, and I was swept away by a wave of grainy darkness. I looked back at my crowd of mourners. Doctor Wertz was not among those mourning for me.

For a long time, the dark sea carried me, showing nothing, relinquishing no answers. I wondered if this was heaven, or hell, or something men had never dreamed of. Sometimes a hand would reach out to mine.

Our fingers would touch and release, miss, miss again, and finally we caught. This person, this guide, tried to drag me to the surface, above the sea, out of the storm, but it was too strong. We were carried along; we drifted together for what seemed like years. My nameless companion pulled me toward other visions that grew in their clarity and haunted me with a stark and rigid sorrow.

■

There was a tall, thin man speaking at a podium. He wore an expensive suit and stood out because everyone else wore white medical coats. For some time, I could not understand the words that he spoke. I could hear only their tone and I was struck by the dry, empty sound that escaped from his expressionless lips. As I listened in reverie to the paper-thin monotony of the speaker's voice, his words presented their significance to me and I listened to them closely. "Doctors, this hospital has operated at a loss for the last three quarters. We aren't a charity, and we can't keep this up."

I watched dispassionately. Most of the men in the room were faceless. I recognized Dr. Wertz, my own doctor, in the third row, and felt a twist in my gut.

"Needless tests. Overhead costs. Over-diagnosis of hypochondriacs. Running this hospital requires that we be good stewards of our resources. Each of you has a responsibility to keep our expenses and costs to a minimum."

One of the younger doctors interrupted. "You mean to tell me that we should not treat our patients to the best of our ability? I find such a suggestion intolerable."

The man in the suit continued; as he spoke, I saw how thin he was, that he had the marks of death on his face. "Dr. Myers, we are all physicians and we have our duty to our patients. We all agree with that. But we also know that fully half of the people we see are just looking for quick cures for minor ills. Overbooking appointments is a proven strategy that weeds out the minor ailments and the hypochondriac complaints. When we make routine patients wait several weeks to see a doctor, the minor ills clear up all by themselves. The genuinely ill come back, and then they receive the treatment they need.

"The hospital administration has prepared a protocol defining guidelines on initial patient intake. In fact, the computer has a simple score based on your patient evaluation. We don't want to turn away the critically ill, but we can't hospitalize every client who comes through the door."

Another doctor spoke up. "I find this procedure potentially barbaric." He was calm and analytical. "It is clear that, by reducing diagnosis to a computer procedure, we are not going to give the best possible treatment to our patients."

The administrator was equally calm. "Of course, Dr. Gustavson, you have the option of returning to private practice rather than working for this HMO. But the Board of Directors has already approved these cost-cutting measures, and they are a required procedure for everyone on staff."

Somehow I could see into the souls of the doctors in the room. All understood what this new procedure meant; five, maybe six, objected. My former doctor was not one of them.

The sea's turbulence swept over me, splashed me, carried me away in a rush of anger and pain.

■

I didn't understand the next vision.

I stood in a car dealership surrounded by convertibles and luxury sedans. As I gazed upon the flashy showroom I was momentarily awed by the presence of it's fantastic machinery. Chrome and brilliant hub cap, engine power and tinted window greeted me with a sparkling magnificence. I approached a huge, shining, black vehicle and climbed inside, sinking into the glory of it's leather, bucket seats.

In a rush of energy, the car seemed to drive from the showroom. I drove by many people and I could see the looks of admiration upon their faces. A pride overtook me that I had never felt before.

For a very long moment I felt no pain and I held no remorse. I drove past my wife and children standing at the side of the road. I drove beyond their pain and I felt only joy, the ecstasy of speed and the beauty of my perfect vehicle.

I do not know how long I drove. I only know that my arrival back in the showroom returned my dispair, my animosity. The cars disappeared before my eyes and the current swept me away.

■

I saw my family once again.

My children played in a field with their dog. My wife, my widow, watched silently. I looked deep into her eyes; I'd always loved her eyes. This day, they were bright, with only a hint of tears. Eventually, she got up and joined them and after a long, long time, she smiled.

I still held the hand of my nameless guide. Patiently, he held me steady as we drifted.

We found ourselves in the car dealer's showroom again. This time I noticed the floor: light green ceramic hospital tile. More than one man on the floor wore a white medical coat.

The current became unusually turbulent and finally swept us away. I left the scene with a raw anger in my gut and I did not know why.

This time, we were carried up toward the surface. The water's blood color thinned; the biting fish retreated. We burst through into the air and suddenly we stood, my guide and I, on a vast plain. Smoke drifted in the distance; The landscape was burned and it's structures destroyed.

He took me by both shoulders, held me tightly, sternly. He was saying something to me, but I could not hear him. And then, with one swift, complete motion, he pulled something from my eyes. I realized that the pain I had lived with for so many years was gone; my physical pain had been replaced by pure emotion, anger, and hatred. My senses were cleared of confusion and my being filled with a welling rage.

■

My guide and I talked. "Am I dead?"

"Yes, John."

"Where am I?"

"This is a world the inhabited by the dead; we are in the shadows of the living world."

"I don't understand."

He was patient with me. He spoke slowly and with understanding. "When someone dies without resolution, they end up here, bound to the places and people that hold them."

"I'm a ghost?"

"Sort of, John. Sometimes we say wraith. People who have led full, happy and complete lives don't seem to be here. The people here are trying to resolve something. When they do, they go on. On the other hand, some people never go on. They hold to this place forever.

"Because I'm here, I must be holding on, is that right?"

"That's right."

We talked for hours. He warned me about others here who would catch and enslave me. He told me how to live and survive. Finally, he left; leaving me alone to watch the shadows of the living.

I was alone now and aware of my circumstances; my anger and my rage were my only emotions. Occasionally I would laugh to myself: *There really were evil, tormented spirits on earth...*My laughter was never genuine, never warm. It was the laughter of a madman.

■

How I ended up at the HMO is something which is still unclear to me. I do not remember how I got there. I simply remember feeling driven to go.

The hospital is a place of death. Orderlies scrub the walls and floors, but I can see the blood nonetheless. Cracked and broken tiles show the decay they try so hard to hide. I could see the death in patients' faces. I was surrounded by a gray haze inhabited by indistinct shapes and muffled voices. None of these nameless faces mattered to me. There was only one who I was drawn to. Only one that I knew I needed to find.

Dr. Wertz sat alone in his office at the HMO. I stepped through the wall and stood before him at his desk for the first time. He could not see me, but some part of him sensed my presence. He looked up, puzzled, then returned his attention to his video monitor and its continuing education course. I waited until he was again engrossed, and then I moved closer. I wanted him to know I was here. I leaned forward, and as I did, I could sense his thoughts. He was incredibly bright, filled with medical knowledge. My anger spilled over onto him. He felt it, was startled, stood up, shivered, and looked around.

I waited until he sat back down, and I lowered myself into his chair. Eventually, he turned off the video monitor and went home checking behind him as he went.

I spent my days and nights waiting for Dr. Wertz to come to work. It was like I was tied to him with elastic chains: No matter how far apart we went, we eventually came back together.

I would wait until he was alone. I wanted to see him, and I wanted him to sense my presence. Sometimes I deliberately avoided him for weeks, lulling him into a sense of complacency, relishing the idea of surprising him. Then I would pounce on him late at night, sit beside him, and let him feel my presence. Sometimes I would find him in a corridor and stand in front of him, forcing him to walk through me, sensing for a fleeting instant my hatred and rage. It worked best at night when he was alone.

Several times during the gray haze between encounters with Dr. Wertz, I asked myself why I did this, and I never satisfactorily answered. I drew a form of pleasure by hurting the man who brought about my death, but at the same time I was empty, frustrated that he didn't understand what was happening to him. In the beginning his blind disorientation added to my pleasure, but with time, my need for him to understand grew. I needed for him to know what he had done.

■

Eventually, I decided that I should go to Wertz's home. When I stepped outside, I saw death in everything: In buildings, in vehicles, in the faces of those walking.

It took me three days to reach the home, hiding in the shadows, learning to fear the dead beings that inhabited the streets.

His house was a well-kept mansion with a manicured lawn and a three-car garage. I crept in during the day when he wasn't home. I hid in the far corners of the house waiting for him. His wife came home first, a beautiful woman with only a hint of pain on her face. Wertz came in about eight, and I watched them eat dinner and talk of symphonies. I waited patiently until he was asleep, and then I slowly, carefully, lay down on the bed inside of him and dreamed...

I flew a kite on the March winds and laughed as it careened against the bright white clouds of spring. I grew up; I started a factory job and graduated to management. I courted

my wife-to-be, picnicking beneath bright
summer skies. I saw my children as babies,
youngsters, and finally teens. Then I saw the
doctor's office, and myself. And as my person
changed from a whole, healthy man to a
cancerous invalid, and finally a raging dead
man, he knew who I was and he knew what he
had done. He woke up screaming, his face rigid,
his heart pounding.

I spent a good deal of time in the Wertz
household following that incident. I was not
satisfied with simply one instance of
recognition; I wanted him to live with the
knowledge of his evil...if he could. Time after
time I dreamed him my rage, and time after
time he was robbed of more of his sanity. When
I left the home, there was very little left of the
man.

Eventually, Dr. Wertz stopped coming to
work. Someone new took over his office. I was
reduced to wandering the hospital halls alone.
I tried haunting the accountants at the HMO,
but they are dull, faceless people with no
concept of the gravity of their crimes. Time has
worn me down.

My guide visits me from time to time and we talk. He has told me of the heavens and hells on the far shores of the turbulent sea. Time has dulled my rage, and I often wonder about oblivion. If I were to dive in, I might come up on the other side, and if not?

END.

GLIMPSES OF BEFORE

john H. Steele

ustin's last thoughts were not of bitterness, surprisingly enough. "Don't go. You can't leave me here," he told Randi.

"I'm just going home for a few days," she answered as she stuffed clothes into her overnight bag, ignoring such niceties as folding. "You know these earthquakes wreck my nerves, and I'll never get any work done. I might as well get out of San Francisco. I can see these buildings going over like dominoes."

"A three-story brownstone is not going over like a domino," he pointed out. "Besides, what'll I do?"

"Come with me."

"You know your mother doesn't want me there, and what about the job? I'm still waiting to find out about that restaurant job. Can't you use that nervous energy here? Paint some fucking dominoes or something."

Randi stopped packing for a moment and pulled her dark hair back out of her face. "If you don't want to deal with my mother, don't come. I'm going."

"Go then. See if I care."

She stuffed in two more wadded-up shirts and zipped her bag. "Look, I'm not your babysitter, for Christ's sake." Her tone softened. "I love you, Justin, but I need to get away."

And so, despite his protests, she left. The next day Justin found out that the restaurant job had fallen through. What else was there to do but stop by the liquor store?

His last thoughts were not of bitterness or abandonment. Instead his mind turned to childhood, playing stickball in the wide alley behind his father's bar. The ball ricochetted off a trashcan, and Justin was running after it. As he dashed into the street, he could hear his mother's voice telling him always to stop and look both ways. The massive Buick was barrelling down on him. He froze as the seconds stretched into hours. The tires screeched. In that instant, Justin wanted to take those steps back, to undo them, but he could not.

That car had been able to stop.

Strange last thoughts, of deliverance, when he wanted to be angry — angry at himself, angry at everyone, angry at life. Justin did not ponder this for long; his life was being stripped away a layer at a time. The bitterness was already gone. The forgotten love was next, then his thoughts, memories, name, his entire sense of self, all stripped away, mercilessly, completely.

There was release. He was floating in warm water. The soothing massage washed over him, much more potent than a hot bath. He could feel himself flowing into the pool, merging, ceasing to be separate from it. What had been before was no longer. Heartbeats. Ebb and flow. Escape.

The floating continued for... how long? Time also was washed away, lost to the tide. There was only basking in the moist warmth, and peace. The calm was enveloping; so complete, so without contrast, that it lost meaning.

Eventually, slowly, there was movement. It was less satisfying than the tranquility but still not unpleasant. The gentle swaying, however, became a rocking and then a spinning. He saw brief flashes of rooms, ceilings spinning —

evenings of revelry ended, but the consequences only beginning. He could see fingers clutching at the sheets of a bed, circles that would not end. The spinning became faster. The calm, all he wanted, was being sucked away like dirty water down a drain. He felt a cold breeze. It was not skin and nerves that felt; there were no goose bumps, yet he was chilled. The wind blew through him. It penetrated every hidden place, picking him apart, exposing that which should not be seen, sparing nothing.

Then he was plunging, being pulled and thrown down into the depths. Farther and deeper — speed, sound, motion, colors — always falling. The pressure of the Tempest was all around him, suffocating, crushing. He was being pulled in every direction at once; terror gripped him. The calm was so distant, timeless years, distanceless miles away. If only the storm would pull him apart. If only he would explode. Surely that would be better. That must be where the calm lay, the sweetness of Oblivion, an end to the chaos.

He realized suddenly that he was not alone. Among the roar and the swirling din were voiceless screams that were sensed but not heard, flailing souls that whisked past, always just out of reach. He tried to go to them, but they passed so quickly, and he could control nothing.

There were other voices also, familiar voices. Embrace the Void, they whispered. Peace lies this way. You have it within. This is truth. The voices dripped of honey. Reassurances swirled about, forming an eddy against the chaos. They beckoned. Follow this way. But there was a blackness. There were teeth behind the enticing lips, yet it would be so easy to succumb to the entreaties. An end to suffering. A lover's voice, caressing in the night. An end to fear. A mother's voice, and suckling at a breast.

An end to all. The crone's voice, crumbling to dust.

He was not strong enough to refuse them. The call of Oblivion was powerful. He might well have gone that way, but he was being pulled in another direction. There was something incomplete that would not let him go yet. They tried to hold him; they scratched and clawed, and he wanted to be embraced by their talons, but the eddy was sucked away into the distance. He heard the once-sweet voices screech and curse, raging against him. He mourned their passing as one mourns a grudgingly surrendered vice — pornography carried to the trash heap and set afire.

He was once again careening through the chaos, first this way then that. All around were more of the voiceless screams floundering in the sea of souls. Some wailed for lost pasts, others bemoaned horrific futures. Many simply howled madness. This, perhaps, was another escape — the safety of insanity, the abandoning of fettering, burdensome reason. But Oblivion lay along that road as well, and he was being pulled elsewhere still.

Gradually the screams and the deafening roar of the Tempest began to diminish, to recede if not to disappear. There was a darkness now, and a quiet of sorts, but it was far from the calm of before. It was a pregnant silence. He felt a tension, as if the cacophony of the storm and the screams was only held at bay, not far away at all, ready to rush in again at any moment. He began to visualize points of light, small flames. The light did not shine forth to dispel the darkness; rather, the darkness tolerated the light, allowed it to exist, not to be swallowed. The flames held no warmth. The dark and the cold permeated all.

Each flame was atop a smooth white candle. No wax ran down their sides. He felt drawn toward these glimpses of the old world, the human world. He could not have turned away had he wanted. There were hundreds of them, or were they endless? The flames flickered, although there was no breeze here. He could still feel the tension pressing in upon him, the hovering storm trying to get at him, never far away.

His vision expanded. Next to the nearest candle was a glass full of bourbon. At this sight, a parade of images and sensations steamed through his consciousness. He saw three boys, young teenagers, scrunched behind trash cans in an alley splitting a stolen six-pack of beer, Pabst Blue Ribbon. The brick walls on either side of the alley seemed insubstantial, fading in and out. The scene was familiar, yet distant somehow. It tugged at him, but only fleetingly, then was gone.

The alley was replaced by a car. He felt he knew the car, yet details — year, make — were just beyond his reach, not quite available, not quite important. The car was rocking from the movements of the two older adolescents in the back seat. Their gyrations and contortions meant very little to him. On the floorboard was an empty flask. It held his attention more than anything; sparkling, it called to him.

Then the car too was gone. Where it had been was a woman. She was lying at the bottom of a staircase cradling her right arm against her body. He could not make out her face; her features were blurry. She stank of whiskey. Red tulips covered the wallpaper next to the stairs.

The images began to pass more quickly — a balding man; a cozy restaurant and bar; a woman with obsidian hair and stark white skin. Each vision brought questions closer to the surface, but like the shimmering and dissipating visions, the questions were not fully formed. They were not whole; they were germs of ideas, remote nagging itches. He was connected once again, vaguely, tangentially, to what had been before.

The aroma of the bourbon brought him back to the candles, except now there was a glass by each candle, hundreds perhaps. He was aware of a thirst growing within him, a thirst so great that all those glasses might not quench it. He saw a hand (his hand?) reaching for the first glass. He had noticed no physical body up to this point, and he could discern no connection with the hand except that it was doing his will. He picked up the glass. The pungent odor poured from it, almost visible. As he held the glass, it began to crack. The whiskey dripped out. Then, as the fissures widened, it streamed over his hand, more liquid than the glass could possibly hold. As the last of the bourbon drained out, the cracks became jagged and sliced into his hand. He still was not sure that it was his hand. He had not felt the smoothness of the glass, the hard comfort that he almost remembered, but he could feel the sharp pain. There was no reflex to drop the glass as it became increasingly fractured and more shards bit into the flesh. The alcohol burned as it entered the wounds, but it was a sensation, an indication of being. Soon blood also dripped from the hand. The fragments of the glass were grinding each other smaller and smaller, constantly peeling away skin, embedding themselves down to the bone, until they all sifted through the red fingers. The smell of blood mingled with that of the whiskey.

He reached for the next glass which slipped in his grasp as it became smeared with blood. Once again cracks appeared and the bourbon began to flow out. It poured into the lacerations on his hand and bubbled and spit. More blood welled up from the cuts. This glass also broke apart and cut deeply into him. One sharp edge entering the palm extruded from the back of the hand. Other shards again were grinding their way down to the bone. The second glass crumbled away and was gone, leaving only the sticky, dripping, tattered hand.

He did not want to drink, but he reached for another glass. The results were the same. Again and again and again he picked up glasses only to have them crumble and cut him. The pain was intense, but it was so vital. The slice of the glass, the searing burn of the whiskey pulled memories closer to the surface. They made him more real.

How many glasses? It seemed to go on for days, one after another after another. There were always more. They did not diminish in number, nor did the pain lessen; it stayed sharp and clear. The hand disintegrated. One finger dangled below the rest, connected only by a thin muscle or tendon, a last bit of gristle. Most of the skin was peeled away. Soon the hand that reached for the glasses would be skeletal, picked clean of flesh as much as if vultures or rats had gnawed it down. He was giddy with the pain. As the last bits of flesh were sliced away, his vision began to fog. The glasses were gone. The candles began to sputter and then to blur. They were vague forms of light again, not discernible shapes. The glowing areas shrank until, one by one, they disappeared completely.

There was darkness.

The violence of the Tempest was not far away. He could hear it; he could imagine it flooding in to engulf him once more. The thought evoked fear, but fear, like pain, was familiar and comforting in a way. It gave him a point of reference.

He was in a room. It had not appeared suddenly; he simply was in it. His vision was cloudy. He wanted to rub his eyes — did he have eyes now? He was not sure — and wipe away whatever obscured his sight. The room seemed to be a basement. It had that damp, underground feel. The walls were a dingy cream color, the floor drab grey cement. On one wall thick wooden steps led upward to a closed door. The room was empty.

It had been empty, but no longer.

A man stood in the room. There was a strange familiarity about the human form. The man's face was blurred, his features indistinguishable. He knew this man, this man who radiated anger, contempt, disappointment, disapproval. All these things he could feel, he could almost remember, yet he still longed to fall into the man's arms and weep, to be held, to be safe and lose himself, to be wanted.

"Your mother was an idiot, a whore, and you're little better." Words. Human speech. The man spoke.

He wanted to respond. He wanted to speak.

Hold me. What is happening? Make me safe. I want to be warm. I want to be whole. But the words would not form.

"You always were a whiner. You could have been a little girl, always running to Mommy. We were happy before you. I wanted a son I could be proud of."

A son. A father. *Father.* Hold me. If only he could reach out.

"I should have tied you in a sack and thrown you in the bay like a dog. Everything would have been okay then."

Hold me.

"You were all she cared about. She couldn't love both of us. You needed this, and you needed that. Always you."

The scene of the woman at the bottom of the stairs came back to him — the red tulips, her shattered arm, her pain. His mother's pain.

His father pushed her. She smelled of whiskey. He threw his drink at her and then pushed her down the stairs.

Rage welled up inside.

"Why don't you use it? You always were a gutless little bastard."

Use it? He realized there were two hands (disembodied? his?) holding a shotgun pointed at his father. This time he could feel the cold steel. He wanted to put it down. How could his father have hit her?

"Go ahead, shoot!"

The shotgun roared to life. No! Sparks rained from the barrel. He felt the kick, but he had not pulled the trigger. He had not fired. For only a moment he saw his father's eyes clearly, unobscured, wide with surprise, then the image was blurry again. The shot ripped apart his father's chest and stomach. Shredded flesh and blood splattered all around. But he had not fired.

"So this is the thanks I get for trying to support a family, a wife and kid. Fucking ingrate. Always wanted to blow away the old man, huh? About time you had some guts, chickenshit son of a bitch."

He could not look away from his father's churned innards. He had not pulled the trigger. He just wanted to be held. This was not how it had happened, or was it? Something was not right. Blood still gushed from his father's body, the gaping hole in his front. A pool of scarlet was spreading, covering the entire floor. His father's shredded heart kept pumping out more and more, as if it wanted to fill the entire room, floor to ceiling, with its venomous blood.

He moved toward the stairs. He was not sure how he moved or what he moved; he still could

perceive no body of his own. He just knew that
he was moving away from his father.

"Go on, run! That's all you ever did! Might
as well keep running!" his father screamed. The
walls of the room were becoming insubstantial,
blurring and melting away. Only the steps were
solid, and the door. From behind the walls the
Tempest poured in. Waves of voiceless screams
crashed in about his father, drowning his curses.
The torn body was out of sight, buried by the
storm. Swirling chaos filled the room. The door
opened before him. He was through and it was
closed, the sea of souls lapping at the other side.

He was in a restaurant, a small bar. He knew
this place, a human place. His vision was still
clouded. Large patches of blurriness floated
slowly through his view. There was a large sign
on the wall. Why was the sign not outside? The
familiar setting was slightly askew. "Parker's" was
the sign, with a flourish from the tail of the "s"
that underlined the other letters. Parker. A
name. *His name.* His name was Parker. His
father's name was Parker. He felt pieces coming
together, more complete but far from whole.

Through the dimness he could see the narrow
room. The brass rail along the edge of the bar
shone. The mirror behind the bar, bordered by
various bottles of liquor, reflected the sparse

light. The room smelled like whiskey. Across from the bar, a man sat in one of the booths along the wall. Below a severely receding hairline the man's forehead glistened with sweat. He motioned for Parker to sit. Parker was at the table, across from Uncle Vinny. From where did that knowledge come, that name? But he knew it was true. Occasionally Parker caught clear glimpses of Uncle Vinny — the whiskers on his neck and chin, the paunch, the hair sprouting from his ears.

Uncle Vinny chuckled as he spoke. He always chuckled for the benefit of others. "Well, Sonny, looks like the fat lady's singing this time. Hell, she ain't just singing, she sat right damn on top of us!" His rumbling laugh was mixed with the thick coughing of cigarettes not given up soon enough.

Sonny was not Parker's name. It was just what Uncle Vinny called him. He was sure of this.

"It's tough, I know, Sonny," Uncle Vinny's voice was softer now with concern but still deep baritone, "but it'll be better for the family, for your mother, bless her heart."

Parker wanted to respond to his soft, kind man who was. . . who was dead, who had died while Parker was in college. Parker's. It was his restaurant. There was no one else. Words eluded him still.

"I've got the papers. All you have to do is sign them, Sonny. Think about your mother. You'll both be taken care of."

There were papers on the table, and a pen. Had they appeared? Had he not seen them before? Taken care of. Someone would take care of him, and his mother. Hold me, Uncle Vinny? But why was the sign inside? Why were the barstools upholstered in blood-red? They should be green.

"Just sign them, Sonny. Trust me."

Trust. Be taken care of. Sign.

"No!" There was another voice, another person in the room, but Parker could not see him.

"Begone!" hissed Uncle Vinny in a whispery voice. "He is mine, miiine."

"No," answered the voice. It was calm, powerful.

The papers burst into flame. The pen melted away. Uncle Vinny scurried from behind the table. He had six spindly arms ending in claws protruding from his corpulent body. "Mine, miiine," he hissed. A thin, forked tongue snaked out from between his sharp teeth. "Mine!"

"Go!"

Uncle Vinny dropped to the floor and scampered away, a fat cockroach fleeing the light, muttering and whining as he went.

Footsteps coming closer. Shadowy form standing above him. The restaurant was fading away — bar, mirror, bottles, scent, tables. All that remained were Parker and the hazy figure before him. It reach toward him with two hands.

Suddenly the haze, the perpetual fog, lifted. In front of Parker stood his father, not the spiteful vision of earlier, but a more accurate, realistic embodiment. His father held in his hands the caul, the death mask that Parker had unknowingly worn, that had distorted his vision and his understanding. Or perhaps it had protected him. Parker had a body himself, hands that were not sliced and peeled to the bone. He threw his arms around his father, but his father did not respond, and he was cold.

Parker took a step back. He could see his father now. He had a tight smile, and those dark, piercing brown eyes. "I truly reap what I have sown," said his father. "Justin."

Justin. Justin Parker. His father, Leonard Parker. With the names came words that had to be spoken, that would not be denied. They burst out as if they had been held back, dammed, for eons. "I didn't pull the trigger. I didn't. I just wanted you to hold me; and Uncle Vinny, when he died I had to take over with the bar. There was no one else, and I tried. I did everything I could, but I couldn't do it. I wouldn't sell, and I wouldn't sell, but I couldn't hold on, and we went under, and it's a fucking parking lot anyway, and we got nothing." The words would not stop. Tears were streaming down his cheeks. "And there wasn't money for the nursing home. Her mind was gone, and I couldn't help her, and I couldn't afford to put her anywhere. Part of me died with her, and I loved her, and I loved you, Daddy, and I didn't pull the trigger." His body was wracked with sobbing. He felt spent. No more words were choking his throat. He buried his head in his father's shoulder. He wanted him to rub his back or stroke his hair softly, but there was no comforting response from his father. Lacking in life, even more lacking in death.

"I know you didn't pull the trigger," said his father. "The spectres invade your dreams, your memories here. Whatever you saw before wasn't me, and that wasn't Vinny. It just wanted you to sign. It wanted your soul."

Justin stepped back. His father may have saved him from the Uncle Vinny creature, but there was no warmth, no life, no completeness to be found here. There was something else still tugging at Justin. He could feel it more distinctly now that he knew a bit more about what had been before.

His father spoke again, "There is power here, Justin. It won't be like before. You can help me. Let me teach you. I can be powerful, important. You can be important here."

Justin took another step back, away from his father. This was not what was calling him. Something was wrong. He saw the death, the hunger in those deep brown eyes.

"Come with me, Justin." A thin facade of patience was wearing away from his father's face. "Don't be an idiot. You were always a loser before. It can be different now. Come with me." Sympathetic hands reached out to Justin. He could see the white fingers with bulbous knuckles, the pale face, ichor dripping from the chin. "Come with me, Justin. Trust me."

Trust me.

Justin stepped farther back. The previous vision of his father had been false, but some truth had lurked within it, making it more believable. "You pushed her," said Justin. "You pushed her down the stairs."

"Forget the past, Justin," slavered his father. "We can make a difference here. You can finally be worth something."

"You pushed her down the stairs," continued Justin, "and I didn't pull the trigger. *You did*. You did it to yourself. You made me feel like it was my fault, you bastard."

"I removed your caul, Justin. I awakened you. I brought you into this world too. You owe me. You owe me!" His father's eyes were bulging, blood vessels about to burst. He stank of bourbon.

"No!" Justin turned and ran.

He could here his father screaming after him, "You'll regret this, boy! I'll make you regret it! You'll pay!"

Justin was running from a wave. A giant crest of the Tempest was behind him, a tidal wave of chaos and loss, and he could not escape it. It crashed down upon him, carrying him with it. The despair, the regret, overwhelmed him; they tore at his soul, trying to gain entry. . . his father's death, the muzzle in his mouth, the shotgun blast, the note accusing him; Uncle Vinny's final heart attack, bankruptcy, the parking lot; his mother's deterioration and death; his father's drinking; his drinking; so much failure, so much pain. But there was something more, something important that was missing. It pulled him, something at which he had not even guessed. That was how he avoided the pull of Oblivion. He knew he was not done yet. The storm tossed him mercilessly, still reaching for his heart. He withdrew into himself and shut out the hopelessness.

Eventually he noticed the silence. He was not sure when it had begun and when the din had faded away. The Tempest was not so close now. Its absence, or at least its remoteness, was soothing. Justin was in a room in the real world, or as close as he could come to the real world — the real world cloaked in the shadows of death. He was in an apartment that he knew in a brownstone in the Mission District. The Mission Delores was a mile or two away. The parking lot on South Van Ness that used to be his bar was only several blocks farther.

The large living room had been turned into a studio. Brushes, tubes of paint, canvases, easels, and other painting paraphernalia were scattered about. Several of the canvases Justin knew were finished or partially completed pictures, but to him they all appeared blank white. They were not alive to him. The carpet had been pulled up to make spilled paint easier to clean. Littering the floor were a surprising number of empty forty-ounce beer bottles and several empty Jack Daniels bottles. The room reeked of stale beer and liquor.

The kitchen was much as he remembered it, as was the hallway to the bedroom. The bathroom door, on the right side of the hall, was closed. As he watched, the door bulged and then receded, pulsating slowly as if it were a beating heart. Justin turned away.

He heard the footsteps coming up the two flights of stairs. Randi was home. She was the painter; she was the one with a vision of life. He had moved in after the restaurant had closed two years ago. She had cared for him as he had slid into self-pity. He could see now, only now, how much he had hurt her in the past.

Up the steps — forty-five, forty-six, forty-seven, forty-eight — keys fumbling at the lock. She had left late Friday night, after the earthquake. Said she had had enough of the ground moving, enough of San Francisco. She had driven to Rio Dell to be with her family on ground that was stable. He had known she would come back, but he had felt abandoned at the time. Two days of heavy drinking and everything had tumbled down upon him, all that the Tempest had found and more.

The door opened and Randi stepped in with her bulging overnight bag. She never would get a real suitcase. She set the bag down and turned on the light. Justin had not noticed that it was off. She pushed her jet black hair out of her face. Her fair skin was touched with blush on the cheeks. The loose sweater hung from her shoulders, her small breasts barely noticeable; her skirt brushed the floor. She saw the bottles, the mess. Her mouth crinkled with concern like it did when she stared at one of her paintings in progress. Justin wanted to reach out to her, to touch her. She shivered and crossed her arms against her body. He wanted to take back everything he had ever said, everything he had done. How could he have hurt her in so many ways over the years? How could he have been so blind?

She began to walk across the room. She seemed to move so quickly. Justin allowed himself a wry smile — the quick and the dead. Randi walked toward the hallway, toward the rhythmically pulsating door which Justin could not face. He saw her pass, but he saw more: he saw within her. Inside her belly there was movement, the first stirrings of a child. *His child.* She could not even know yet. Dear God, what had he done? He had not known. He wanted to scream. How could he have failed her more? Give him another chance! Everything would be different this time.

She walked past the bathroom into the

bedroom looking for him. The light was on in there now. In a moment she would come back and open the bulging door. He knew what she would find —the old, giant bathtub, his body bloated, veins opened to the once-hot water, globules of congealed blood floating. How could he have done this to her? It had been Halloween, and the call of the voices and of the full moon had been so powerful.

There was no scream. He merely heard her soft voice say, "No, baby. No." She came into the living room and leaned against the wall. She was changed; she was defeated. Justin could see death about her — extreme pallor; skin aging and falling away; the smell the rotting flesh; and for just a moment her left eye seemed to glow eerily red. As he watched, her stomach began to swell. He could see the baby growing, struggling, tearing its way out into the cruel world. It did not break straight out. Instead it climbed upward, gouging its way through her chest, into her neck. Her body convulsed. Her mouth was forced open from within as she vomited blood and chunks of torn flesh. The semblance of a child climbed out, clawing apart Randi's cheeks as it did.

Then the vision was gone. Randi leaned against the wall, shades paler than she usually was, hair hanging in her face. The child, a boy, rested in her belly. Her eyes were clear except for the tears beginning to form. She slid down the wall until she was sitting with her head on her knees. She began to cry quietly. Justin sat on the floor next to her. Why this torturous limbo? Why couldn't he just burn in Hell? He would have eternity to find out. He was bound somehow to her, and to the unborn child, both of whom he had failed so miserably. He wanted to cry as well, but he could not. He was filled only with emptiness.

REAPER VERSUS REAPER VERSUS REAPER

Edo van Belkom

"I trusted her," spat Sonny Manganesi, twisting his white-knuckled hands back and forth along the arc of the steering wheel. "I fucking trusted him, too."

Sonny clenched his teeth and shook his head as he turned onto the Golden Gate Bridge, heading north out of San Francisco.

"I'm gone two weeks... Just two goddamn weeks." He shook his head. "I can't believe it."

Sonny had gone to New Jersey to help with the arrangements for his uncle's funeral, then stayed there another week to get the man's affairs in order. When Sonny was satisfied that he'd done all he could and that his aunt would be able to get along by herself, he booked a flight back to San Francisco. He'd come home a day early, on Hallowe'en night, with a dozen roses in one hand and a gift-wrapped black silk teddy for his lady in the other.

He had been hoping to surprise her.

Well, surprise!

He'd crept into the house, silent as a cat, and padded his way toward the upstairs bedroom. He'd stopped for a moment outside the door, listening to the sound of what he thought was her sleeping, then pushed the door open ever so slightly to peek inside the room.

She wasn't alone.

And she wasn't sleeping.

Sonny stood there in the doorway for a few minutes, watching the two of them do it, listening to her moan and say the same things she'd said to him so many times before.

"Oh, yeah... You're the best... Oh, god that feels good!"

Anger flared inside Sonny like the hot end of a missile. But rather than bursting into the room and saying something stupid like, "What are you two doing?" he silently stepped back from the doorway then left the house, got into his car, and vowed to return — with his gun.

He kept a shotgun in the cabin he owned up

on the Marin Peninsula. The double-barreled shotgun, ironically enough, had been a gift from Sonny's uncle on the occasion of his sixteenth birthday. The gun was a few years old now, but he had kept it in perfect working order and it would be more than adequate for the job.

Sonny had been afraid that he'd lose his resolve to kill them during the hour-long trip out to the cabin and back. But now, halfway to the cabin, his rage and need for revenge were more powerful than ever. The image of the two of them doing it was still fresh in his mind and he still felt like stepping back into that bedroom, switching on the light, and pulling the trigger.

Blowing the two of them apart — for good.

Brake lights suddenly blinked on up ahead.

"What the—" Sonny was forced to slam on the brakes as an old shitbox Chevette suddenly slowed down in front of him. "C'mon!" he said, pulling into the left lane and stomping on the gas.

His black Firebird surged forward.

"My two best friends!" he shouted at the driver of the Chevette as he passed. "My girlfriend and my best friend, doing it... in my bed... probably using my condoms!"

He focused on the road again and saw the fog rolling in, washing over the bridge like a heavy, dark cloud.

Shit! thought Sonny. As if my night isn't black enough already.

Despite the fog, he kept his foot pressed down hard on the gas, making the car's big-block V8 roar like some enraged animal.

The Firebird punched into the wall of fog — Sonny couldn't see more than a few feet ahead. But his foot still pushed down on the accelerator, as if the car's screaming engine was the voice of his anger.

He kept his eyes focused on the road, but by the time he saw the red rear lights of the semitrailer it was too late.

The speeding Firebird slid under the back of the trailer, the truck's thick steel bumper shearing off the car's roof.

And cleanly severing Sonny's head from the rest of his body.

■

The Repoman stood on the walkway at the side of the bridge, leaning back against the railing. He crossed his arms over his chest, his jacket sleeves creaking together with the distinct sound of leather against leather.

His hair was greasy, long and blond, pulled

tightly back and braided behind his head in a rat's tail. He had a thin wisp of a mustache and a slight beard trimmed into something that looked like a goatee. His face was a road map of fresh cuts and old scars, and even though the night's darkness was complete, his battered eyes were covered by a pair of dark wire-rimmed glasses.

He had the look of a fighter, a hunter, a scavenger... a survivor. He was someone who would do whatever it took to get by in the Shadowlands, no matter how despicable or reprehensible it might be.

He stood on the bridge at the edge of the fog, waiting for the dead man to stumble out of the wreck.

A newly arrived Larva was a valuable commodity in the Shadowlands and there were a lot of things a skilled reaper like the Repoman could do with the newly dead. He could try to convert the Larva to a specific cause or faith, he could befriend him and make him part of his Cohort or gang, or he could simply feast on the dead man's hapless little soul.

All these options, but not one of them was right for the Repoman. First of all, he wasn't much for causes or faiths, and he didn't believe in anything but himself. He preferred the life of a loner, so he wasn't really part of a Cohort and the pleasure of soulfeasting might be intense, but it really didn't last very long — not long enough to make it worth his while, anyway.

No, he'd do with this Larva the same thing he'd done with countless others before — claim it as his own and sell it on the open market to the highest bidder.

At last Sonny Manganesi stepped out of the fog. Wisps of vapor hung from his form and his entire body shone with a faint white glow — the glow of the after life.

"Hey," the Repoman shouted. "Over here!"

Sonny stumbled forward like a drunk, looking around for the source of the voice.

"I said, over here!"

Sonny moved toward the Repoman's voice, tripping on the curb at the edge of the road and nearly falling against the handrail. "Who are you?" he said.

"I'm the grim reaper, pal."

"Oh yeah," replied Sonny sarcastically. "And I'm Little Bo Peep!"

"Pleased to meet you, Bo." said the Repoman, the tone of his voice was dead serious.

Sonny stood there, eyes squinting stupidly at the Repoman through the plasmic caul covering his face. The caul was a sort of protective mask, strands of yellowish, iridescent matter that wound and twisted together to form a thick mat of netting. It covered the aquiline nose and high cheekbones of Sonny's face like another layer of skin.

"You're not kidding me, are you?" asked Sonny, grabbing hold of the handrail and hanging on tight.

"Do I look like the kind of guy that would joke about something like that?"

Sonny moved closer to the Repoman, twisting his face around so he could see more clearly through the caul. "No, I suppose not."

Cars drove past slowly, cautiously entering the fog as if it were a bank of toxic clouds.

"So you're telling me that I died in that crash?" Sonny asked, gesturing into the fog with a wave of his hand.

"How else do you get up and walk away after getting your head sliced clean off?"

"Is that what happened to me?" Sonny said, a tinge of sorrow in his voice. "I don't remember much about the accident. I really couldn't see anything in that fog."

"I couldn't either," said the Repoman. "But I saw you when you turned onto the bridge. Top half of the car was missing... So was your head. After I saw that I hopped on the next car and rode it all the way to the edge of the fog."

"You could see that I was going to die?" asked Sonny.

"Sure I could, the Repoman sees death as if he were looking through a window into the real world..." The leather-clad reaper took a look around. "See that old-timer in the Buick, there? See that growth on his head?" He pointed toward a car being driven by an elderly man with a large, purplish growth bulging out of the side of his head. It pulsed as if it were alive, being fed by a throbbing network of thick veins and arteries. "Cancer," said the Repoman. "Probably kill him in another year, maybe two."

Sonny turned to look in the direction of the car, but he couldn't see much through his caul.

"So you saw me... dead? Before it happened?"

"The way you died, it was hard to miss."

Sonny's hands darted to his neck, searching for a wound or fresh scar tissue and other than needing a shave, his neck felt clean and whole. He turned to the Repoman. "But I can't be dead yet. I can't be!" he shouted. A wave of purple rage pulsed through his caul, leaving it a slightly darker shade of yellow. "Not when she's with him... They're the ones that were supposed to end up dead. Not me!" He leaned forward and looked out over the dark waters of the bay. "If

I'm dead, that means... they'll end up staying together."

The Repoman said nothing, giving the Larva enough time to come to grips with the fetters that were tormenting him.

"They'll be fucking each other..." said Sonny. "Again and again..."

The Repoman smiled, exposing a set of dirty, jagged teeth. This one's fetter is strong, he thought. He could feel the pain and anger radiating from the larva like pure energy. This one's soul would fetch a good price on the open market, a high price — maybe even one of the best ever. "You stick with me, kid," the Repoman said at last. "And I'll make sure you get the chance to set things straight."

"You can do that?"

The Repoman nodded.

"He's lying!"

The Repoman spun around, turning in the direction the voice had come from.

Sonny turned as well, but more slowly, as if still trying to get his bearings.

"Don't believe him!" the voice said. "He doesn't give a damn about you. He'll tell you anything, anything you want, just so he can sell your soul to the highest bidder." The voice belonged to a large black man wearing a pair of white leather high-tops and a blue sweat suit with the word BOMBERS printed in bright yellow letters down the left arm and leg.

The Repoman recognized the wraith as Coach Wardell, a Ferryman reaper who caught Larvae and helped guide them through the Shadowlands. He had a round, jolly kind of a face that made him look like everyone's pal. Well, he wasn't the Repoman's friend; the Repoman didn't have any.

"He's mine, Coach," said the Repoman. "I found him first."

Coach Wardell stepped between two cars slowed in the traffic crawling around the wreckage on the bridge and moved closer to the Repoman and Sonny. "Finding a Larva first can hardly be considered a claim to his soul."

The Repoman laughed mockingly at the other Wraith. "Fuck you, Coach. I found him first and he's mine." His lips stretched back into a malicious grin. "If you want him, you're going to have to take him from me."

The Repoman bent his right arm, then snapped it straight, and a two-foot length of steel chain slithered out of his jacket sleeve into his hand — a relic from the real world.

Coach Wardell lifted the front of his sweatshirt and pulled a bowie knife from the waistband of his pants. He held it before him, the point of the blade centered on the Repoman's heart. The knife was a relic as well, a payment to Coach Wardell by a traveler upon the safe conclusion of his journey.

"Well, all right," said the Repoman, looking at the knife. "Let's party!"

The Repoman began swinging the chain in front of him in a wide circle. He lunged forward, hoping to catch Coach Wardell with the chain, but the Ferryman moved quickly out of the way.

The Repoman lunged forward again, but Coach Wardell's knife slashed through the air, catching the chain on its sharp steel blade.

The chain whipped around the blade and held. The two weapons were locked, and the reapers were suddenly joined.

Coach Wardell yanked the Repoman closer, grabbing a fistful of black leather jacket with his free hand.

The two pushed and shoved at each other until Coach Wardell's strength and size finally gave him the upper hand. He tried to free his knife, but it was too tangled in the chain to be of any use. He spun the Repoman around and pushed him away with all the force he could muster.

The chain slid away from the knife, and the

Repoman stumbled backward into the slow-moving bridge traffic. He lost his footing and fell to the pavement in front of an eighteen-wheeler and was unable to get up before before the truck's huge front wheels rolled over his chest and legs.

The Repoman screamed in agony as he felt the full weight of the nine wheels on the right side of the truck crushing his body flat against the pavement.

Coach Wardell stood by, his body tensed, the knife poised to strike, waiting for the truck to pass so he could finish off the fallen reaper.

The Repoman lay lifeless on the pavement as the last of the truck's wheels rolled over him. Then slowly he began to recover, his body beginning to regain its shape. His chest rose up to fill out his jacket and his stomach expanded until it was once again tight against the waistband of his jeans.

Coach Wardell moved in, the tip of the knife leading the way. As he lunged to stab the prone Repoman, the Repoman's right arm shot up and the chain whipped around the Coach's beefy neck.

The big wraith reached up with his left hand, trying to pull the chain loose, but the Repoman held it tight, using it to drag himself to his feet.

Coach Wardell opened his mouth to breathe, or perhaps even to scream, but the only sound that escaped his lips was a sick, wet gurgle.

The Repoman jerked the chain, pulling the Coach forward and making him stumble. Then, before the Coach could regain his footing, the Repoman gave the chain another hard yank, pulling it even tighter around his neck.

Coach Wardell's eyes began to bug out their sockets. Brown skin began to bulge through the links in the chain. And dark red blood began to run down his neck, turning black as it soaked into the blue fleece of his sweat suit.

Finally, Coach Wardell dropped his knife and began clawing at the chain with both hands in a frantic attempt to remove the choking hold.

It was the reflex the Repoman had been waiting for.

He pulled hard on the chain and knelt to pick up the knife. Then he gave Coach Wardell a little slack so that the larger wraith could scramble to his feet and remain still for a moment.

The Reapoman reared back and drove the knife deep into the Coach's throat.

Coach Wardell's mouth opened in a scream, but the sound was drowned in the continuous soft, wet gurgle that bubbled up from his neck.

Blood ran freely down the hilt of the knife and leaked from the corners of his mouth, but Coach Wardell continued to grab at the chain, tearing his own wounds.

Eventually, the Coach's efforts slowed.

He fell to his knees, then toppled over, face-first onto the asphalt, his fingers tangled in the chain around his neck.

The Repoman knelt down, took a firm hold of the knife's hilt, and began sawing, cutting through muscle, tendon, and bone until his head came away from the rest of his body.

Once that was done, the Repoman pulled his chain free from the bloody stump, then stood back and watched Coach Wardell's body slowly dissolve and his head fall screaming into The Tempest — the nightmare realm of chaos and destruction beneath the Shadowlands.

For just a short moment, the night seemed deathly silent, with even the breeze whispering its way quietly through the wires and cables supporting the bridge.

The Repoman took a deep breath, gathered up his chain and returned it to its place in the sleeve of his jacket. Then he looked at the bowie knife, a fine relic that would empower him in future battles. He wiped it clean on a pant leg, then tucked it into the waistband of his jeans.

"Now, as I was saying..." The Repoman turned back to the walkway. "You stick with me, kid, and I'll make sure you get the chance to set things straight."

But the words escaped into the fog, unheard.

The walkway was deserted.

"Kid?" said the Repoman. "Where are you?"

He looked up and down the bridge.

Nothing.

Finally, something caught his eye.

The glint of something yellow a dozen yards away.

He ran towards it, slowing to a stop when he realized what it was.

Sonny's plasmic Caul, lay face down on the pavement, rocking gently back and forth in the breeze.

THE END

For the Coming

Joseph M. Shaughnessy

The Bough, 1994

Serin, Prince of Smiles, Architect of Haunts, Prime Mover of Despair, kneeled in absolute stillness and sniffed the raw, greasy air. He reflected on the lovely, black, primordial days of immaculate darkness when Yerba Buena was a bountiful garden fertilized with despair and overflowing with possibilities. *What a prosperous time for the Bough that was!* thought Serin.

Rising, Serin stalked inside the antechamber north of his lair within the Bough. He stopped, stretched, held his gnarled hands outward, and slammed his body down to the cold earth. Abruptly, he shifted his form into that of a maggot. Arching and writhing on the muddied earth, he settled himself and became completely still.

He lay still through the night, contemplating the majesty of his own baseness, the regal splendor of misery personified. His mind and soul became wholly undivided, singularly black. Serin smiled in deep satisfaction.

In the cold, early hours of the dawn, having regained his human form, Serin sauntered from his grotto to a flint-hewn stairway a short distance from his chamber. He spun his way through the rock, moving upward, until he reached the summit, bursting forth in splendid fashion. Serin had perfected this grand entrance, and though he had no audience at the moment, he delighted in it just the same.

From his perch at the highest point in the haunt, Serin surveyed that which lay below him. He watched the robotic motions of the patrol team as it approached the southwest perimeter in search of a yet-unclaimed Lemure. He was teaching some pupils to "reap," to claim unharvested Lemures' souls in his name, and had chosen a young female subject for the exercise.

She is so beautiful, Serin observed. *I will delight in her trust and revel in her degradation! I select my chosen so precisely.*

He spoke in a barely audible hiss, "Yes, that's it, my children; approach her slowly, be gentle…she will come to know our full horror in time…."

Serin stretched his jaws wide open and smirked with delight as he beheld his followers encircle and subdue the Lemure. She resisted at first, recoiling in horror at the grotesque appearance of the patrol team. But the contingent had been well schooled by their master. Again and again they whispered the sussurant chants of Serinic dialectics:"seringohiontachagusgohaillain… seringohiontachagusgohaillain." The mesmerized victim relented and followed willingly toward the inner sanctum of the Bough in perfect cadence with the chants of her captors.

Well, Serin reflected, *we have her, and there are so many more. But there is one for whom I will wait no longer….*

He transferred his weight and settled into a crouching position, turning in the direction of a festering swamp that Serin knew well. In the living world the swamp was occupied by a dwelling, the basement shelter of Serin's desire. *It is time to bring sweet Lalo home*, he thought.

Serin casually licked his misshapen upper lip with a knotty worm of a tongue as he thought of his prize, of the pupil he had cultivated for

so many years. It is time, my delicious, time to
come to your father. Come and rest. Dream of me.
Experience me. We will be such good friends....

San Francisco, 1994

The cellar air was repellent, a potpourri of
mildewed furniture, damp books and Lalo
Montpar's sweat-soaked jeans. Lalo held the
crumpled plastic bag up to the light, attempting
to determine exactly how much cocaine
remained. He twisted uncomfortably in the well-
worn leather chair, which squeaked in resistance
to his awkward movements. Exhausted and
sodden with perspiration, he knew that he could
not keep up the insane pace of his latest binge.
He had been without sleep for almost four days.

It had been years since he had truly slept. His
departures from consciousness were tumultuous
crashes into disorienting, cloudy stupors. Lalo
feared his dreams — their increasing frequency
and intensity, their seductive whispers, which
seemed more real than the dismal miasma his
life had become.

Often, from within the shadowy crevices of
his slumbering mind, a masked creature
appeared, enticing Lalo with a glorious vow: *I*

will give to you the World of the Shadows, a world where you will be sovereign king.

Though he knew it was but a dream, Lalo could actually perceive the sensations of domination and rapture, savor previously unthinkable successes that had proved so elusive throughout his waking life. Every fiber of Lalo's consciousness craved acceptance of the masked being's offer.

For the pact to become binding, however, an offering was required in exchange — one that repulsed Lalo with horror.

He did not want to believe that he was capable of doing what the creature demanded. He did not want to believe that he was capable of forsaking the only truly precious gift enduring in the scarred and abandoned shell of his existence.

In the dim shadows of his basement dwelling, Lalo fell deep into the horrors of restless sleep, accepting his dreams, knowing that they would come.

Lalo stands in a courtyard with his four-year-old daughter, Sarah. Misty clouds of vaporous dew, smelling of rosewood, fill the air and filter the light, dimming and softening the image of his little girl. The flowing tresses of her hair sweep about her shoulders, luminous with a flaxen iridescence highlighted by rays of light sifting through the mist.

She sees him, giggles and hurries toward him. With outstretched arms, Lalo reaches out for his daughter.

And then the horror...gnarled, misshapen hands, fingers ruptured and torn, encrusted with rags of scarlet flesh, strike out and seize Sarah around her delicate throat. The loathsome grip tightens, restraining the child, pulling her away from Lalo, who stands frozen, unmoving.

The mists part, revealing the entity who holds his daughter. The creature's face is cloaked with an exotic, demonic mask. Ripping apart the mantle of his robe, the creature reveals a gelid mass of tissue, braided and entwined with bone and crimson gore. It hisses: "Give to me this child's chaste and undefiled soul, and I will ordain you as king among kings, with minions to serve you as lord and master. I will give to you the World of the Shadows, a world where you will be sovereign king."

The magnificent passion, the unrelenting sensations of power and fulfillment course through Lalo's being. Lalo gazes at Sarah, a corrupt leer playing upon his lips. The small child, writhing in the beast's grip, reaches for her father as Lalo steps forward. With a hushed voice he seals Sarah's fate:

"Creature, as you promise this bounty, I accept. She is yours."

"Daddy," screams Sarah. "Please, Daddy! No! Please, Daddy!"

Ignoring the child's pleas to her father, the beast snatches her from the earth and thrusts her into its pectoral mass. A blackened heart emerges from the bloody tissue that envelops her.

"Aaaahhh, I so hungered for a young virgin soul," sighs the beast. "Thank you, Dear Lalo — I know that you will bring me many more!"

In a moment, both creature and Sarah are gone, and in the dream Lalo cannot remember who she was or how she looked or her name or the color of her hair. Lalo spins around violently, trying to remember his loss. An abyss of pain rips at the fabric of his soul. He begins to wail, then scream. Then the beast reenters the dream. It removes the mask, yet its face is indiscernible except for a wretched twist of lips forming a grotesque smile.

The demon whispers, almost sweetly: "I am the Hideous Rhymer, Serin, Prince of Smiles. We are bound by covenant and for you I will return."

With that, he vanishes, and in his place vapors of surrealistic graffiti surface and rise from the cellar floor:

I saw the silver cord emerge
At first as in a dream
The creamy choir of angels danced
Their beauteous smiles gleamed

The Prince of Smiles took awhile
Yet finally the cord was wound
Around each delicate angelic neck
Heaven rebounds in strangled sounds

Lalo awoke, numb with chill. He twisted himself into a fetal position, clutching his arms around his knees, coiling deeper into the leather chair.

The thought of Sarah stiffened his spine. Sarah would be the final offspring of the Montpar family. Somehow he knew this was true. Lalo would have no more children, and his natural father had died two months before he was born. His stepfather was a spineless facade of a man who had inanely managed and thereby destroyed what remained of the once extensive Montpar business empire.

His mother was nothing: a semblance of a being, seeming always to be in the background of his life, on the outskirts, seldom touching, seldom speaking. He could never recall his mother being much more than that. If she had ever experienced happiness, Lalo had not seen it.

Happiness, he pondered. *Have I ever known true contentment or tranquillity? I have felt a sick and twisted joy when watching the pain I inflict upon others take its course…but have I ever really known what it means to be free of this darkness that torments me?*

Lalo reached back into his memory, to the year 1983. To the only period in his life when he could remember real joy and happiness. He was about to move to Japan with his mother and stepfather, who were attempting to salvage Montpar shipping concerns.

His natural father, according to family and business records, had been the consummate deal-maker, and was on the verge of reestablishing Montpar business interests as formidable enterprises when he had suddenly died of massive heart failure.

About a week before leaving for Japan, his stepfather made it clear that Lalo would have to fend for himself, as he would be immersed in the task of "doing business and making deals" and would not have the time to watch over Lalo. That statement would not have seemed so utterly ridiculous to Lalo if his stepfather had the least clue about how either business was done or deals were made. His stepfather's concerns were not about Lalo having to fend for himself in Japan, but his anxiety over the appalling reputation Lalo had earned for being a vicious delinquent throughout his young life. He had just finished probation for a three-year stint under court supervision for a series of robberies he had committed, and neither parent had the energy or inclination to keep up with him.

San Francisco International Airport, 1983

For the last month Serin had been intensely scrutinizing Lalo and his family, obsessively chronicling Lalo's moods, movements, and conversations. It was apparent to him that Lalo would be journeying outside Serin's realm of dominion — into the Dark Kingdom of Jade, in fact.

Serin observed Lalo's preparations for departure with a mixture of anger and weakness. He had attempted to influence or delay the exit, but his capability to do so was limited. Though virtually omnipotent within the Bough, his authority and control over those in the living world were less absolute.

In his mind his right to Lalo's soul was based

on the contract he had formed with Paul Montpar. The fact that he had reneged on his portion of the deal was irrelevant. He had no desire for Lalo to move out of his sphere of influence, but following him was out of the question: he did not wish to risk a possible invasion of the Bough by the minions of the Jade Kingdom.

Serin leapt up on the wing of the 747, which was awaiting takeoff clearance orders from the control tower. He slowly moved along the top of the craft, toward the cockpit. Serin wanted to examine the markings on the faces of the flight crew to ensure that any indications of immediate death were not present.

If the pilot is going to die, Serin thought, *I must not let Lalo go down with him…. Who knows what Reaper might find him in the wreckage of a plane so far away from my kingdom?*

Satisfied that the pilot was not in any present danger, Serin doubled back, sniffing the air for Lalo's scent, smelling the oily fear and unctuous anxiety of the passengers within.

He slid down the side of the plane until he was outside the window where Lalo was seated. Pushing a pointed finger through the thick glass, he gently pressed his fingertip against Lalo's head. A sickly sweetness coursed through Serin:

away from the Bough's influence, Lalo's true personality was emerging.

"Arrogant boy!" Serin screamed angrily, though none could hear him. "How dare you believe that you are anything but what I desire! How dare you believe that you are capable of anything save serving my design! I am your architect! And I own you. You will return to me, for I own the soul of the one who made you! I own your real father — he gave you to me, as you will give me Sarah!"

The 747 began to taxi down the runway, and with a thunderous surge lifted gracefully off the ground, quickly moving out over San Francisco Bay. Serin vaulted off the airplane, turning wild somersaults in the air, cackling and cursing Lalo in the same breath.

As the plane left the runway, Lalo began to examine his reasons for going to Japan. He had dreaded that he would be stuck beneath the strict supervision of his stepfather and had been relieved upon hearing that he would be "fending for himself." Lalo had eagerly anticipated the opportunities presented by a whole new world of strangers. These people would not be suspicious and guarded, as were so many of his current and former acquaintances. He had spent the few weeks considering all of the wonderfully wicked possibilities that fortune had place within his reach.

But, looking out of the small window into the majestic sky, Lalo began to experience wholly unfamiliar feelings: sensations of cleanliness, purity, freedom. He did not understand the nature or the source of this change, but it was as if his old nature were sloughing off of him the farther he traveled from San Francisco. He could be something other than a thief, something other than cruel, something other than a user and abuser of all he encountered.

Japan, 1983

Lalo spent the first two weeks in Japan in a state of euphoria and confusion.

Lalo saw little of his parents, but barely noticed their absence. He roamed the streets of Tokyo, marveling at the sights. He felt exhilarated, playful, and, most profoundly, capable of existing at peace with others and himself. No longer did he feel challenged by every person he met. He felt...good.

During the third week, while wandering throughout a section of town he had yet to explore, he observed a tall Caucasian man carrying two elongated cloth sheaths into a building a few yards ahead. Lalo stopped in front of the building and examined its immaculate facade, upon which a sign read in English: "Tenshin Shoden Katori Shinto Ryu, founded 15th century. Damien Kirkland — Master Swordsman." Directly underneath were a series of Japanese characters, which Lalo assumed simply repeated what was above in Japanese.

Lalo entered the building, stepping into an enormous, beautifully illuminated hall. Directly ahead, he saw 16 men kneeling, heads bowed, each with two swords placed in front of him. They appeared to be statues, unmoving, apparently waiting for someone. An observation area was located to the right of the hall; here, a small group of people were already seated. A large sign above the seating area read: *Visitors welcome. Please remove your shoes and be seated.* Lalo took off his shoes, placed them in a rack with several others, and found a seat near the front of the observation area.

A few minutes passed, and then a man stepped out of a room at the back of the hall. He swiftly and silently assumed a kneeling position in front of the class. The students bowed deeply. The man returned the bow briefly and then jumped straight up into a formal posture. Each class member followed his example.

Lalo sat mesmerized. The grace and beauty of the movements, the obvious demand for discipline, and the power and respect the man in front of the students commanded was extraordinary. He knew that whatever this were, he wanted it. He listened intently as the man began to speak:

"Good morning," said the man, addressing the guests in the observation area. "My name is Damien Kirkland. I see that we have quite a few visitors today, and many appear to be European or American. For that reason, in deference to our guests, I will conduct our historical studies in English today. When we began to practice our forms and movements, I must revert to Japanese, as there are no words in English to describe the absolute beauty and power of *kenjutsu*." Many of the students shook their heads knowingly.

"Before I begin, do any of our visitors have any questions?" asked Kirkland.

Lalo looked around, then raised his hand and stood.

"Yes?" queried the teacher.

"What do I have to do to join up? When can I start?"

"So eager! Do you know anything about our art?" responded Kirkland, softly laughing.

Lalo shook his head no.

"Well, I suggest you listen for awhile, watch what a study session is like, and if you are still interested, see me after the class. I must warn you, much of what you see today will be slow and methodical. This is not a Bruce Lee movie, and we don't break bricks with our hands!" With this, he smiled and motioned for Lalo to be seated.

For the next two hours Lalo listened with rapt attention as Damien Kirkland recited the history of the Japanese swordmaking art, which predated Christian history by over two hundred years. The most magnificent swords were personified or even deified: a tradition, he explained, which still exists presently.

"Swords are awarded denomination with as much prudence as a parent choosing the name of a firstborn child. Many have been honored as *kami*, extraordinary beings. The sword is the avenger, the protector, the healer and the prayer-giver. Even today, our divine emperor could not have ascended to the imperial throne without possession of the Sanshu no Shinki, the Three Sacred Regalia, which includes the most revered and magnificent of all Japanese swords, the Kusanagi no Tsurugi."

After Kirkland finished his lecture, the

practice session began. Lalo watched the meticulous motions of the students as they mirrored the sublimely graceful movements of Damien Kirkland. He knew he had found a sacred truth that could lead him closer to an understanding of who he was and what he wanted to be.

After the class, he waited for what seemed like hours for the appearance of Damien. All of the other observers and most of the students had gone. Finally, Damien strolled out toward where Lalo was seated. Smiling, he spoke:

"You still here? I thought you would have fallen asleep by now...."

Lalo spoke rapidly: "I want to study with you, sir. I want to move like you do, I want to know what you know...."

"Whoa," Damien interrupted, "slow down, my friend. I can sense that you more than *want* to study; you *need* to study. I have a good feeling about you. Can you be here tomorrow at 10 in the morning?"

"Yes, sir." Lalo stood, grinning.

"I'll see you then. We will talk about what you expect, and then I will tell you what I expect. Besides, I need some help keeping this place clean, and I think that you would be a perfect candidate for the job," Damien said.

"Now go home; I've got a wife and kid who just can't wait to see their dad! *Konichi wa!*"

Lalo ran all the way back to his parents' rental house. He could not sleep that night and was waiting at the school by 8 a.m., as he was for the next six months each and every day. He virtually lived at the school, training, cleaning, helping in whatever capacity Damien requested. Damien took to the boy, and Lalo's parents were delighted when Damien asked if Lalo could move in with him and his family.

For the next six years Lalo rigorously studied *kenjutsu*, or sword art. Through the prescribed disciplines of *kenjutsu*, Lalo learned how to counter all other weapons in combat. Damien was an energetic and skilled teacher, and Lalo became highly proficient with both *odachi* (long sword) and *kodachi* (short sword). Damien looked upon Lalo with pride and love, and marveled at his swift understanding and mastery of the most difficult techniques.

For the first time in his young life, Lalo fell in love. In love with himself, in love with *kenjutsu*, and, most importantly, in love with Karina Kirkland, Damien's daughter.

With Damien's enthusiastic blessings, Lalo and Karina were married. As a wedding present, Damien bestowed upon Lalo a priceless treasure, a Nihon-to, believed to have been forged by the master smith Amakuni around A.D. 700. Lalo was stunned; he embraced Damien, and wept through his words:

"Thank you...father...thank you for everything."

"Ah, Lalo," responded Damien, "I love you like a son. I have given you my daughter, my favored sword, and now, a final gift." He handed Lalo a brown envelope, which Lalo opened immediately. As he read the documents, his mouth fell open and he gasped: "You want me to return to San Francisco to open up a school in your name? Why?"

"Because, Lalo," Damien responded, "many of the great masters have opened *ryu* throughout America, but the greatest are located in San Francisco. Yamaguchi has his son teaching Goju Kai there. There also are some of the very best wang chun and kung fu schools in the world. Does this disappoint you? I thought you would have been delighted to return home."

"No, sir, I am truly grateful...my parents have been back there for almost two years. I just never imagined I would have had to return.... I don't know why or what; I just have this feeling that I should stay here, with you, in Japan," Lalo sighed.

"You are basing your future on your past. The past does not equal the future. You can be whatever you want. There is no need to fear. Karina will be with you, and I will stay for a few months to help you get started. Your parents will be proud of what you have become," Damien concluded.

"You honor me with this request. You are father, brother, and master to me. I do not wish to appear ungrateful. I am honored. Of course I will go." Lalo bowed toward Damien.

San Francisco, 1989

Serin grinned. Through his extensive network in the Shadowlands he had learned that Lalo was returning. Serin's mind whirled with the possibilities. *I wonder how difficult it will be to overcome the virtuous dung that pretender of a swordsman has corrupted my sweet child with? Not too terribly difficult, I would imagine. Eventually, they will enter my domain, and I will be waiting for them!* Serin returned to his chamber within the Bough to make preparations for Lalo's arrival.

Montpar Manor, 1989

As soon as he was on American soil, Lalo changed. He became combative, surly, even hateful. He resisted visiting his parents at Montpar Manor, finally relenting when both Damien and Karina convinced him that it would be the proper thing to do.

On the morning of the trip to the manor house, Lalo successively engaged in violent arguments with both Damien and Karina, who was now pregnant with their first child. He alternately pleaded with and screamed at them, begging and demanding not to go. They were equally insistent, and eventually Lalo gave in. "Fine. We will go," he yelled, "and the both of you can go to hell!" He telephoned his parents and told them that they were on their way.

As Damien drove the group up the winding road toward the manor house, Serin crouched in wait. In his hands, poised high above his head, was a sword made of the finest Stygian steel. The discorporated souls used to forge the blade groaned and wailed as Serin slashed the sword to and fro.

Serin began to hum a song he had recently composed:

"Come closer, noble swordsman; I have a prize for you.... I'll wager a flock of fettered souls that I'll cleave your soul in two!"

Serin leapt downward from a granite perch overlooking the ocean and landed on the hood of the car. The sword sliced downward, through the metal of the auto and into the skull of Damien. Though no physical wound was inflicted, Damien screamed as searing images of malignant death filled his mind. He lost control of the car, swerved off the road to the right, and slammed into a large tree.

Lalo examined Karina, who was moaning and holding her forehead where a small red welt had arisen. Peering over the front seat, Lalo saw the cracked and crushed form of Damien slumped over the steering wheel. The blood gushing from Damien's skull indicated instant death.

Lalo lived in a state of confusion for the next few months, retreating into his mind, uttering mumbled fragments of thought. When Karina gave birth to Sarah, they moved from their small apartment into Montpar Manor. Within a week Lalo began disappearing into the cellar for days at a time. He bought a motorcycle and began disappearing into the night, saying nothing to his wife or parents, only to return days later, drunk, drugged, and incoherent.

For weeks at a time he stayed at home and made a sincere effort to control his dark urges. He grew attached to Sarah during these brief periods of time. But Lalo's love for his daughter did not stave off his absences or his drug use.

One morning, upon his arrival home from an extended binge, Lalo found that both his wife and child were gone.

San Francisco, 1994

God, all of that seems so unreal, so long ago...Damien, Karina, Sarah, thought Lalo, returning from the distant memories of his past to the grimy reality of his current life.

Gazing into the fading light of day from the cellar window, Lalo could barely discern the outline of the family crypt, which was to be his final resting place. The crumbling Gothic structure was an obscene monument to the dead Montpars, emblazoned with the family crest and motto: *AUT VINCERE AUT MORI.*

Either to conquer or die, mused Lalo. *Well, I have yet to conquer shit. Is death all I have left to vanquish? At least the crypt is a great place to hide the Harley, and hey, I am an excellent addict. At least I conquered something! At least I succeeded in something....*

He let out a small, tinny laugh as he leaned forward to pick up the film-streaked mirror. Gently balancing a razor between the thumb and forefinger of his right hand, he began to scrape the layers of dust into uniform white lines. Satisfied that no more residue could be summoned from the dust, he set down the razor and picked up the well-used straw. With two short, quick blasts, Lalo inhaled.

Sweet cocaine, he whispered to himself. The initial rush of warmth and well-being spread over him, incestuously creeping downward to surround his groin and thighs with a tingling, honeyed intensity. For a moment he enjoyed the feeling. Coca filled the emptiness, the loneliness.

He knew that this was a delusion of the most brutal type: even as the "white lady" inflamed his passions she left him incapable, unable, impotent. The chain reaction began, and as the lustful surge withered, his fears increased, and the frightened child in his mind demanded more.

Cocaine can keep me awake and alive, he thought. *My heart beats loudly, wildly. I know that I am insane with passion and if I am this alive, death cannot come near me. I can't die. Pain, sickness, pain, sickness, death. It cannot master me. It has no power over me as long as I can keep the dreams away. I must stay awake. I must get more cocaine. What I have left will maybe last the day. And when evening comes I must be prepared to fight off the night. So what to do? Ah, maybe a little bit of thievery. What's another theft or two in the grand scheme of this magnificent life of mine? Shit, on my résumé, if I ever prepare one, stealing would come right after drugging and just before lying!*

Lalo spun around in the leather chair and performed a perfectly executed, though maddeningly slow *mae geri*. Extending his leg with a graceful and practiced power, he moved toward a brief phantasm of light that seemed to glimmer about three feet from his reddened eyes. "Missed," he said aloud. "Christ, here I go again, seeing crap fly by...."

Lalo reexamined the wrinkled baggie, disregarding the hallucination as a function of his habit and confirming his fear that he was nearing the end of his supply. "Well," Lalo spoke aloud, "I had better think about getting the hell out of here and finding someone to donate funds to my heroic quest! If there was cocaine in the Holy Grail I most certainly would have found it!"

Lalo stood, and his heart clicked, the valves laboring to correct the incredulous signals sent by a dope-infested brain. The nosebleeds and the clicking sound in his chest were occurring more frequently, so Lalo tried to rationalize these odd noises and health problems in order to continue his present binge. He figured that all of this came with the territory of snorting, smoking and occasionally shooting up over an ounce of cocaine each week. He was healthy — for an addict.

He suddenly sensed something — no, *someone* very near to him in the damp cellar. He felt as if someone were caressing the base of his neck. He twisted around toward the sensation, but saw nothing.

Am I hallucinating again? he silently wondered.

It happened again — an intense, frigid chill.

"Am I dying?" he implored in a frightened voice. *What is this?* his mind silently screamed. *Am I going to die right now, right here in this piss-smelling pit of a basement? What is this? I am not ready. Dear God, I really want out of this. Why am I so afraid? Why do I bring myself so close to the edge?*

Lalo needed something real. He balled his fist into a *seiken*, the traditional punch of Karate-do, and thrust it into his open hand, unwittingly mocking the salute he had once earned by studying *kenjutsu* for so many years. But his skills, as with so much of his life, had faded. He unclenched his fist, realizing that the only reality left for him was a white powder.

He steadied himself against the chair and began to cry uncontrollably. He saw his broken reflection in the puddled leather seat, which glistened like a cracked mirror.

Somehow, Lalo knew that the reflection was not his own. In terror and revulsion he picked up the keys to his bike and headed for the door.

Lalo effortlessly wove his 1983 Harley-Davidson FLT Glide through traffic. How he had maintained possession of the motorcycle baffled him; he had tried to sell it, tried to trade it for coke, and even left it on the side of the road during a police chase years ago. Each time the bike somehow remained with him. It was a glorious monster of a machine, 94.25 inches long, 59 inches high, with a majestic Vee twin four stroke 1340 cc engine. He made a right turn on Polk Street, searching for a target.

The Underworld

Serin perched like a gargoyle between the handlebars of Lalo's Harley. He loved the power of the bike: the incredible noise, the fantastic vibration, the rich scent of burning gasoline… Looking over his shoulder, he watched Lalo with glee as Lalo scoured the street, oblivious to Serin.

"Oh Lalo, how confused you are," Serin cackled. "What you do not realize is that you are the prey and I am the hunter. That poor soul ahead is merely bait."

Lalo spotted a man just ahead of him. He raced down the street and parked the motorcycle on the opposite side of the road. Opening the saddlebag of the Harley, Lalo extracted a section of lead pipe. Serin bounded off the cycle, racing ahead of Lalo's victim. Doubling back on foot, Lalo quickly caught up with his target.

With great strides Lalo overtook him. The pipe whistled through the air and crunched into the victim's skull. Pushing him into an alleyway, Lalo quickly rifled through his pockets, removing a wallet. Reaching inside the inner pocket of his victim's light-blue suit jacket, he removed a folded wad of bills, a treasure trove beyond his expectations. From there, a watch, a wedding band, and a small signet ring were taken. The man began to move, uttering garbled pleas for his life. Lalo swiftly cracked the pipe across his forehead. He slumped and was silent. Lalo moved quickly out of the alleyway and onto Polk Street, where he hastily crossed over and headed for his motorcycle.

Ah, my sweet — such talent, such pain. So close to me you are, and yet closer still will you be...soon, soon, soon.... Serin watched Lalo mount the Glide and ride off.

In the recesses of Battery Park, Lalo bought all the cocaine that was available and settled a debt to his dealer, Ramón.

"Hey ese, all of dis cocaina para te?" inquired Ramón.

"Sí, mi amigo," replied Lalo.

"Be careful, hombre, dis is good flake. Very pure. Vaya con Dios."

"I truly appreciate your concern," mocked Lalo.

Serin waited for Lalo, clinging to the underside of an overpass. He had timed his lope through the Shadowlands with remarkable accuracy, taking the form of a jackal as he raced parallel to the motorcycle. He had imagined this next encounter for many years, only waiting for the time when the mark of death, visible to those from the Underworld, was most evident. Deep lacerations crisscrossed Lalo's face, extending down his limbs and to the tips of his fingers and soles of his feet.

Serin knew that once the sensation of hopelessness was strong enough, Lalo would easily succumb. Now, watching the drug deal completed, he leered wildly and sang, in shrill tones, some of his favorite verses from an epic written by Johnny Vegas, the poet laureate of the Bough:

Serin, Prince of Smiles, evil, dark and dank
love and lust to him are one
heart and death a brother's song
from him life withers as does the sun.

The Prince of Smiles held the blade
between his gnarled hands
he split the god from nape to ass
and stopped to slit the glands!

"How glorious I am," screeched Serin, as he raced toward his lair.

Montpar Manor

Lalo sat on the floor in the basement, using the murky light from the window above to measure out his fix. He had already snorted two thick lines of it, and thought about preparing some freebase when he realized the best high would come from shooting it up.

How much of this should I cook? he thought. *I guess I could probably handle at least a quarter.*

Serin moved toward Lalo, peering intently into his face, examining the vivid marks that now completely obscured his facial features.

You can handle much more, Serin urged in silence. *Feel the coldness of the room; feel the coldness of my touch.*

Lalo shuddered. He dipped the spoon back into the bag and added almost twice as much as was previously there. *Screw it. I will get good and high. I'll be awake for a week, and then I can deal with all the bullshit.* He added a small amount of water to the powder and began mixing the solution, placing the spoon directly over a thick wax candle burning in front of him. Holding his breath, he plunged the needle into his vein, releasing the entire contents of the syringe into his arm.

Dropping the syringe, he watched as it appeared to float to the ground. He crossed his legs and untied the rig, allowing the screaming trainload of cocaine to course through his body.

"Oh my god, oh my…Sarah," he gasped.

He reached back for his wallet, which contained his only photograph of his daughter. His heart spasmed, buckling him forward toward the grimy basement floor. For 20 seconds he was fully conscious, though unable to move. He began to drift, mumbling his last coherent words: "Sarah, Sarah, Serin…"

Shadowlands

Like two birds, light reaches out,
shuddering; rags of mist cover me.
I am startled, afraid, now shivering.
Am I so old as the comet,
that I should now descend into the sadness of
eternity
after the brevity of life?
The great dark majesty surrounds me,
such anguished isolation,
the furnace of my soul stokes upward toward the
light I sense is there but cannot see. This place is
faint yet familiar, something like the told stories.

Lalo awoke from his dream, feeling immensely refreshed. In the misty place between sleep and awakening, all things are possible.

Sarah, Sarah, I need you my baby, I love you….Today is the day. I will go to see your mom today and I will demand my visitation rights. No more drugs. And I will get a job and pay back all the people I have harmed….

A boisterous giggle filled the room; voices shrieked with laughter. Lalo snapped out of his reverie. As he looked around the cramped and dank chamber, comprehension slowly returned.

It had been many weeks since Serin had brought him to this place, though Lalo could not entirely account for the passage of time. He now knew Serin to be the creature from his dreams, who in subsequent weeks had assumed the role of captor, mentor, and constant companion.

From the beginning of his time in the haunt, Serin had visited upon him one crushing vision after another. He now knew that these were "fetters," memory chains that compelled his soul to be intrinsically constrained to his reaper. Serin had delighted in revisiting the failures of Lalo's life. He had taken him to Montpar Manor, to the aging crypt where Lalo's kin were buried, and to the site of his own burial. Only his mother was present with the priest.

Then, too, there were the painful recollections of his life, from the sale of his fetal soul to the severe images depicting his ruined relationships with his own progeny. Again and again he would be forced to watch her: Sarah, playing, singing, becoming muddied in the yard while frolicking with the puppy…and not once had she asked about him, or thought about him.

"You call out to your daughter now," Serin mocked, "and lament over her absence, yet you were never there for her. How abysmally stupid to yearn for something that never was. You were never a father to her, yet you believe you were special to her, and she to you. You are an addict and a thief and a liar, and so special for all of this. You were destined for me, and I for you. We will be one."

As Lalo's thoughts became more focused, he pulled at the cloudy mass that covered his face. This covering had been affixed to his face since his first day in the Shadowlands. He could not remove it, and shuddered at the thought of what might lie beneath the hardened, chalky bulk that covered his features.

Peering through the murky light, Lalo observed the magnificent relics that had been buried with him in the crypt. The razor-sharp Nihon-to sword, which he had concealed in the tomb shortly after Damien's death, stood gleaming before him. But even more remarkable was his Harley-Davidson, which he had so successfully concealed in the mausoleum for so many years. The powerful machine loomed in the darkness, its splendor more terrific than in life.

He reached into his back pocket and removed the torn lizardskin wallet, worn thin and barren. Peering through a ragged opening in the caul, he gingerly removed the laminated photograph of his daughter. He spoke to the photo as if its subject existed within the four corners of paper and plastic:

"My baby. I am sorry. I am so sorry, Sarah. These words choke me. I tried to be a good father. I could have been. I want to be your daddy. I am your daddy. Do you even know that? I have not seen you for such a long time, since you disappeared with your mother that long weekend. I barely knew that you had gone, until I was out of money, out of dope, out of women wanting both. I staggered home to find the house silent, empty, devoid of life.

"At first I was relieved. No more nagging. No more responsibilities. Within hours I had sold the TV, the cocaine flowed, and faceless women took the place of your mother. I remember that in the early hours of the morning on the second night, I was alone and wandering through the house hallucinating, staring down tree-people and imaginary dogs. I stumbled over your bike…I can remember glimpsing with utter certainty the horror of my life.

"Now I only have this picture left. I can see the thin razor cuts in the lamination. Another plate for my coke. I am disgusting. I truly am a pig."

"Talking to yourself again, my son?" It was Serin's queer articulation that caught Lalo's attention. "Have we still the pangs for our own flesh?" he continued.

"Do we want to visit Sarah today? Do we want to see how well her new daddy treats her?" Serin taunted Lalo. Strangely, Lalo felt little of the pain he had experienced in the last few months. Lalo sat upright, then stood. He searched for the familiar pangs of regret and felt nothing.

Serin spoke to him again, softly, gently. "My child, I have shown you the terrors of your life. You know that I will reap dear Sarah, no matter what it takes. The choice will be yours today. Would you not prefer her to be here with you than relegated to the chains in which your father and you will be bound if you deny me?"

Lalo followed Serin to a large dais in front of the Great Hall of the Bough. Masses of the faithful dead had gathered. A sea of death spread out before him. Serin left him at the side of the stage and gracefully ascended an elaborate pulpit depicting Serin's mythical strangling of Heaven's angels.

Listening intently, a smile formed beneath Lalo's caul as the Prince of Smiles began to address the multitudes:

"The cross on the chest and the devil in the deeds!" Serin spoke, his voice rising, grower stronger and more spirited. "It is the guise we must perfect, my children. All of you, from legionnaire to despot, must continue to reap and make us strong. It is the principal obligation of each and all of you to uncover and procure fresh souls that enter these Shadowlands! These are our riches. We must reap them in abundance. We reject the imbecilic Code of Charon, and I spit as I say his name! Though he is purported to have given the first order to the chaos of the Underworld, and is hailed as a great leader, I say he was a sanctimonious fool, a common ferryman, and we are proof that our way is the way to survive and flourish in this world."

The assembled jumped to their feet, wildly chanting *LORD, LORD, LORD!*

Serin held up a single finger, and the great hall grew still.

"Many of you came to me from the worlds beyond this one. Many came from other haunts, where I delivered you from your enslavement or tortures. How many of you did I free when I destroyed the walls of Alcatraz?"

Loud yells from 300 wraiths in the far corner of the hall: "Us Lord!!!!" Again the deafening roars of approval and gratitude. Serin gestured to the group and gracefully bowed.

"Have I sold a single mane? Have I banished any to accursed Stygia?" A universal acclamation filled the hall. "I condemn the Hierarchy! When my wrath is finally unleashed, when I lead my insurrection against those pious pukes who have the gall to name themselves my superiors, my fury will be a Maelstrom which will make the storm of '67 seem like a soft summer rain!"

The masses were delirious with excitement. Many of those present had survived the Great Maelstrom of 1967, the very gale which swept away Charon, unharmed and protected by Serin. They knew that Serin had the power to make his rhetoric a reality. All that was left was the unveiling of the Named One, the coming of the wraith who would marshal Serin's forces.

"And others, branded or outlawed, did I not open my arms and bring you into our home?"

Some of those standing closest to Serin now raised their hands and howled. Many bore strange marks seared into their foreheads. "Yes Lord, you, it was you, thank you lord!" the marked rejoiced.

Serin waited for the pandemonium to subside. What was left of his heart swelled with a demented pride; he knew that he had the undivided allegiance of the incredible gathering before him.

"I have entered a sacred covenant with each and every one of you. I have promised many things. I have promised you a leader, one with thunder in his heart and steel in his fists. I knew that I must seek a modern man, shackled with dark fetters of past and present times which weigh heavier than a thousand destined for Oblivion. Three decades ago I found my Chosen One, the one whom I have found worthy. For years I have watched and counseled this one, have delighted in his capacity for hatred, loneliness and despair!

Serin paused. The Great Hall was silent. All looked from Serin to Lalo.

"And now, the reason I have called you forth today!" Serin shouted.

Serin motioned to a minion, who brought Lalo forth and forced him to kneel in front of Serin. All knew that Lalo would now be uncauled, and at this moment none but Serin knew exactly what lay beneath.

At Serin's feet, Lalo kneeled, absorbing all that encompassed him. The sensation was overwhelming.

All of my years of drug use could not equal the high I am now feeling, thought Lalo. *I am the high.*

To the right of Serin was a gilded table upon which lay a dragon-handled mirror and the magnificent Stygian sword Serin had so effectively wielded on Damien.

Serin placed a hand on Lalo's shoulder and gently raised him off the floor. He turned him to face the masses, lowering him back to the floor. With one hand he selected the sword from the stand, strode forward, and forcefully slammed the jagged point deep into the floor in front of the kneeling Lalo. Serin picked up the mirror and placed it in Lalo's hands, positioning himself directly behind Lalo, who remained motionless, perfectly calm. Lalo knew what lay behind the caul now. He finally understood, for the first time in his existence, exactly what he must do.

"For the coming of your leader, kneel in adoration!" proclaimed Serin, tearing off Lalo's caul.

The hordes of wraiths gasped aloud, stunned. Slowly, deliberately, all began to drop to their knees, balling their right fists into open left hands.

Lalo looked at his reflection and saw the hideous grin staring back at him. He knew that he did not need the mirror to observe his own features, that he need only look upon Serin to see his own face.

He bounded to his feet, yanking the sword from the floor. He spun, facing Serin for the first time uncauled. Serin stepped back and lowered his head, sweeping his arm forward. Lalo raised the blade above his own head, struggling for a moment with the path that lay before him — and, striking downward, imbedded the point of the blade into the floor at Serin's feet. He dropped to one knee and bowed reverentially, gently placing the worn and laminated photograph of Sarah in the gnarled hands before him.

"My father, thy will is mine."

THE TIES THAT BIND

Kevin Andrew Murphy

t was autumn, and the leaves would have been brown had there been any. There weren't, and cold sunlight slanted down, illuminating a Saturday more dismal than most. I had always detested the Mission District, even in life, and the soot, grime and uninspired graffiti did little to alter that opinion.

However, I had an appointment. The wheels of time turn slowly, but it is possible, when one is dead, to catch glimpses of their future positions. I had paid those whose foresight was better than mine to tell me when and where I might find a certain man; a living man whose acquaintance I had made some years earlier, and of whose service I currently had need. This was a man who had met with Destiny and other weird and otherworldly things.

It was an acquaintance I intended to renew.

Peter came down the sidewalk towards me, boots clomping in not-quite-military precision. He'd changed a great deal in the three years since I'd seen him last. He was more gaunt, with dark circles under his eyes, hair long on top and shaved round the sides, and he'd affected a little ring in his nose and weighted clamps for earrings. A Goth now, though I might have expected as much. The mark of Death was gone from his face, but the scars were still there, showing in the shadows beneath his eyes.

Not that they mattered. Death may be a fearful and jealous mistress, but even *La Morte* has been known to relinquish Her claim when confronted with the proud and haughty visage of Destiny, who takes precedence before even the most dreaded of ladies. Those whom Destiny claims are Hers alone, and though the rewards of such a liaison are often great, it is seldom a simple relationship.

I have never claimed to be a great man. But I do hold in high regard my ability to recognize a greatness in others — or at least a potential for greatness. There are some who hear Destiny calling and answer readily and then there are those who run from it, screaming in denial.

Then there are those who merely recognize it as it rushes by and, if they are quick enough, they can reach out and grab it by the coat tails.

Peter walked right past me, paying me no more mind than do any of the living. It's a rare man who can see ghosts for the Quick have an instinctive fear of the Dead, and shutter their minds away from even the slightest glimpse of that-which-lies-beyond. However, this man, as I knew from experience, could see me as plainly as he could the rest of the world. He just wasn't paying attention.

"Peter, hold a moment."

He paused, listening, then continued down Tenth, hunching into the collar of his pea coat.

I caught up a second later and tapped him on the shoulder with my cane. "Hello, Peter. Remember me?"

His eyes narrowed, gray mirrors that reflected the Shadowlands, and I saw the spark of recognition. "Fuck you. You're dead. Leave me alone." The words came out in a fierce whisper and he turned away, loping off at a swift pace.

"Peter — wait." I had to jog to keep up.

"Get the fuck away from me. I've had enough of everyone thinking I'm crazy. I don't need this shit."

"Wait, Peter. Wait. Peter — Do you want me to tell everyone else?"

He stopped and glared, and the whisper came out in a sharp hiss. "You're a fucking bastard. I ought to beat your face in."

I tried to smile as ingratiatingly as I could. It is always paramount to appear in control, especially when dealing with those who view you with disfavor.

Peter broke eye contact and continued on down the sidewalk, rounding onto Folsom. He spoke again, louder this time, as if he were only talking to himself. "I'm going to Mary's, and I'm gonna get myself a fucking burger, and a fucking table by myself, and I don't wanna talk to anyone."

I followed him down the street and into the restaurant. He didn't speak a word the entire time, and I chose to respect that.

Hamburger Mary's is the type of San Francisco eatery that has been around since the Summer of Love — exposed wood and posters and little bits of stained glass and bric-a-brac. It's one of the jewels of SoMa, the South of Market area, staffed by gays who call each other "Mary," though not nearly as much as they do in City lore. It's a nice, casual place, where the staff is neither on display nor in hiding, and aside from the shadows on the faces of the doomed and the dying (and there's a fair number at Mary's), the feeling is good. As much as anything in the Shadowlands could be.

Peter got a little table in the back and pretended I wasn't there until finally he kicked the chair opposite him out just enough so I could sit down. I waited till he'd finished looking over the menu before I said anything. "Peter, I need your help."

"Fuck you." His lips formed the words, but he didn't voice them.

I've heard that there are some wraiths, mostly Norwegian, who are so scandalized by vulgar language that it sends them screaming into the Tempest. But I'm not Norwegian, and it certainly didn't apply to me. "Peter, listen — I wouldn't really tell everyone that you're a Topper, but I need your help. I have a friend, another wraith, who's lost every connection to this earth except his grave. He was one of the plague victims, the miners they buried out in the potter's field by the Port Authority Building. They've rediscovered it, and the City plans to dig everyone up, cremate them and cast the ashes into the Bay."

"That will be a monument," Peter said softly,

looking at the grain of the wall. "The City likes that sort of thing."

"Probably. It doesn't matter, it wouldn't be the same. Once the fetter is broken, Frank will be lost."

"Fetter? What is he, a fucking horse?" Peter glared back at me. "You talk weird even for a ghost."

I took off my spectacles and began to polish them. "I beg your pardon, Peter. A fondness for legal terminology has followed me even into death, and while it has served me in good stead when dealing with the various Guilds and Hierarchies the Dead have seen fit to amuse themselves with, I do have an unfortunate tendency to slip into the vernacular. My apologies." I placed my spectacles back atop my nose and adjusted the ribbon. "By fetters, I refer to the ties that bind, the reasons a person has for living that are so strong that they continue to hold true even when that person has ceased to live. And when a fetter is gone, your reason for living — "

" '—s your reason for leaving. Don't ask me what it means,'" Peter finished for me, singing. "ABC, 'The Look of Love.' Know it."

"Exactly," I said, continuing blithely onward even though I hadn't the faintest idea what he was talking about. "Yes, well, when a fetter is broken, your reason for living *is* your reason for leaving, and the ties that bind can hold you no longer. The body is one of those, for what could be a more obvious reason for living than that which holds life itself, even when that vessel is broken and the spirit no longer infuses the divine machine?"

I think I was beginning to lose Peter, for he was playing with his napkin and humming the song he'd just recalled, interspersed with snatches of verse: "I don't know the answer to that question . . . if I knew, mmm-mmm-mmm-mmm."

When you're dead, you grow used to the living paying you no mind, but I knew Peter was deliberately ignoring me, and I'd never had patience for that sort of thing. I snapped my fingers quickly in front of his face. "Peter, pay attention." He glared at me and I continued: "If Frank's fetter is destroyed, he'll fall into the Tempest. And by that I mean neither a mundane rainstorm nor the Bard's play, but a maelstrom of spiritual energy that will suck him down to Oblivion, if he isn't caught along the way by various fiends, who will enslave him or worse.

"And that's why I'm here. Frank would be scattered with his ashes, and if not destroyed outright, he'd be made a slave. The miners left so little that's tangible, but their legend is strong. There are spirits who want that power, who are willing to sacrifice Frank and others like him in order to seize it."

Peter's mirrored eyes looked at me, and I'm still not sure whether he was looking to the core of my soul or just looking right through me like the rest of the Quick. It was that sort of look.

He broke it off as his burger came. It was a big sloppy one, with fried bread on each side and lots of juice and trimmings, so thick he had to go at it with a fork. I could feel his hunger and the savor as he took a bite, and I reached out to share a bit of the real experience.

The knife flashed in Peter's hand and he whacked me with the flat of the blade. "Get your fucking fingers off my food, you rotten ghost bastard. You're gonna give me a case of grave rot." He took the knife and polished it clean with the napkin, then on second thought set it aside and took the clean one from the setting on my side of the table. "And now you've got everyone thinking I'm a fucking loony. Hey," he said, sitting up straighter and looking right through me this time, "I'm practicing for a play. Gotta problem with that? 'Alas poor Yorick. I knew him well.'" He slumped back down and locked eyes with me. "'He was a dick.'"

"Sorry." I glanced back at the two women who were looking at Peter with over-mascaraed eyes. They shrugged after a moment and went back to their lunch.

Peter went back to attacking his hamburger and swallowed it in big bites, juice running down his chin. "So," he said around a mouthful, "this friend of yours loses his place. So what? Why doesn't he just go into the light along with Carol Ann and the rest of you assholes?"

I'd never heard Ascension discussed so quickly and crassly, and I wasn't expecting his next remark: "Okay, fine, you can't, you're stuck, you're here in Purgatory and I'm stuck here with you and I have to listen to you whiny bastards 'cause I'm the closest thing you've got to some *Poltergeist* midget psychic. Fuck that. If I knew how the hell to get into the light, I would have done it a long time ago, and the only reason I haven't bumped myself off yet is that from everything I've seen being dead sucks even more than being alive. What do you want me to do? I can't stop City Hall, and once they get it into their heads to build a monument, there isn't anything in this world or the next that's gonna stop them. So what do you want me to do?"

Peter wanted the cards on the table, and I

had to give them to him. "We were hoping you could dig up Frank's body and move it elsewhere."

"You want me to go grave robbing."

I tried to put the best face on it. "Well, yes, if you could, please."

Peter attacked the french fries, not saying anything for another minute or two. "Why don't you go find some girl who just died and get her to ask her boyfriend to do it?"

Believe me, I'd tried, but young wraiths are jealous of their fetters, and even if you get them to ask, most mortals balk at the idea of grave robbing, especially at the request of the dead. "I think you know the answer to that, Peter. It's a terrible thing to be chained as a thrall. The chains are forged from the broken souls of the Dead, their shattered promises and dreams. Frank doesn't deserve that sort of a hell. No one does. You can save him."

"What do I look like? Fucking Amnesty International?" Peter contemplated a french fry and licked a drop of ketchup off his nose ring. "How much is he paying you?"

"What?"

"Don't give me that shit — How much is he paying you? You're not Casper the Friendly Ghost, you're Thaddeus Winters, the Greedy

Bastard. I know your rep and who you are, and you're not doing this out of the goodness of your heart. What's this fucking Frank the Dead Miner paying you that you're threatening to write my phone number on every bathroom wall in the Otherworld?"

I fussed a bit with my gloves, making sure the buttons were secure at the wrist. "Frank is older than me. Not in life, but in death. He's the shade who removed my caul after I died." I glanced back up. "He's my Reaper, and I owe him a great debt."

Peter looked at me, his mirror eyes seeing into the darkest corners of my soul. "Don't give me that shit. I bet you paid him off a dozen times, or at least got him to agree that you paid the debt and that he even owed you."

There are many frightening and terrible things about death, and people like Peter are among them. "You're right. I've treated him abysmally, and not as one should treat a friend or Reaper. But if his fetter is destroyed, then he'll be taken by the Regents of the Skeletal Lord. I know this. And Franklin knows where my fetters lie from the early time we spent together. And if I'm taken as a thrall, I'll be forced to tell my new master everything. And that includes everything about you, Peter." I

paused, letting it sink in. "A Topper is a precious
and wonderful thing to the Dead. A mortal who
can see and touch us without charms or effort,
and who doesn't risk being consumed by the
Shadow. . . ."

"You don't know what the fuck you're talking
about." He stabbed the ice in his Coke with the
straw and it rattled like the chains of Stygia.
"The Shining sucks worse than Stephen King
ever imagined, and you bastards nearly got me
killed a dozen times over. I've seen my Shadow,
and that's something no living person should
ever have to do."

"The mark of Death isn't upon you anymore,
Peter."

"No thanks to you, asshole." He stabbed the
ice again. "I bet Shirley Maclaine never had to
deal with this shit. Housewives in Oregon get
two-thousand-year-old medicine men as their
spirit guides. I nearly die, what do I get? Some
fucking Robber Baron lawyer. Who the hell
wants to talk to you?"

I shrugged. "Do you want ancient wisdom or
competent legal advice?"

"Fuck you."

He was evading the issue. "If you really want
to go on the talk-show circuit, Peter, you can
tell them I'm a law-speaker from ancient

Lemuria. That should appeal to the credulous masses. It's not as if anyone could prove it regardless. But who knows? If I'm taken along with Frank, then your name will be sold to the highest bidder and there's no telling what number of dyspeptic old medicine men's shades may show up at your door — if that's really what you want."

Peter stirred his Coke, avoiding my eyes. "Listen, I'll think about it. But it won't be easy digging up a parking lot."

"The asphalt is already broken, and the bones are lying exposed."

"Says you," Peter said. "You wraiths see the future. I only see the present, and I don't need you to tell me things have gone to hell 'cause I already know they're going there. Anyway, tomorrow's Halloween. I've got things to do, and there's no way I'm messing around in a graveyard on Halloween night — too much weird shit going down without digging up dead men's bones on top of it."

"We don't mind."

"Frank ain't the only one buried there, you know, and there's nastier things than you ghosts out on Halloween night. Anyway, even if you and Frank are the only things that go bump in the night tomorrow, you aren't the cops, and if the cops don't have everything guarded, I'll have to stand in line behind the weirdloops who want to sacrifice cats and read Crowley to each other. Everybody knows where those graves are, so fuck that shit." Peter threw a handful of bills on the table and stood up. "I'll be at the House of Usher on Tuesday and the Temple on Thursday. You know where to find me." The hem of his coat whipped through me as I sat there and Peter stormed out of the restaurant.

I was quite proud of Peter. He'd done a lot of growing up since last we'd met.

■

Frank was where I'd left him, his customary perch in the Washbag, the Washington Square Bar & Grill. "How did it go?"

I shrugged. "Better than expected. He didn't say no."

Frank smiled. He still looked like the boy he'd been when he died, seventeen, with golden hair and green eyes. His miner's shirt was gone, replaced with a 49ers T-shirt, though he still had the same rough-worn denim jeans. It was a well chosen ensemble, nothing the drunks would find remarkable when they caught a glimpse of him in the bar's mirror. My own suit and cravat were of course a trifle old-fashioned, but this was San Francisco, and in a city where men wore tea dresses and women wore lumberjack shirts, it would take far more than that to raise any questions.

As they also said of the City, the miners came in '49, the whores in '51, and there, beside Frank, was Grace. She'd died in 1951, not 1851, but for all the century of difference between them, they made a couple. Grace had traded her semblance of a bloody murdered harlot for the dress of one of the movie queens of the late '40s of this century, and her auburn locks were immaculately curled and styled.

She twined her fingers with Frank's and moved closer to him. "You've got to help Frank, Teddy."

I moved up to the bar, sharing a draught of one patron's Anchor Steam. "I fully intend to, Grace. And drop the little-girl-lost tone; I've a feeling that's part of what got you killed in the first place."

Grace gasped, playing her part immaculately, and I saw the Shadow look out of Frank's eyes for a moment. A danger. "I beg your pardon, Grace. That was a very uncivil remark, and unbecoming of a gentleman. I'm just a bit overwrought. Peter is a very difficult man to deal with."

Frank's eyes returned to their customary green, and Grace dimpled. "Okay," she said in her best baby-doll voice. "I know it's tough getting living guys to believe in you." Her lips formed a tiny moue. "And not much fun even if they do."

Frank nestled closer to Grace, comforting her. "Don't worry, Grace. Thaddeus says the guy's a Topper. He'll be easier to talk to." He looked up, plaintively "He is a psychic, ain't he? We're not just wasting time?"

I glanced about, making sure that the rest of the Washbag's patrons were both living and interested in other matters, then leaned over and shared another draught of Anchor Steam. "Peter," I said, softly and distinctly, "in my personal and professional opinion, he is no mere sensitive, nor strong enough to warrant being called a Topper. Oh, I have no doubts that he may have started life as such — there's a certain fey and otherworldly quality about the boy. That sort of air only comes about through long experience — but after what he has been through and the talents he has evinced . . . no. He is a magician, a potent spiritualist — though frankly, I don't believe he's realized it yet."

"A magician?" Grace asked. "You mean like

Copperfield?"

"No, Grace," I said, biting back several choice remarks, "not like Copperfield, nor Houdini. A true magician, a Magus, one of the wise men whom we have come to know as the Magi — though I believe they now call themselves mages to keep from offending the fairer sex such as yourself." I touched the brim of my hat in deference. "Magician, witch, sorcerer — it all comes to the same thing. They know we are here, and I know you've heard the stories and the warnings: necromancers and spiritists, living men who can drag the Dead before them and force them to do their bidding. Conjurers who trap souls in bottles, and dark priests who can send them to Hell. Soothsayers and oracles who see more of the worlds beyond Death than the Dead themselves.

"Euthanatos, I've heard they call themselves, the 'Good Deaths.' Hollow Men. Strange and arcane Orders and Brotherhoods." I held out my cane, pointing to one after another, as if representatives of all of these were before me.

I let my arm fall and shrugged. "It really does not matter. We gain our power when we realize that we are Dead. They gain their power when they realize the world is a stranger place than they imagined. We take our own in hand for our own reasons, and they do the same.

"Sometimes one falls between the cracks. A duckling goes astray to be raised by wolves or a fox by magpies. Pick a metaphor; I'm sure there's a better one. But Peter nearly died once, and It was there that he met with the Dead — myself included. He has been doing his best to avoid us ever since, though unlike most who tread upon the hem of the Moon-Angel's robe, he cannot forget what he saw, or stop seeing it. And as dour and taciturn as he is, I see little reason for him to have ever made the acquaintance of other mages — or for him to have taken up their tricks or their politics. And as he is living, and wishes only to be left alone, he won't give a fig if he knows the location of your bones . . . even if he is the one who helped to move them. This leaves him our best and brightest option."

Grace put on an innocent look and batted her eyelashes. "Could we maybe meet him? If we ask him nice-like, well, maybe . . ."

I considered Peter to be one of my own secrets, but I'd already let most of my hand show. And desperate times . . . "It is a possibility. He won't do it tomorrow, but he's mentioned two likely rendezvous points: the House of Usher on Tuesday and the Temple on Thursday. I can only assume they're nightclubs. I'll need to do more research."

Grace brightened. "They are. The H of U is at Thunder Bay in Berkeley, and the Temple is at the Oasis. They're Goth clubs. And if he's going to them, I'd bet anything he'll be at the Waydown tomorrow."

I had not considered Grace as a source of information. "The Waydown?"

Grace nodded. "It's what they call the Old St. Francis Church in the Haight. Some of the underground clubs go there, and it's where they're holding the Necrotic Neurotic Halloween Ball tomorrow night."

"Necrotic Neurotic?" I'd heard of the Exotic Erotic Halloween Ball, but still . . .

Grace dimpled. "It's a Goth thing."

Frank smiled again, looking at Grace. "Well, at least we've got something to do for Halloween." He looked back to me, and I saw the fear in his eyes. "It beats waiting for them to dig up my bones and burn them."

I nodded in assent. "Agreed. Speaking from personal experience, I must say that having one's bones incinerated is less than pleasant."

■

The Old St. Francis proved to be in the

Ashbury Heights near Mount Olympus. Fire had blackened the exterior, and the marble statues of St. Francis and his little animal friends had had their heads knocked off long ago. Someone had thoughtfully replaced them with grinning jack-o'-lanterns, however, and girls dressed in cobweb lace were happily running about festooning everything that didn't move with orange and black crêpe. Flyers done up, black on purple with illustrations in the style of Edward Gorey, proclaimed the coming revel with phrases like "It's a Dead Man's Party!" and "Every Day is Halloween!"

We felt right at home.

Grace had felt it an engaging idea to appear in the manner of our deaths, and she now looked like a murdered whore circa 1951 (though far less grisly than I'm certain she'd looked originally), while Frank looked like a miner fresh in from the gold fields (as opposed to the cholera ward). I told them I died of smoke inhalation, as I did not particularly wish to retake my aspect as a charred corpse from the Great Fire. However, my top hat and spectacles lent me a dignified air, and I noted at least one or two of the mortals had affected similar apparel.

Dusk fell, the fog rolled in, and the revelers began to arrive on motorcycles and in cabs and limousines. There were of course several who arrived in hearses, as might be expected, though the most stylish by far was the young lady who rode in (presumably from just down the block) on a penny-farthing dating to somewhere between Frank's death and my own.

Peter had not shown as yet. To brighten Frank's spirits somewhat, Grace decided to explore the inside of the church. The Old St. Francis had caught fire in the '20s as I remembered, and there had never been enough money to repair the damage or enough interest from the local Catholic diocese to do anything other than hold onto the land as an investment. All attempts at chain link fence had of course been cut to bits long ago, and last I'd heard, hippies had used it as a crash pad.

Their heirs, the Goths, had now made it their own, and the Deejay had set up atop the altar. The crucifix that had no doubt hung behind it had been removed, replaced by speakers and a crucified medical skeleton wearing an iron crown. Loud morose music pertaining to Lucrezia Borgia blared out of the apse, while the main portion of the nave was now arguably the dance floor, though no one was dancing as yet. At present, it was occupied by various cliques who milled about, snubbing one another, whispering behind each other's backs, and generally behaving as if they were members of some baroque court. Lucrezia would have approved.

The west transept had been set up as a lounge, the last of the pews mixed with couches and odd furnishings, while the east transept and choir loft had suffered the worst damage from the fire and now stood open to the sky. Moonlight poured in, filling them with rich shadows, and this seemed to be the smoking area, for the cherries of cigarillos and clove cigarettes winked on and off in the darkness, a cloud of smoke hovering in the charred remains of the choir loft.

At the fore of the church, the baptismal font blazed with witchfire, flames dancing on the surface as drops of molten sugar fell in from the brandy-soaked sugar loaf suspended in the silver tongs above; an old-fashioned German *feuerzangenbowle*, tended with painstaking heresy by a young man with black hair and tiny blue spectacles who dispensed the flaming punch into paper cups and goblets and whatever drinking receptacles were proffered. I stood by, sharing the pleasure of the young Goths in what for them was a new experience.

"Great party, huh?" a girl asked me, sipping

her punch.

"Um, I suppose." I looked at her carefully. She wasn't dead or damned, which only left the third alternative: drunk.

"Ooh, what a cool cane. Where'd you get it?"

"I died with it, though originally I believe it came from the Orient."

"Cool. I like the little ball in the dragon's mouth. I hope I die with something half as neat." She took another sip of her punch and wandered off, spilling blue flames onto the floor.

Goths are very intriguing creatures. To look Death in the eye and appear blasé about it is something most wraiths only aspire to.

But I kept my vigil at the baptismal font and was rewarded an hour later by the appearance of Peter. He'd switched nose rings for something smaller and more subdued, but aside from that was identical to his appearance the day before.

"Hello, Peter."

He paused, then studiously ignored me, getting a flaming punch, tossing a handful of bills into the collection box, and going off with a quartet of three girls and a boy.

I followed, having to wait it out as he and his friends danced to various songs which proclaimed that Bela Lugosi was dead and that Joan Crawford had risen from the grave. She hadn't to the best of my knowledge, unless someone had mistaken Grace for the dead actress. At last Peter tired and I was able to hook him off the floor with my cane.

"Hey, wha — "

"Peter," I said, "I would like to have the pleasure of introducing you to my very good friend, and Reaper, Franklin Deere. Franklin, this is Peter, the young man I mentioned. Peter is only a few years older than you were when you died, so you should have a good deal in common."

Frank, a well mannered man in spite of a lowerclass upbringing, immediately doffed his hat and held it to his chest, smiling and leaning forward, extending his hand for a handshake. "Pleased to meet you, Peter."

Peter only looked at Frank's hand, then back at the two of us. "You assholes want everyone to think I'm crazy?" he whispered. "I don't shake hands with ghosts."

I saw a hint of the Shadow twist behind Frank's eyes, and I placed a hand on his shoulder. "Steady, Frank. We must excuse Peter. Young men of his generation were never tutored in the finer points of etiquette."

I placed my cane against Franklin's cheek and the dragon's pearl glowed black for a second, the

Shadow ebbing. Though I have seen many useful and magical artifacts since my death, I must say that I consider my cane to be the finest. In life, I paid little mind to the old Chinese gentleman who sold it to me, and less to his talk of dragons and pearls and the forces of yin and yang; in death, I wish I had, for though the real cane is as charred as my body, the touch of its spiritual remnant has proved anathema to the Shadow and the forces of Oblivion.

Not that my *memento mori* was much aid in dealing with a petulant psychic or fledgling mage. But then, serendipity provides assistance from the most unexpected quarters, and I observed Peter smile (or at least cease frowning) and look to the right of Frank and myself.

"I'm Grace," Grace said, and I noticed that the trace of blood had disappeared from the corner of her mouth and the bruise was gone from her cheek. "If you don't shake hands, maybe you'd like to dance. Teddy doesn't understand stuff like that . . . He doesn't know what it is to have fun. Just power and politics, that's him. But don't worry, we're . . . "

"Peter," a girl said, coming up behind our Topper.

"Yeah, let's dance!" Grace said, grabbing Peter by the hand and pulling him onto the

dance floor along with the girl who'd come to
retrieve him. The black lights gave the few
specks of brightness an eerie pallor, but Peter did
indeed begin to dance, or at least gyrate, with
Grace. Frank's paramour, I must admit, was a
lovely figure of a woman, and she'd picked up
on the flow of all the modern dances . . . or,
should I say, lack of same, as there seemed to be
no recognizable form or choreography to the
Goths' random cavortation.

Frank beamed with pride beside me. "That's
my Grace. She knows what my momma always
said: You catch more flies with honey than you
do with vinegar."

My mother had also had a number of sayings,
mostly to do with painted women and the harlot
of Babylon, but I was not about to complain. If
Grace, and her various methods of persuasion,
made Peter amicable to what he wouldn't
countenance when confronted with either
threats or reason, then all to the good.

The drunken girl beckoned me at one point,
and Frank noticed and hooted, shoving me onto
the dance floor as he joined Grace and Peter and
their partners. The music went on and on,
bleating incessantly about how every day was
Halloween, which while certainly a pleasant
thought, was very far from the truth. I

manifested slightly, enough to give my partner a turn or two I knew from the fox trot, and the dance went on for some time before I could escape.

Grace and Frank followed a few minutes later with Peter, slipping out through the gap in the wall of the east transept. Someone had set up a projector and the wall of the church was illuminated with a twenty-foot-tall transvestite in a green dress and rubber gloves.

"Give 'em to Magenta . . . she knows what to do with bloody rubbers!" chanted the Goths in the weed-choked garden, and Peter sidestepped a number of people garbed in rather more gaudy attire than most of the assembled company. I walked straight through a blond man clad in nothing more than a gold lamé jockstrap and he shivered, I knew, from more than just the night's chill.

We slipped out through the gates and away from the Old St. Francis, its hilltop an island in the sea of fog that had overwhelmed the city. Peter led the way down into the mists and we walked a long while in silence until he found a suitably private alcove.

He leaned his back against the shop window. "Okay, you guys found me. Now give it to me straight without Thaddeus here adding his lawyer bullshit."

Frank stuffed his hands in his pockets and looked like the shy boy from the gold fields. "Well, it's like this, Peter. Thaddeus has a lot of people who don't like him, and a lot of people who want to get at him and get the secrets he knows. And I know where Thaddeus' fetters are."

"And Frank's too nice to tell anyone, even though Teddy's just a bloodsucking lawyer who deserves what he gets," Grace put in, glaring at me. The bruise reappeared on her cheek. "He'd sell Frank out in a second if the tables were turned."

Peter's mirrored eyes surveyed the three of us, then he whistled, soft and low. "Now the whole story comes out — Thaddeus screwed the Hierarchy, and now they're out to get him, and they don't care who they fuck up along the way."

I surveyed the head of my cane, perusing the skillful carving and the intricate whorls of the ivory. Pity, as I mentioned, that its powers were completely useless in the current situation. "In a nutshell, yes."

"You're an asshole, Thad. But then, we already knew that."

I was not expecting the punch, nor the force of it. Pain exploded through my gut and I doubled over, falling to the tiles of the alcove, which stank of urine and human sweat.

Through the haze of pain, I heard Peter's voice. "And you, Frank, are too goddamn nice for your own good. Fuck. I swore I'd never play midget psychic again, and here we go." There was another kick in my stomach, then Peter hoisted me to my feet. When they got to use it, the strength of the Quick was frightening, and I was not used to the idea that mortals could touch me, let alone hurt me. But then, Peter was not your usual mortal, or even your usual psychic. "Now wake up, you bastard. We're gonna get Frank's bones and put them somewhere safe, then you're going to apologize to Frank for fucking up his life."

"Death," Frank said.

"Whatever. How's that sound?" Peter shoved me back against the glass and pressed the head of my own cane into my throat.

"Fine," I whispered.

"Then you're gonna go to whoever you screwed and give 'em what they want, so they take Frank out of the loop, so he doesn't have to deal with shit from assholes like you."

"Fine."

"Good, now swear it on something so you can't weasel out."

"Charon's Scythe," Grace suggested, damn her.

"Charon's Scythe. Yeah, that sounds good. Swear it on Charon's Scythe that you'll apologize to Frank and do everything in your power to keep him out of the shit you've brought on yourself."

"Let him down, Peter," Frank said. "He can't breathe."

"Since when do the Dead need to breathe?" Peter asked, but did relax his hold and allowed me to take my cane out of my throat.

I paused and straightened my cravat, gathering what shreds of dignity I still possessed, then held forth my cane in the manner of a ceremonial mace, not, I'm sure, that any of the three would have recognized the symbolism. "All right. I, Thaddeus Anthony Winters, do swear by Charon's Scythe that I will do all within my power . . . by fair means or foul . . . to remove the threat to Franklin Deere posed by my enemies. And I do also hereby apologize to Franklin, my Reaper, for the heartache and grief I have caused him and his." I lowered my cane and stamped it three times on the ground. "So let it be witnessed.

"Is that sufficient?" I asked, looking to the three confronting me.

In answer, there came a thunderclap, rolling through the ether. A moment later, there was the sound of firecrackers and bottle rockets and the tolling of a church bell.

Peter looked at his watch. "Midnight."

Grace smiled with malice. "On the Eve of All Hallows. I think your oath has been witnessed."

"Full moon too," Frank remarked and a chill passed down my spine.

Let it not be said that the men of the Winters family make unimpressive oaths. And, take this as a warning — One does not meddle with the pawns of Destiny unless one is willing to come under the influence of that austere lady oneself. Peter, as I said, bore Her mark, and to deal with him was to deal with Her.

However, as might be expected, I felt more than a touch of foreboding, and was generally subdued all the while as Peter found his car and drove us to the Port Authority Building.

Fog shrouded everything, thick as a blanket and twice as dense, and it was an hour before we arrived. Frank led the way to his grave site, which, despite what Peter had said, was broken open and covered against the rain with a rotting tarp. There were no police out and about, or if there were, they were well concealed by the fog.

"This it?" Peter asked.

"Yeah." Frank walked around. "Under this tarp here."

Peter pulled the canvas back, and the smell of mildew and decay wafted up. Bones lay there, partially exposed, with bits of string and wooden pegs and the other props of the archaeologists' trade set into the earth around them.

The fog swirled as Peter stepped over one of the cords, and the moonlight coalesced before him, becoming a twisted parody of a human form, skin pocked with decay and rot, and eyes empty sockets filled with the Shadow.

The figure laughed and Peter leapt back. "Holy fuck!"

The spectre leered. "I've been called many names. That one will do as well as any." It looked to Frank, the Shadow of its eyes open in a lightless void. "Hello, Franklin. You've come back. Open yourself to the Dark and we shall kill this mortal, then feast on the souls of your three companions as we drag them to Oblivion. You hate the lawyer for what he has done to you, and you envy the whore for having sampled every night the pleasures you only dreamed of before you died. You know it's true. We spoke of it before your death. Died a virgin. What a shame." The spectre held up its hands and the fingers lengthened into claws. "Let's share the pain."

Its voice was hypnotic, like a siren, but it was Grace's scream that broke the spell. "Frankie! No! Don't listen to it!"

Franklin's eyes had changed from green to black as his own Shadow was drawn out, so I had no time for subtlety. I hooked my cane around his neck in a throttle hold, and the dragon's pearl spun in a black void, consuming the darkness.

The spectre turned its attentions to Grace. "Hello, Grace. Terrible, isn't it, that you could only find a man to love after one had already killed you? Poor Grace. Not even a man. Merely a boy, a virgin, and one who'd remain so forevermore. That's it, isn't it? You could never love a man who could hurt you, rape you, take his hard stick and make you bleed like — "

"Peter!" I called out. "Kill it!"

He had taken up one of the archaeologists' shovels and held it in a fighting stance. Unfortunately, I fear that his training consisted mostly of bad action movies, for his swing only hit it a glancing blow.

The rotting horror paused for a bare moment, suddenly realizing that this was a mortal who could indeed harm it, then darted in and out, barely touching him with its claws, but laughing, playing with him like a cat. "Hello, live meat. Happy Halloween. Come to play with the dead, have you?" It cackled and feinted at him again, watching him jump back.

I hoped Frank could deal with his own inner demons, for I had a more immediate and external one to deal with myself. I disengaged my cane from Franklin's neck, then grasped the handle and twisted, unsheathing the blade.

A gentleman never goes anywhere without his cane, and there are good reasons for this. I feinted and lunged, the phantom slashing back and screaming as it lost half a paw. "Hello, Thaddeus," it said. "Don't you — "

"Frippery and nonsense," I shouted back, "I've had quite enough of your second-rate badgering. You may terrify Frank and you may horrify Grace, but you are no longer dealing with an inexperienced boy or a battered woman." The first rule of debate and of swordsmanship is to never allow your opponent an opening, and to always take the offensive. I pressed my advantage as best I could. "You are nothing more than some tedious creature of the Void, some weak spirit without enough sense of identity to hold its own when it met its Shadow. You are pathetic, less than nothing, and would be beneath my notice except that you have dared to annoy those under my protection."

I drew blood again, or at least putrescent ichor, but then the fiend managed to slip a paw past my guard. "Pompous ass!" Blood welled up on my side. "Everyone hates you! You have nothing more to defend yourself than words and hot air!"

"That, and a good sword," I said, slashing the creature down the side. It screamed, pus oozing from the wound. "As for the opinions of others, I don't care a whit, especially for the opinions of creatures such as yourself."

I would like to say that my rapier wit, or at least my rapier, finished the beast, but that is far from the truth. At the moment when I was about to sally forth with a new and deadly offensive, there came a sickening crunch, and the spectre began to discorporate, screaming. Almost as quickly, a webwork composed of tiny bones appeared about it, twisting and confining, then abruptly taking it . . . elsewhere.

I have seen wraiths go not-so-gently into that good night, and even the final end of spectres, but this was like none of them. It was old magic and arcane magic, and I recognized the bone motif as the hallmark of the Skeletal Lord, the lord of disease and pestilence. The lifeweb set to catch Frank and the others had taken its first victim.

I stood there, panting, trying to staunch my wounds, my sword still at the ready. But when I looked around, I saw Peter and Grace standing over a recently excavated and shattered skull. A hole in the brainpan would have been sufficient to release the spirit and ruin the fetter, but Peter had been a bit more thorough. The spectre had not been destroyed, only severed from its connection with the Shadowlands, then caught by the magics of the Skeletal Lord.

Frank crawled over, his eyes once more green. He reached his hands out to touch the bits of crumbled bone. "Miles. It was Miles. I knew him. . . ."

The encounter with the spectre had shaken me very badly, but not as badly, I knew, as it had Frank. Now was not the time for harsh words. "Even the best of us can succumb to the darkness, Franklin. I'm sorry you lost your friend."

Grace comforted Frank in ways I never could while I wiped my sword off on one of the tarpaulins, the black ichor turning to dust. I sheathed the blade.

Peter looked at me, the strangest mixture of expressions upon his face. "Don't be so dumbfounded," I said. "Fencing was a common skill for men of my class, and now that I can safely admit it, I must say that my skill with the blade does not match my command of the language. And you were right about additional complications. If you could see to retrieving Frank's bones, I'll tend to my injuries."

I sat down rather heavily. The pain from the wound the spectre's claws had left was intense, but began to ease as Grace used her gifts to bandage them. "Thanks for helping Frank, Teddy."

I wished she wouldn't use that name. "Think nothing of it, Grace. We all do what we must." I closed my eyes. "Clever of you to destroy the beast's fetter while I kept it busy."

"Peter was the one who did it," Grace said, but I knew it was she who had told him where and what to look for. I had been seriously underestimating the woman's capabilities, for all that she downplayed them so well.

I opened my eyes. Peter had taken up the shovel again and was digging about, and I could see from the cast of his features that he had allowed Frank to slip inside him, as Frank knew how to handle digging tools, and knew the precise location of his own bones as well. One by one Frank's bones were freed from the earth and placed atop the tarp.

"Do you have all of them?" Grace asked, coming up beside them.

"Yeah, everything, plus a little dirt," Frank/ Peter said, reverently folding the canvas over Frank's remains and gathering them up in his arms. Frank slipped out of Peter's body, leaving Peter to hold the precious fetter alone.

Peter stood there, looking at Frank. He was still shaken from his encounter with the spectre, and though there were no physical marks on his body, the psychic wounds were probably near as great as my own. "Where do you want me to take them?"

Frank was at a loss for words, as I saw him no doubt realize that just setting them in the corner at the Washbag would not do.

"And no, you can't stay at my apartment," Peter said. "You seem like a nice enough guy, Frank, but I have enough trouble with living roommates without having a dead one too."

In the distance, I heard the moan of a foghorn, sounding its beacon across the Bay. "I'm sure anywhere relatively safe and secure would be fine, Peter. Preferably somewhere no one is liable to go digging, and where the other wraiths are more pleasant company." After the debacle with the spectre of Miles, I understood why Frank had been having so much trouble with his

Shadow.

"You could be buried with me," Grace said.

"Really?" I inquired. "And where might you be buried, Grace?"

She looked shyly at her feet and scuffed a toe through the dirt. "Nowhere near here. Sorry."

Frank hugged her anyway. "It's all right, Grace."

"Well," said Peter, "we can't just stand around here all night, and I'm not going to wait for that fucking thing to come back. How'd you like to be the patron saint of the Goths, Frank? There's a reliquary back at the Waydown just waiting for some bones."

"Safer than many places," I said, "and there is the added bonus of having your bones honored. It should prove more satisfying than taking corpus from local football games, if less entertaining."

"Settled, then," Peter said and walked off through the fog.

The Goths at the Waydown were enraptured with Peter, for he had won some unspoken contest to be "more morbid than thou." To not only rob a grave . . . alone, and on All Hallow's

Eve . . . but to then treat the stolen bones as
saint's relics was an idea that captivated one and
all, and the various cliques became united in
purpose to share some of the glory and pooled
their knowledge and resources as they prepared
Frank's bones for the reliquary. One girl knew
that relics were to be washed in wine, while
another donated a white silk scarf for the
cerements, and a boy wearing enough crosses to
outfit a sidewalk vendor in Barcelona had on
him a Latin prayer book, including last rites,
prayers for the dead, and requests for the
beatification of saints. It now being All Saints
Day by an hour or so, it seemed to be a perfect
time to go about the process, and the Goths
queued up to enter the sacristy while the deejay
felt it appropriate to put on the rave mix of
Orff's *O Fortuna.*.

After what we had just gone through, Frank
especially was sorry he couldn't stay for it, for
the power in such a ritual was great, even if
Peter's associates didn't know exactly what they
were doing. However, there were still things to
be done, and places to go and people to meet if
I wanted to fulfill my oath, which was what
Frank and peripherally Grace wanted as well.
Also, a plan was forming, based on suppositions
I could make and on the interesting manner of

departure of the spectre, Miles. With luck, it would cost me very little to see this matter to its close.

We prevailed on Peter to drive us again, and he was intrigued, or at least shell-shocked, enough to go along with the idea. I promised I would make it worth his while.

Now, there are some things those not of the City do not generally know. One is that, with the exception of the Military Cemetery at the Presidio and the old graves at Mission Dolores, and the odd potter's field or plague monument (such as Frank's), no one is buried in San Francisco. All of the graves were moved to Colma just south of the City, and the Necropolis there is one of the jewels of the Hierarchy. The Citadel of the Presidio is the heart of the old guard's military force, but the heart of pride and politics is the Citadel at Colma.

How do I describe the splendor of Colma? It is a grand and glorious nihil, filled with the avenues and palaces of the dead, and each of the nine cemeteries is dedicated to one of the Nine Legions. Cypress Lawn is the province of the Legion of Thorns, and was my home until the Insurrection. That happened in the '60s of this century, and consisted of the Renegades (or Loyalists as we prefer to be called) breaking free from the Hierarchy (or Usurpers as we Loyalists like to call them). As I said, the Dead have devised all manner of petty politics to amuse themselves, and the whole shambling monolith of robes and titles and masks is a medieval scholar's wet dream . . . and something of which I was admirably suited to take advantage, being, as I am, a classically educated gentleman with legal training.

Peter parked a ways down from the gates. It is always disconcerting to realize the discrepancies between the ways reality is viewed by the Quick and the Dead, for Peter — despite being a Topper, a budding necromancer, and no doubt other things besides, and easily sensitive enough to see Frank, Grace, and myself — said he saw only a low stone wall between the road and the graves on the other side.

I, on the other hand, saw the high walls and ramparts of the Citadel of Thorns, the white roses of Death climbing all across the stonework, here and there holding some hapless soul prisoner, who had then been set alight as a beacon.

"Remember, Peter. You are just a harmless and somewhat stupid drunk, and they dare not touch you without bringing a flock of priests and psychic investigators down on their heads. Hop over the wall and ignore what you do see, and Frank and Grace and I will join you as shortly as possible."

"Gotcha," Peter said, uncorking the bottle of wine and passing straight through the seemingly impenetrable ramparts of the Citadel of Thorns. "Hey!" I heard him call from inside the wall. "I've got some wine! Anybody want a drink? It's Halloween."

If you by any chance are living, and wish to enter a cemetery on Halloween night, I'd advise against it, of course, but notwithstanding, if you are still set upon doing it, then Peter's course of action is advisable. Wine poured on the graves will endear you to all but teetotalers, as there are very few who remember the ancient Greek sacrifice, and being a gracious guest usually makes for gracious hosts.

Frank and Grace and I walked by the walls until the gates of the Citadel of Thorns towered high before us, traitors to the Hierarchy impaled on stakes to either side, burning with unquenchable flames. Wraith guardians stood there as well, and their spiritual armor was barbed and fluted and altogether overdone, just as I remembered it. Each of them held three chains which were attached to the collars of an equal number of slavering barghests, the near mindless phantoms staring at us with mad eyes through the grillwork of their iron masks.

All of this was intended to terrify and awe, and it accomplished this quite nicely, at least in the case of Frank and Grace, who clung to each other, dumbstruck. I, however, had already seen it.

"Halt, shades!" cried the guardian to the left. "State your name and rank within the Legion before begging admittance to the Citadel of Thorns!"

I polished my cane, admiring the luster of the ivory. "Nice to see you again too, Herminia. Former rank or current?"

"Current!"

"Currently I hold no rank within this Citadel, as well you know, though I possess the Mark of the Flames, which makes me a victim of happenstance of the highest order. Regardless, I take for myself the name and office of Herald and Advocate, and have business to discuss with members of the Legion. These shades accompany me and are under my protection."

"You are a Renegade!"

"Quite true. Now, Herminia, are you going to set your barghests upon us and report to your superiors that you destroyed a Herald and Advocate and dashed any hopes of reconciliation between the factions, not to mention that you obstructed business which is of direct interest to your superiors, or are you going to allow us within the gates of the Citadel?"

Pomp, circumstance, bluff and bluster. It often becomes tedious, but then the same may be said of chess in the opening moves.   We were kept waiting while messages were sent, and the barghests' chains were rattled so they slavered a bit more so as to terrify Frank and Grace, but the whole effect was ruined when several older wraiths riding in carriages and motorcars wished to exit the Citadel, drunken from Halloween revelry.

"Thaddeus!" cried one woman I knew of old, and I waved as they rode out the gates.

"Hello, Penelope! Charles! Walford! Happy Halloween!"

"Give 'em Hell, you old bastard!" Charles called, waving a bottle of champagne from the back of the Nash Rambler. He was inebriated as usual.

"Never fear, I will! Give my best!" I waved after them, tipping my hat to the ladies, watching them disappear into the moonlight and fog.

Herminia and her fellow guard were left at

the gates, and I smiled at them. "Rotten luck, isn't it, having guard duty on All Hallow's Eve? What say you escort the three of us to Lord Montalieu and we'll see what we can do about getting you relieved for the rest of your shift?"

"Silence, traitor!" Herminia barked, then exchanged a quick glance with her fellow guardian. "You and your companions may enter the Citadel of Thorns. Proceed directly to Lord Montalieu and beg his mercy if you value your souls."

Herminia stepped aside, reining in her barghests, and I shepherded Frank and Grace inside.

"Teddy," Grace said, clutching my arm. "Wha — "0

"Don't worry, Grace. Everything is proceeding according to plan." I disengaged her fingers from my arm and led the way down the grand avenues of the Citadel, in search of Peter.

Little had changed in the intervening thirty years, though there were fewer citizens and more thralls, although I'd expected as much. I took Frank and Grace down the avenues, and we collected Peter along the way, much to the annoyance of his new drinking companions.

But drunks wandered where they would, and the shades could hardly stop him from following us.

At last, we came to the grand portico of the mausoleum of the Regent of the Emerald Lord, or, more mundanely, Lord Montalieu's house. I rapped once with my cane and Peter jumped. "Holy fuck! The grave just opened up."

As I mentioned, the perceptions of the Quick and the Dead are quite different, and where Peter said he saw a grave yawning forth in Shakespearean fashion, I only saw the door being opened by Brandon, Lord Montalieu's manservant.

He was dressed in finery befitting the festive evening . . . assuming that it was still the Court of Louis the XIV . . . and he goggled as he saw me.

"Hello, Brandon," I said. "My, my. You haven't changed a bit. Now, if you could escort us to Lord Montalieu? I believe he's already received some word about me, probably warning him of the appearance of a rebel spy, though I told Herminia at the gate that I was a Herald and Advocate. My companions are nothing quite so grand, though I will vouch for their character."

Brandon recovered nicely, holding open the door. "If you will step this way, Mr. Winters. Lord Montalieu will receive you in his study."

Brandon led us down the halls, past parlors where the dead danced and musicians played in an exultant *danse macabre* . Lord Montalieu was holding his annual ball to which he invited only his most staunch supporters and those who held the most dirt on him, excepting, of course, wraiths such as myself. It was something the Goths would have given their ankhs to attend, and Peter was looking at everything in alternating wonderment and terror.

Brandon also did an excellent job of taking us by the circuitous route, allowing Lord Montalieu time to be briefed and ready himself so he wouldn't look surprised at our arrival.

We were ushered into the study and Brandon made a sweeping bow before the desk. "Reverent Lord, this Renegade has begged audience with you, and has also brought with him these two shades and this mortal. He claims to be Herald and Advocate."

"Which I am," I added, "though honestly we're here on private business this evening."

Montalieu gestured. "Leave us. I know this shade."

Brandon bowed low and slipped out, and Montalieu arranged himself behind the desk. I believe he'd been the dean of a French boys' school several centuries back, or at least he gave that impression: cultured accent, penchant for scholastic robes, and, most telling, a tendency to play with rulers when agitated. The ruler was already out on his desk and he was beginning to nudge it.

I raised my cane in salute. "Happy Halloween, Monty. Allow me to introduce my companions: Franklin Deere, Grace DuBois, and Peter Cameron."

Frank and Peter grinned idiotically, but Grace had the presence of mind to curtsy. "Pleased ta meet ya."

Lord Montalieu surveyed the three of them, his gaze lingering on Peter. For a mortal to enter the Realms of the Dead was a thing almost unheard of. Unless, of course, the shade whose grave had formed the Gateway was a spirit of almost boundless power and erudition, or the mortal was a potent sorcerer and shaman.

Even if he had the power (which I seriously doubted), Lord Montalieu had not invited Peter into his home. This left only one possible explanation (though I think only the two of us realized it) and I was not going to enlighten him further unless he came out and asked.

One also does not ask a mage what he is doing in one's home so long as he is being civil and reasonably well mannered. Peter, in fact, was acting like a shy and nervous schoolboy, and this was something I knew that Lord Montalieu could deal with: "Be seated. This is not a formal audience."

Frank, Grace, and Peter sat down on a hard wooden bench . . . another quirk that made me think that Montalieu had formerly run a boys' school . . . while I took the one comfortable chair facing the desk.

He gave me a withering look, but did no more, studiously ignoring Peter. "What do you want, Thaddeus?"

I went for the formal mode of address, for that was the mood he was in, regardless of what he said. "I crave as boon, Lord Montalieu, something easily within your power."

"Yours is not the place to ask, Renegade. You might at most beg for your existence and my mercy."

"You might also go to the Emerald Lord and speak to him of your loyalties and a certain matter which transpired, oh, about fifty-four years ago, but that's not very likely either." I leaned forward in the chair, resting my hands and chin atop my cane. "Let's not mince words, Monty. You would like to get me in your power, to ensure my silence and the silence of my agents with regards to various matters, and you've had more than one gambit to that end. Noteworthy among which is maneuvering for my Reaper to be lifewebbed by the Skeletal Legions, then arranging for his last fetter to be destroyed so he would be caught by the magic of the Skeletal Lord, who considers him his property, justly or not. A thoroughly amoral and reprehensible act, Monty, and just the sort of deed I'd expect from you. Also, rather ineffectual. My own fetters are well protected and relatively indestructible, and discovering them would prove useless to you and simply annoy me.

"Troubling Frank is another matter. I'd like him left out of this game, and am willing to pay for it. Pay well."

Montalieu looked at me, and I could tell that he had not considered this option. "Perhaps . . ."

"No, Monty, the moon, the stars and the sun are out of the question, and so is what I'm certain you're thinking of. Past business is past business, and there is some information I would only be willing to part with for the steepest of prices. However, I have just recently come by a new bit of information. Scandal. High scandal and near treason with regards to the Skeletal Lord himself, or at least his Regent, knowledge dangerous and near useless for me to possess, but of great value to a wraith such as yourself, especially a Regent of the Emerald Lord."

He paused, considering. "What, exactly, do you want done regarding this wraith here?" He pointed the ruler at Frank.

"Simple enough. We want him left out of your maneuverings against me, and we request that you use your influence with the Skeletal Legions to get them to quit actively pursuing their claim on Frank. His fetter has already been removed from their current machinations, so you needn't worry about getting them to desist in that plot."

"Removed?"

I smiled. "Removed. We'd also appreciate if you would spread the word that you would be very displeased if anyone else tried to get to me through Franklin. And Peter Cameron here is merely a silly drunken mortal, but he has proved useful to us, so we'd also like it if his name could be put on the list of those mortals whom the Legions are not to bother under any circumstance. It's quite a trivial thing to ask really — the Dead are forbidden to trouble the Quick as it is — but you know how things are in these trying times. Peter would be happier, and we would rest easier. That should be sufficient."

Silly drunken mortal, eh? The look spoke, but I retained my same expression, and Peter continued to look young and nervous, despite the nose ring and the mere fact of his presence.

I know Lord Montalieu was beginning to entertain the possibility of some third option — perhaps that I had learned some arcane rite that allowed mortals to rend the veil between Life and Death and crash his party or that the Ashen Curtain had worn thin of its own accord, and this was one of the wonders that heralded the Day of Judgement — for Peter certainly did not act the part of a mage, let alone a dreaded necromancer.

The living are not the only ones who shutter their minds away from that which disturbs them, and Lord Montalieu turned back to the simple and easily understandable business of intrigue and blackmail. "Possible. Certainly possible." He laid down the ruler and steepled his fingers. "But first, I would like to hear this 'scandal' to n which you refer regarding the Skeletal Lord."

I twirled my cane once between my fingers, remembering how useful it had proven against the spectre. "The Skeletal Lord has seen fit to destroy a number of fetters belonging to those who died with his mark, namely, the mark of pestilence. Among those, as you know, is Frank.

The Regent of the Skeletal Lord set up lifewebs to catch the souls as they fell into the Tempest, one for each of the miners in the potter's field.

"One of those was a nephwrack, a foul and hideous spectre consumed by its own inner Shadow. We destroyed its fetter, but before it could dissolve into the Tempest, it was caught in a web marked with the sigil of the Skeletal Lord. It is forbidden by the Covenant to take creatures of Oblivion as anything but beasts for the blood pits. But if you know the Regent of the Skeletal Lord, and you do, that spectre will instead just be chained as a thrall and forced to work as any other wraith."

Montalieu rested his fingers atop the ruler. "Do you have proof of this?"

"Certainly. I have the name of the spectre, and any wraith with skill in the proper arcane arts can ascertain who, where and what he is. We can give you that information in exchange for your promise." I laid my cane across my knees. "As this is All Hallows, will a binding oath suffice?"

"Indubitably," said Montalieu. "It is agreed then?"

"It is agreed." I stood and we clasped hands, speaking the particulars of the pact. "So let it be witnessed!"

"So let it be witnessed!" cried Montalieu, and as we did, there came a thunderclap and a ripple through the ether.

As I expected, Peter's Patron had been keeping an ear to the proceedings. One does not, as I mentioned before, meddle with the pawns of Destiny unless one is willing to play Her game.

"It is witnessed," I said.

Montalieu looked with shock at the way Fate had taken note of our bargain.

I just smiled. "The spectre's name is Miles. Miles . . ."

"Kirk," Frank supplied, looking shaken.

"I don't suppose you'll be inviting us to join in your festivities, will you, Monty?"

He gave me another withering look.

"Ah well, then, we shall just have to find our way out. But in any case, it's been a pleasure doing business with you, as always."

I tapped my cane to my hat in salute, and Lord Montalieu barked for servants to escort us from his home, and from the Citadel of Thorns.

Ah yes, it was always a pleasure doing business.

Finis

THE PARDONER'S TALE

Jackie Cassada

 ll manner of thing shall be well
By the purification of the
motive
In the ground of our
beseeching
—T.S. Eliot, "Four Quartets"

Angyr stalked the streets with the ease of a panther, prowling through the fetid wisps of fog that filled the spaces between buildings and lay, thick and congealing, along the byways of San Francisco's Shadowlands. All around him clustered the frantic hordes of the quick — desperate mortals intent on cramming as much gratification into their brief lives as possible. Hard core revelers were out early. Although Halloween was still two nights away, the round of parties and celebrations had already begun in earnest, tinged by the thrill of fear and uncertainty that hovered tangibly over the city in the wake of the evening's quake.

The trembler had done more than start a few fires and topple some outworn structures. The borders between the living and dead worlds, already thin at this time of year, were stretched to the breaking point by the shifting of forces deep beneath the ground. Angyr did not know for certain, but it seemed that even now he could be seen by mortal eyes. He suspected, though he did not yet have occasion to experiment, that if he reached out to touch a passing stranger, his phantasmal body would make solid contact with corporeal meat and bones. The black clothes and silvery chains he wore as a matter of custom, along with the slender black whip coiled softly at his waist, made him almost indistinguishable from the once-a-year masqueraders. To them, he was just another gothic joyrider in search of his own particular danse macabre.

He smiled as he caught a faint reflection of himself through the bars of a darkened storefront window. The long black hair and black eyes were his own. The face he wore once belonged to someone else. A gift in payment for a service rendered, the mask shaped itself to his features as if he were born with it. It was a good face, hard and angular, a killer's face. Or a hunter's. His own face bore too many marks of pride for exposure. Hard experience had taught him to hide his true face so that others could not read his character.

In a soft leather-looking bag that hung from his shoulder he carried his other mask, the full-face Pardoner's helm that he wore when performing the duties of his guild. The bag also contained an iron lantern, the symbol of his membership in the Guild of Pardoners. Angyr was never without these tools of his trade, but given the reputation the Pardoners had for prying into the soul's darkest corners, he rarely displayed either mask or lantern openly.

With a confidence spawned by frequent treks throughout San Francisco, he headed south from the Presidio, traversing the shrouded mists. Alot of wraiths were out tonight, taking advantage of the fog that eased their passage through the streets of the city. The Hierarchy's Legions, however, were conspicuous in their absence. Rumors of an impending Renegade attack on the Citadel kept most of them close to the Presidio. "Hey, Angyr! What's the going?"

He turned at the sound of his name, startled by the sudden intrusion, and then relaxed as he spotted the ragged, misshapen figure that had sidled up next to him. Damned Spook, he thought, biting back the words before he could give them voice. It didn't pay to rile the city's pulsetakers and rumor-sellers.

"I'm busy, Shaky. You want something?" His voice was harsh, with a practiced steeliness. Long ago he'd learned that weakness didn't pay, not in his line of work.

The malformed, dirt-covered wraith brushed back a patch of thinning hair with a trembling hand and laughed, a hoarse cackling sound that conjured up thoughts of disease and contagion. Involuntarily, Angyr backed away.

"Me? Want something? I always want something. But so do you, Pardoner." He whispered the last word so softly that Angyr had to replay it in his mind before he was sure he had heard it. He looked around nervously, hoping no other ears had overheard Shaky's words.

Shaky laughed harder. "Oh, yes, I know what you do with that whip and that other mask of yours, Angyr. But your secret's safe with me. No one else knows — just me and whoever taught you how to rape our minds. But it might cost to keep me quiet."

HE'LL TELL. The familiar inner voice of Angyr's Shadow taunted. **HE KNOWS YOUR SECRETS. DO HIM! YOU'RE STRONGER. DO HIM NOW!**

Angyr clamped down on the voice, willing it to silence. As a Pardoner, he had studied the intimate workings of Shadows, and his Shadow in particular. Fighting to control the dark inner demon that resided in every wraith was the Pardoner's highest calling. Angyr knew his Shadow well, and tonight he had no time for its constant temptations.

"What do you want?" he asked Shaky, exasperation leaking from his control as he resigned himself to the inevitable.

"Not much. A favor sometime. A big one." Shaky's body seemed to vibrate with excitement. "Investing in futures, you might call it." The Spook drew himself up into a semblance of height. "One thing I'll give you gratis. There's a big storm coming and you'll need to be quick if you want to find *her* before it starts."

Fear, like a rush of cold air, settled on the back of Angyr's neck. Of all his secrets, she was the one he most wanted to keep.

"Get lost, Shaky. You'll get what you came for," he started to say, but the Spook was already gone, swallowed up by the fog.

Angyr quickened his pace as he approached The Haight, keeping his eyes opened for anyone or anything that might be trouble. This was Renegade territory, and he played a dangerous game every time he entered it. Although he thought of himself as a Freelancer, treading a fine line between the factions who constantly tried to lay claim to the city, some might think otherwise. As a Pardoner, he did the occasional anonymous job for the Hierarchy, usually a quick and dirty soul-search to extract information from a suspected Renegade or Heretic. Often the poor soul didn't know he had something the Legions wanted. He also worked for the Renegades, on the rare occasion when any of them admitted that they needed his help. Neither group knew — or so he hoped — of his work for the other side. His Pardoner's mask helped preserve his anonymity, that and the Guild's reputation. No one wanted to get too close to someone who could look directly into the soul and ferret out its darkest secrets. Pardoners usually walked alone.

He shrugged off his thoughts as he turned onto Haight Street and opened himself wide to the blast of sight and sound that assaulted him when he ventured here. Two worlds existed in this place, each one as vibrant and, ultimately, as sad as the other. Clubs like the I Beam and Nightbreak emitted pulsating throbs of the latest music, drawing crowds of quick and dead inside their electric wombs.

But beyond the sonic waves that penetrated the barriers between the living world and the Shadowlands, another sound traveled through the air. From buildings that used to be house clubs twenty years ago, the music of another time wafted into the streets, unheard by mortal ears. "Take another *little piece of my heart*," a soulful voice wailed into the night, carrying a message of pain and hunger and final release. "*We can be together*," answered another abandoned hulk of a building, its soaring harmonies promising revolution and eternal freedom.

Angyr fought the urge to stop and bathe himself in the echoes of a paradise that lost itself nearly three decades ago. On any other night, he might have surrendered to the wild innocence that still persisted on the backside of Haight-Ashbury's shroud. The melancholy pull he felt from the ghostly melodies of the past filled him with memories of another self, a young idealist whose dreams had died in violence. He had called himself by another name in those days. He sometimes thought that if he listened long enough, he would hear the whispers of that forgotten name carried on the winds of time.

Tonight, however, a different music — Juniper's music — pulled him into her haunting wake. He had followed the call of her voice on other nights when the mists allowed him access to the living world. Tonight, when full moon and approaching Hallows closed the gap between life and death, the warmth of her songs exerted a power he found impossible to resist.

If he was lucky, she would still be in the Park, so Angyr walked west, turning his attention to his search for Juniper. Old hippies and new agers passed him by as he entered Golden Gate Park near the carousel at the Children's Playground. A bag lady in a stained rain-coat and mismatched shoes paused suddenly in front of him, and he jerked to a stop. For a moment their eyes met, and he noticed that although her right eye was milky with cataracts, her left eye glowed a baleful, bloody red. She stared through him, unseeing, and bent to rummage inside one of her tattered shopping bags. Angyr smelled the stench of death about her, and quickly moved on.

He found Juniper in the Shakespeare Garden, arms wrapped around her battered guitar, singing to the flowers. No one else was around, but he approached her carefully and stood quietly behind her until the song was finished.

"They say you should sing to plants to help them grow," she said without turning around.

"Old wives' tales," Angyr said. "People like you should know better than to believe in them."

"Ghosts are old wives' tales, too." She smiled at him and held out a hand, turning to look at him.

Angyr shook his head. "Not tonight. I feel I've taken too much from you already."

She dropped her hand. "Why did you come here then? Just to look at me, or to talk? You usually want more than that."

"I came here because you were here. Because you called me here, somehow."

"I was thinking of you earlier," she said. "I guess you heard me."

She stood and began walking, urging Angyr to join her along the path that wound through the garden.

"Why do you always dress like that, all in black?" Juniper asked. In all the times they'd met since the first time he realized she could see him clearly, she had never seemed to pay attention to his appearance.

"Don't you like it?" Angyr asked, and knew he wanted more than anything to hear her say she approved.

"It's so stark," she said. "It makes you look gaunt and cruel and dangerous." She laughed softly, and Angyr could sense her secret delight at flirting with someone from the other side. He stopped himself before he went further into her feelings. That was Pardoner's work, and tonight he was just Angyr.

"Maybe I am all those things." Angyr stopped suddenly. "I am dangerous, you know."

Juniper continued walking until she found a bench. She rested her guitar on the ground by her feet and waited until Angyr caught up with her.

"They say life's dangerous. Why should death be any different?" she asked. She motioned for Angyr to join her on the two-seater. He was careful not to touch her when he sat.

"Can you see me as well as I can see you?" There was a plaintive note in her question, and Angyr studied her carefully, seeing long brown hair and sad grey eyes, faded jeans and an old army coat over an embroidered peasant blouse. In any other city, he supposed she would be a misfit, a throwback to an older generation of flower children. Here, though, she was just another part of the patched-together scene of punks and retros. Again he stopped himself before he could look too far. He didn't want to see any more of her than he did right now. If she was marked with death, he didn't want to know it. Not yet.

"I can see you," was all he answered.

"A storm's coming soon," she said. "It's going to be a bad one."

Angyr nodded.

"We call it a Maelstrom," he said. "I need to be undercover before it hits."

"A maelstrom," she repeated, lingering over the word almost lovingly. Then she looked puzzled. "I didn't think things like that could affect you once you're dead."

"Maelstroms aren't just storms," he said. "They're more like purges. They sweep through a place and destroy — or change — everything that can't get out of the way."

"Like hurricanes?"

"Worse," he said. "Maelstroms are alive."

Juniper shivered, pulling her army coat tighter around her slender body. A sharp gust of salty wind blew through her hair. Angyr felt the wind, too. It touched his cheeks, penetrating his mask, and left a cloying film in its wake. A hint of a scream teased at his ears. Where Juniper heard only the distant moan of the approaching storm, Angyr thought he could discern the frantic whispers of the shattered spirits on the fringe of the Maelstrom — the advance guard sent by the malevolent storm to scout out the territory before the shock troops arrived.

He looked quickly about him at the trees that edged the park, backlit against the bloated moon. Already they seemed bent to the point of breaking.

"What's it like on your side?" His voice was tense with urgency. "The trees, tell me about the trees."

"The wind's picked up," Juniper said. "The trees are bending a little. It's kind of neat — neat and scary."

THE STORM'S GOING TO WRECK THE CITY — BOTH CITIES. SHE'LL DIE. SO WILL YOU IF YOU DON'T LEAVE NOW. LEAVE HER, OR GRAB HER JUICE WHILE YOU CAN! The voice beat furiously inside Angyr's head, bringing a sudden panic to the surface. He forced his instincts deep inside of him, using his training as a Pardoner to wrestle his Shadow into submission.

A flash of white pierced the darkness overhead. A low rumble of thunder soon followed. In the instant of sudden illumination, when the sky exploded with the lightning's flare, Angyr's vision scanned both worlds. To Angyr, the lightning had a face, many faces, all of them tormented. Eyes crazy with hunger stared greedily down at the storm's intended battlefield, sighting their targets. Gaping mouths gave forth distorted groans, sounding in the mortal world like moans of distant thunder. Angyr had never looked into the face of a Maelstrom before. He had never been this close to one without being securely under cover.

Caught by the unexpected lightning, Juniper started, lurching into Angyr, making sudden contact with his ghostly form. Unprepared, Angyr felt her body like white-hot liquid searing his corpus. As he had suspected, his world and hers had moved close enough together to give him nominal solidity. And her touch scalded him.

NOW! His Shadow roared in his skull. **SHE'S FULL OF JUICE AND YOU CAN HAVE IT ALL. TAKE IT NOW!**

This time he surrendered. A howling blackness filled him and Angyr knew only the sweet taste of fear, youth and desire — her desire for him. He drank swiftly, greedy for the taste of her, mindlessly drawing her life energy into himself in excruciating consummation of his primal needs.

Then, without warning, a massive body slammed into him, bearing him to the ground and breaking his connection with Juniper. The inner darkness faded and Angyr found himself pinned beneath the weight of a hulking wraith known as Flatface, one of the many Renegades who frequented the Park. Hovering over both of them stood Shaky.

"You can get off him now," Shaky was saying to his companion. "He's back with us."

Flatface lifted his bulk from Angyr's prone body.

Still buzzing with stolen energy, Angyr pulled himself to his feet. Juniper lay half-collapsed on the bench. Only the shallow rise and fall of her chest indicated that she still breathed. Angyr walked toward her and knelt by her side, careful not to touch her fragile form. He stared at her, afraid that if he looked away, she might cease breathing. Almost without thinking, Angyr's training as a Pardoner took over. His vision pierced the barrier of her flesh and focused on the soul that lay helpless before his scrutiny. He blanched at what he saw.

The marks of her passions were there, plainly written for him to read. Like himself, she bore the stigmata of pride — a pride that held itself aloof from mere mortals, that regaled itself with love for someone who didn't exist in the world she knew. Other traces marked her as well, a slash of desire, a broad band of what he recognized as love. But those passions were already known to him, made brutally clear as he leeched their essence from her. Even now he felt their energies boiling inside him.

It was the other thing he saw that filled him with dread. The taint of death lay upon her, hovering over her like a jackal waiting for the feast to begin. Ruthlessly Angyr probed deeper and deeper into her soul, searching for signs of sickness or disease, for any natural cause that would explain the mark of death engraved upon her. Angyr plunged into her memories, sifting through the useless ones until he found what he wanted. A lonely child gifted with music had grown into a young woman filled with strange longings for a world just beyond her grasp, a world that held out a promise of mysteries explained.

He saw their first meeting through the filter of her senses. What had been to him an unexpected reconnection with a world he had very nearly left behind was to her the inevitable materialization of her desires. She had willed a ghost to come to her and Angyr had appeared.

With that memory, Angyr found the root of Juniper's impending death. Unwittingly, he had planted the seeds of her desire, a desire which had steadily grown into an overwhelming passion. She had come here tonight determined to find a way to bridge the gap between herself and her ghostly lover. And he had almost made her dream come true. In one irrevocable moment, his Shadow had put the mark of death upon her, transforming a formless desire into inevitability.

"Cut it out, Angyr!" Shaky's trembling voice penetrated his concentration. "Save that Pardoner shit for later, if there is a later. She's just meat. We've got real trouble staring us in the face."

Angyr whirled around, ready to strike out, but Flatface was there, anticipating his move with the reactions of a veteran of the Blood Pits. An enormous wrist grabbed Angyr's arm and held it rigid, locked in an unbreakable grip. Angyr let himself relax. "It's not her time to die," he lied. "I have to do something to help her."

"This is more important than some little meat-chain, Angyr. You bought my silence tonight by promising me a favor. I was going to save it. I figured you might do me some good with your pals in the Hierarchy..." Shaky paused.

"You did get that last word, didn't you Angyr? Or do you want me to say it again — loud — so Flatface can comprehend my meaning?"

"I heard you the first time." Angyr tried to keep any sign of emotion out of his voice. He looked again toward Juniper.

"Getting back to that favor," Shaky continued. "I'm calling it in, now!" Shaky looked from Angyr to Flatface to Angyr again. "Flatface wouldn't be too pleased if he found out what you are and who you hang out with in your spare time."

"What's it to me?" Angyr asked, glancing upward at the impassive figure who held him as if he were a dirty rag, liable to be tossed away at the slightest signal. "He already saw me do my 'Pardoner-shit' just now. I think the secret's out."

"He saw, but he won't know what he saw unless I spell it out for him," Shaky replied. "And if he knows, he won't like it. He's met some of your friends up at the Morgue before."

"So what's the favor?" Angyr pulled at his arm. Following a nod from Shaky, Flatface loosened his grip.

"What do you think I want? Open your eyes! Can't you see what's going on?"

The storm had intensified. Constant rumbling thunder filled the mortal air as dark, bilious clouds whipped across the sky, covering the moon. In the Shadowlands, the low moaning had grown to a shrill scream. The wind that ripped through the mists tasted like corruption. The trees thrashed wildly with the rising of the storm.

"The Maelstrom," Angyr said. "It's almost here." He shouted to make himself heard.

"Exactly. Word is out that it's coming from the Citadel, that it's no normal Maelstrom. It seems they're tired of sending the Legions out to shut down the Renegades, so they've harnessed the storm to take us out once and for all! It's an invasion!"

"Since when did you become a Renegade, Shaky? I thought you went with whoever paid you — like I do." Angyr felt a grim satisfaction at seeing Shaky flinch. It didn't take a Pardoner to recognize what made the pathetic little wraith tick.

The tortured screams rose to a constant howl as the winds continued to accelerate.

"Since I got left out in the cold," Shaky replied, timing his speech so that he could be heard in between the shrieking winds. "Just like you've been. You're not exactly sitting pretty in a safe place, are you, Angyr?" Jagged lightning crossed the sky, searching for a place to anchor.

"I don't care which side any of us is on," Angyr shouted. "We've got to get to shelter!"

"What we've got to do is fight this thing!" Shaky answered, and for once his voice was full and steady." And you're going to help us! That's the favor I want from you."

"You're crazy! You can't fight a Maelstrom! It's too big!"

"We're going to try," Shaky said. "Or we'll lose it all. It's not just the Renegades, Angyr. It's this park, this whole damn city. If the Legions can't have it, they'll make sure no one else has it either."

"What do you think I can do about it?" Angyr asked, although he thought he already knew what Shaky wanted.

"Flatface and I are going to the Temple of Music." Shaky pointed to the ornate band shell that lay due north of the Shakespeare Garden. "Come with us. It'll give us some cover. When the Maelstrom hits, the three of us will fight it."

Angyr shook his head. "It'll never work. We'll all be sucked away," he said. "Besides, what can I do against such a strong Maelstrom? What can either of you do, for that matter?"

"You know what you can do, Angyr. The Maelstrom's full of spectres. You can cleanse them." Shaky's voice had dropped to a whisper, but Angyr heard him anyway. "It's what you Pardoners do." Shaky's face took on a crafty look. "You and me and Flatface should make a great team. We have our secrets, too."

"The storm's going to break over the whole city," Angyr said. "What are you going to do about the other places? We can't be everywhere at once."

"We don't have to be," said Shaky. "We've got people spotted all across town. We'll beat it back however we can. We've been rounding up troops all evening, getting ready for this, so don't think you're special. You're just available — and you owe me one.

Me and Flatface, we've got this part of the Park to defend. And now we've got you to help us. Right? A deal's a deal."

Shaky jerked his head once, towards Flatface. The big wraith tensed, all his attention now focused on Angyr.

Angyr shrugged. "It's your favor," he said, glancing again to where Juniper lay, her life still glimmering faintly inside her. "Go on to the band shell. I'll be there as soon as I can. I've got something to do first."

"Make it quick," Shaky snapped, his cringing posture replaced by an air of command. "Move your corpus, Flatface." The pair sprinted through the garden, in the direction of the band shell.

Angyr turned to Juniper. Closing his eyes, he focused his will, gathering up the excess energy so recently absorbed. Carefully he placed a hand over Juniper's chest, where her heart struggled to keep her alive. This time, when he touched her, the energy flowed from him. It was the energy of death he poured into her, but he hoped it would be enough to kick her back into life.

She stirred, and opened her eyes.

"Is it over?" she asked in a dreamy voice. She smiled up at him wistfully. Angyr choked back the harsh words that welled up inside him. He wanted to scream at her for wanting death so badly.

MAYBE SHE WANTED IT, BUT YOU ALMOST MADE IT HAPPEN. Angyr's Shadow insinuated itself into his thoughts. **YOU COULD STILL GIVE HER WHAT SHE WANTS. YOU CAN USE THE EXTRA JUICE ANYWAY.** He shoved the voice away from him.

"You fainted," he said to Juniper, trying not to betray his growing panic as the first rancid drops of rain began falling in both worlds. "Let's go to the band shell. We've got a storm to fight."

He watched her stagger to her feet and steady herself. Once again, he stared inside her soul.

The death taint was still there, but fainter now. He didn't know how much time he had given her, but it was something. Together they set out for the band shell. "Wait," Juniper said, and retraced her path to the bench. She rescued her guitar from where she had left it on the ground, and they ran through the garden, reaching the band shell as the skies broke open above them.

Angyr and Juniper ducked underneath the structure's sheltering dome. Shaky and Flatface hovered near the far side of the shell. All around them the winds howled.

"We've got groups stationed all over the Park," Shaky said as Angyr joined him. He gestured past the shell towards some nearby buildings. "We'll all be fighting our part of the Maelstrom at the same time."

"This place is too open," Angyr shouted. His voice echoed off the shell's acoustic lining. "If the wind changes direction, we'll be swept out into it."

"We've got to face the storm to fight it." Shaky said. Flatface grunted something that sounded like agreement.

"Is there someone here besides us?" Juniper's voice carried through the keening wind.

Shaky glared at Angyr. "She's not one of us," he hissed. "What's she doing here? You didn't say you were bringing her with you."

"Just some friends of mine," Angyr said, stretching the word uncomfortably in his mind. He turned back to his allies. "She needs shelter too. It's dangerous for *everyone* out there."

For some time they watched the storm whip past them. Lightning strobed the Park grounds, while thunder rocketed off the insides of the shell. Rain sheeted past them, obscuring details. Inside the body of the storm, Angyr could see vague forms coalescing, haunted faces attached to grasping arms and wispy bodies. A malodorous stench assaulted them from the drafts of wind that buffeted the shell's facade.

"This is crazy," Angyr whispered to himself. "You can't fight a Maelstrom."

But you can battle the creatures inside it, he thought. Something crystalized within him, as he began to rehearse in his mind the ancient formulae for the Ritual of Purification, one of the Pardoners' most carefully guarded secrets, and the power most misunderstood and feared by those outside the Guild. He studied the spectres that rode within the Maelstrom.

A low strumming sound caught his attention, and Angyr turned away from the spectacle in front of him.

Juniper was sitting in the center of the shell's

covered stage, tuning her guitar. As if she felt his gaze, she looked up.

"You look like you're going to be busy," she said. "I thought I'd entertain myself and wait out the storm."

Angyr shrugged. "Suit yourself," he said. "Just don't bother us for awhile."

Once more, Angyr lost himself in contemplation. Vaguely, he sensed Shaky and Flatface making their own preparations and, for the first time, he wondered what secrets they — like himself — kept from their fellows. A faint ionic crackle seemed to emanate from Shaky, as his decrepit body began to remold itself, transforming both his arms into swords and armoring his body with a metallic shell. Flatface's omnipresent bulk took on a Thicker, more ponderous presence. Angyr wondered what preparations he was making.

Angyr's right hand reached for his whip, his fingers deftly uncoiling it from his waist, where a length of slender chain bound it to him. Angyr had used it before in his purification rituals. Tonight, the instrument of cleansing pain would also be a weapon. Angyr tensed, as he began his final preparations. He glanced to either side of him at Shaky and Flatface. The three wraiths stood poised at the edge of the band shell, facing outward towards the storm.

"Let's do it, before I lose my nerve," Shaky muttered.

Angyr nodded. He reached inside his shoulder bag and withdrew its contents. Carefully he placed the iron lantern at his feet. "Might as well advertise," he muttered to himself. He slowly donned his Pardoner's mask, the other half of his hidden self. Angyr felt his Shadow begin to stir. He had expected this, and he was ready for it. Gathering his will into a single focus point, Angyr summoned his Shadow.

THIS IS WHAT YOU'VE ALWAYS WANTED, the voice tempted him. **YOU HAVE FRIENDS OUT THERE IN THE STORM. JOIN THEM! BETTER STILL, GIVE THE OTHERS TO THEM. DO IT!**

"Not this time," Angyr howled into the wind. "This time you serve ME."

Angyr's whip struck out at its first target — himself. He felt the sting penetrate his corpus, lashing out at his Shadow, bringing it under his control.

"We fight together!" he muttered, willing his Shadow to surrender. The world around him exploded in molten fury as Angyr rode his Shadow into the Maelstrom.

All around him, the minions of Oblivion

clustered, taloned fingers seeking purchase. Angyr's whip struck again and again, each blow severing some small piece of corruption from its roots and flinging it out, to be consumed by the storm. Dimly, he was aware of other presences fighting alongside him. Even more faintly, he heard the music. "Love is but a song we *sing, Fear's the way we die,*" Juniper sang, and with her song he felt as if the ghosts of another time joined him. Her voice, their words. "*Turn around, go back down, back the way you came,*" she chanted, and he fed on the energy of her voice.

He dove in and out of awareness, biting back the pain as he felt pieces of himself torn away. He gave his agony to his Shadow, buying time for himself. The howls of madness and fury that surrounded him slowly gave way to shrieks of pain as he chipped away at the grotesque forms that lent their substance to the body of the Maelstrom.

Lightning struck where Shaky had been standing, and he heard the Spook scream. Flatface fought in a deep pocket of silence, grimly shredding whatever piece of the Maelstrom he could tackle. Banger, Angyr thought, as he suddenly recognized the marks of a professional wrecker in the giant's destructive power. He's a member of the fucking Bangers' Guild!

He couldn't pinpoint when it happened, but finally Angyr realized that the winds were beginning to die down. His targets were fewer and fewer, and finally there were no targets at all. The Maelstrom had retreated. In the world of the living, where there had once been a raging storm, only a gentle rain fell. The moonlight glinted off the wet ground like slivers from a thousand shattered mirrors. The black trees stood still and silent.

Angyr felt empty. From his Shadow, he felt nothing. The battle had nearly drained him of feeling.

"He's gone," a dull voice next to him rumbled. Angyr turned towards the speaker. Flatface stared blankly at the space where Shaky had been.

"Gone?" Angyr echoed, looking around at the battered band shell. Shaky was missing. "It took him?" he asked.

Flatface nodded.

YOU'RE SAFE. Angyr's Shadow sounded feeble, but its presence meant he was still whole. **YOU'D BE SAFER IF THE OTHERS WERE GONE, TOO.**

"Give it up," Angyr said, pushing the voice

behind him.

He removed his helm and walked over to Flatface.

"We both look like shit," he said. Flatface shrugged, still looking around him expectantly, as if the act of searching could force Shaky to materialize out of some dark place inside the band shell.

"He won't be coming back," Angyr said softly. "Tell his friends he went down fighting."

Flatface turned without a word and walked off into the night. Angyr watched the fog swallow him up.

"Where are you?" Juniper's voice broke the stillness, sounding weak and frightened. "I can't see you." She lay, pale and waxen, on the floor of the band shell, guitar still clutched to her chest.

"I'm right beside you," said Angyr, closing the gap between them and crouching down beside her. He looked at her closely, and saw what he had feared. The juice he gave back to her wouldn't last very long. Before tonight, she'd had a long life in front of her. His actions had shortened that life to a few months at best.

Juniper's hair was plastered against her face. "I can hear you, but you're so faint!"

"I have to go," he said. "I won't be coming

back to you."

"Why?" In her question, Angyr heard betrayal.

"I nearly killed you tonight," he said simply. "I won't be able to stop myself next time."

Juniper smiled at him. "Then don't."

Angyr looked at Juniper's face, framing her features in his memory.

"Everybody dies eventually," he said. "Don't rush it."

"What's it like, on your side?" she asked.

"It's not what you think," he replied. "You're a lot better off than I am."

Angyr extended his hand toward her and traced the shape of her face in the air.

"I'm not coming back here," he said. "Go home. Sing to your plants. Leave me alone." He turned from her and stumbled into the fog.

As he headed homeward, he saw all around him the signs of the storm's passing. Broken branches and overturned trash receptacles littered the Park. But San Francisco, living city and hidden necropolis, still stood intact. The invasion, if it had been one, had failed.

When he was sure she could no longer hear him, he whispered, "When your time comes, I'll be there."

(end)

BREAKING FREE

James A. Moore

The only thing Bobby Shing could remember about his life, aside from his name and his disgrace at being born a mixed breed, was the way he died. The image of the aluminum baseball bat swinging at his face still haunted Bobby, even a year after his death. Despite the manacles that were locked around his ankles, he knew the time had come to find his murderer. Halloween was just around the corner, and this year he meant to take advantage of Charon's Rules. Last year he'd only been dead a day; this year he could seek vengeance...if only he could break the chains that held him in the bowels of Stygia.

Stygia was everything that Bobby felt was wrong with the afterlife. The massive stone buildings looked like the set from some elaborate Cecil B. Demille movie about the Roman Empire, sturdy marble and granite set in lines that were pleasing to the eye, but someone had apparently decided to let the whole set rot away rather than keep it intact. The marble was cracked, slowly crumbling under its own oppressive weight, the dust and debris littering the streets was thick enough to choke a person— if the person had to breathe, which no one in Stygia found necessary.

He'd heard rumors about the towering buildings that made the center of Stygia, huge edifices with doors that were sealed shut and crusted over with grime; he'd heard that once those mammoth structures were the gateways to every possible variation of heaven and hell. Everything that had been promised by the gods, imagined and real, all locked away and sealed as tight as a funeral drum. Paradise and Damnation, held at bay by heavy iron doors and guarded against entry. One thing was certain as far as Bobby was concerned: They may have barred the pearly gates to heaven, but hell was right here, right now, and he wanted to escape.

Bobby had spent almost a year stuck in the

realms of the dead, forced to do the bidding of the dreaded Smiling Lord. The Smiling Lord was spoken of only in whispers, but what the whispers told was not pleasant; some who claimed to have seen him said he was gaunt, barely more than a skeleton in appearance, and lacerated everywhere. They said that his smile could drive a sane being into the Oblivion, the horrid blackness that threatened to destroy everything in Stygia and every soul stuck there as well, fleeing with fear of what his smile meant. Others who had been in his court reported that there was nothing at all on his dais, just a darkness that sat on a throne of flames and seethed with the need to commit violent acts. The Smiling Lord ruled all who had died by violence, and as a result, ruled over Bobby as well. Bobby had never seen the Smiling Lord, and he had no desire to, either, he had enough troubles with the wraith that ruled over him in the Smiling Lord's name.

William Mathers was the man who claimed Bobby, and the others shackled to him in a long line, as his slaves. Bobby and all the wraiths attached to him by the manacles on their ankles were all Mathers' property; he had purchased them all from a Reaper, a wraith that found the newly dead and then sold them like property to the highest bidder. It was just bad luck that the first Reaper Bobby came across was Lester Boggs, a man who believed in profiting from the misfortune of others. It was worse luck still that Mathers was the one with the most to spend on the day Boggs nabbed him.

October 30th in the lands of the living, called Hell Night in more cities than anyone really knew. There were few times as good as Hell Night for grabbing new souls, normally the poor, homeless slobs and squatters who lived in the buildings that burned down. Somewhere, some psychotic moron was going to light a few old buildings on fire for the sheer fun of watching them burn, and tonight he and the other slaves were going up to the Shadowlands with the sick bastard who called them his thralls. The wraith who ruled over them was greedy enough to want any newly dead larvae for himself. He was also the one holding the key to their chains.

Bobby was the last in a long line of slaves. His ankles were shackled together with some three feet of harsh, black chain between them, and that chain continued off to his left, linking him to a slim, middle-aged woman he had never even met before he was locked in place. Beyond her, the line went on, linking soul to soul in a long stretch of misery and hardship. To his right there was only open space. Bobby believed that, in time, others would be locked into the queue of thralls that served as William Mathers' work force. He dreaded the day when the string of slaves left him buried somewhere in the middle, with hopeless, forlorn entities stretching off in both directions to be lost in the constant gloom of Stygia.

Mathers believed in a hard day's work for his slaves. Normally, he would gather the energies from souls that were too weak to rise above Stygia and back to the world where life was still happening. If Bobby felt for anyone, it was those mindless entities. Some called them drones, and used them for menial repetitious tasks; some used them for the energies they excreted, the very energies of their fading souls. Some, if the rumors were true, fed them to the great void called Oblivion, as sacrifices to placate the entropic energy's merciless attempts to overcome Stygia. These drones were also referred to as the Ectorn and were often seen as nothing more than shambling, nightmarish pillars of pain.

Bobby and those who were forced to work with him collected the Ectorn like rotton fruit, and gave them over to Mathers. What Mathers did with them was anyone's guess, but Bobby hoped whatever it was would put them past the reach of their mental agonies. Even dissolution had to be better than the endless suffering the drones endured.

He kept telling himself that, and sometimes he even believed it. The little lies made what he did more tolerable, helped him stay sane when the writhing shades twisted and tried to break away from his grasp. He tried to tell himself that they had never been human, and when that didn't work, he told himself that he was ending their suffering. He knew the truth had to be worse, knew it in the depths of his soul, but dared not think about it.

Beside him, the woman yanked the chain that joined them at the ankle. He looked at her, his eyebrows showing his curiosity. She pointed with her head in the direction of Mathers who was coming their way. Bobby focused himself, forced himself to stay calm and look anywhere but at his master's face. The mask the man wore was hideous, enough to terrify Bobby. The covering made Bobby see things he didn't like, truths about himself that he simply was not prepared to face. From the side, the mask was just a silvery model of a face, tarnished and crude. But whenever anyone looked at it straight on, it showed them the truth, unblemished and uncensored. Bobby didn't like looking in there, and he suspected that very few others liked it either.

The thralls were all without masks, while the actual members of the Hierarchy of Charon all wore covers over their faces. Without the masks, the full impact of every mark on a person's soul was revealed for everyone to see, and there was a certain power in knowing everything about a person. Whenever he desired, Mathers could look any of his slaves in their faces and drain them, sapping away their free will and making them empty, subservient.

Before the night was over, Bobby wanted three things from Mathers: He wanted the key to break his bonds, he wanted the mask that Mathers wore to cover his own face, and he wanted revenge. If things went the way he planned, he'd have all three before the sun rose again in the lands of the living. The only things that had prevented him from acting were the lack of an opportunity, and the lack of planning. He was waiting for an opening, any small chance to attack Mathers and steal what he wanted from the fiend who held him in bondage.

Mathers stood before them, Whatever lay beneath the coverings upon his face was a complete mystery to Bobby and the others he worked with. All anyone ever saw of Mathers' face were the cold, angry eyes beneath the mask. He wore a thick length of chain around his waist that crossed over his shoulders like bandoliers. While the manacles on all of his lackeys merely held his slaves in bondage, the chains Mathers wore meant something more: He wore his chains with pride, strutting and quite pleased to be burdened with their weight. The heavy chains represented something different for Mathers— they were a sign of station, prestige even.

"Well, you're all looking chipper this morning." Mathers' voice was cheerful behind his false face. His British accent echoed tinnily, making him seem even more alien. "Let's be off, before the night is on us, shall we?" Bobby was excited, knew that Mathers' could see it clearly on his face, and decided he did not care. Part of him knew he'd only been in Stygia for a year but most of him swore he'd been there for centuries. Stygia was like hell: The endless servitude, the endless torture. But somewhere above them—far through the Tempest, the massive roiling clouds of nightmarish memories that completely surrounded Stygia—there was another place, The Shadowlands, where the dead could actually see the living, and possibly even communicate with them. Now, at last, he would have a chance to see the real world again, for the first time since he'd been murdered.

Mathers' stood directly in front of him, his head tilted oddly, as if he were listening to something, hearing a secret told by the wind. Bobby tried to force all thoughts of escape from his mind, tried to focus only on the work ahead. He trembled, certain that Mathers' would forbid him his one chance to see the world of the living again. As his master spoke, Bobby listened intently, waiting to be denied his visit to the Shadowlands and hearing instead a simple warning to everyone. "Some of you have dared the Tempest before, some of you have been through the Tempest just once. So, let's all try to remember that everything we see in there is only illusion. Yes?" Bobby hated the way Mathers' ended his comments like that, with a curious "Yes?" as if a slow student had raised his hand in class to be noticed. "We are not going out to have fun, we are going out on serious business."

Mathers stopped in front of another slave, staring intently at the old man's face. The man shivered violently, wracked with fear and self-loathing. Bobby knew just how he felt; it was fear of Mathers and self-hatred of his own weakness that fueled the rage building within him. "I shall allow you time to play, but only after the work is done. Until then, you are on my time and shall act accordingly. You will not speak to others, nor will you stop and enjoy the sights, as it were. Yes?"

They all nodded their affirmatives, even Bobby. Each felt the chill winds of Stygia pass through them, each knew that no matter what their answer was, the facts would not change. They would still be the slaves of William Mathers. Each knew it, but Bobby refused to believe it. Bobby intended to escape, with or without a plan or the aid of those around him. He would not suffer at Mathers' hands any longer. Even Oblivion was starting to sound like a better deal than working for this masked bastard.

Mathers clapped his hands together briskly, sending a volley of rattling noises off around his person as his chains crashed and jingled. "Well then, we're off." With those words, the entire group was lifted from the gloomy world of Stygia and hurled into the Tempest, linked together and guided by the evil plans of William Mathers. There was an old saying about there being strength in numbers, but that didn't make any difference in the Tempest. The only possible strength to be gathered from moving through the Tempest in groups came from the knowledge that you were not suffering your wracking fears alone. As they moved through the turbulent void, each mind spewed forth its most violent terrors, and everyone got a taste of everyone else's nightmares, free of charge. Bobby endured it all, refusing to allow what he knew were only illusions to stop him in his quest. Instead, he turned the horrors that threatened to consume him into fuel for his anger. Now, tonight, he would be free.

When they broke through the barrier between the worlds of the living and the dead, Bobby felt his hopes sink substantially. This was wrong, so very wrong. Nothing was as he remembered. The buildings were all where they should be, and the streets were still there as well, but everything else was in turmoil. San Francisco was a warm place in his memories, a place where, even on the worst days, you could find someone smiling, someone laughing. Sometimes, even though he knew it was only his imagination, he could swear the city itself was one entity, smiling and happy. Now he felt differently; if the city truly had a soul, it was a soul in mourning.

The streets were filled with debris, the cars looked wrong, older than they should, and not

one of them without dent or damage. Several
buildings were in states of severe disrepair, and
the damage was recent. Something, possibly an
earthquake, had claimed the city; not a mortal
wound, but certainly enough to leave an ugly
scar. Some of the people he saw on the streets
walked apathetically towards their destinations,
moving about like the survivors of some
apocalyptic plague. But almost everyone seemed
healthy, robust and filled with energy, and Bobby
was drawn towards them like a moth to a flame.
"That is what life looks like," he thought. Bobby
was aware that Mathers was speaking, not with
the harsh tones of command, but rather like a
museum tour guide pointing out anything of
interest. The noise of his master's voice became
a mindless droning as Bobby continued to
examine his surroundings and the living souls
around him.

There were a few among the crowds who were
gaunt, drawn and sickly. The palpable aura of
impending death surrounded them, sapping the
vitality of the living and replacing it with a
darkness that matched the feelings in Bobby's
soul. Bobby was repulsed by the pallid ones,
understanding instinctively that they would
soon die and join the masses in Stygia.

By looking closely at the inanimate objects, he could see the same signs of health and entropy upon them. Some buildings were cleaner, less decayed. Others looked ready to collapse at any moment. With the people it was obvious who would be around for years to come and who would soon join the ranks of the dead, but the landscapes were not so transparant. Bobby found himself looking closely in order to notice anything beyond a general state of disrepair.

His eyes had to be playing tricks on him, because one little boy walking past him, tiny hand locked in his mother's larger hand, looked directly at him, his right eye sad and brown, his left eye a fiercely burning red. The boy reeked of death.

Bobby would have recoiled from the boy but the manacles on his legs held him securely. Mathers called out to them all, but he looked directly at Bobby as he spoke. "Welcome to the Shadowlands. Bobby, this is your first return isn't it? Yes, I thought so...this is our world, the closest we can come to the lands of the living. Well, the closest I'll allow you to come at any rate. It's a rather depressing place, but all you have to remember is your mission. You'll find the city is much like the one you knew in life. The differences are all fairly minor."

He pointed, gesturing towards the part of town that Bobby knew best. Again he looked steadily at Bobby. "That is the only real exception." A huge wall surrounded Chinatown, a wall of glassy jade, easily three stories high. "We will stay far away from Chinatown; the place is a veritable den of thieves. Yes?" Mathers strode over to Bobby, his eyes menacing behind the mask. "The Heretics wait there, looking for weak souls to steal for some unholy purpose. We will stay away from the district. You are all too valuable to lose." One hand reached out and ran across Bobby's cheek. "I should hate to part with any of you."

How it hurt not to lash out, how it pained him not to wrap his fingers around that neck and squeeze. Bobby felt his hands open and close of their own volition, and probably would have reached for his "master," right then and there, if not for the cautioning look thrown his way by the woman to his right. She indicated the long, curved blade of Mathers' scimitar, glinting darkly under the bloated moon above. Mathers' hand was resting a little too casually near the gilded pommel. Bobby nodded his thanks. There was time yet—the night was young—and Bobby needed to remember what patience was all about. So close to his goal, there was a part of him that whispered in a cold, menacing voice—how easy it would be to take Mathers out. That part seemed almost suicidal, but after a year of trying to ignore it, the dark voice seemed a good deal stronger than it had been in the preceding months.

The woman next to him knew what he was planning. He could tell by looking at her and by the look she returned. Bobby should have been afraid of that, should have been terrified that she would warn Mathers about his plans. Instead he was comforted by the knowledge. He was not alone, and that somehow helped soothe his anxieties. He studied her face for a moment, searching for signs that she would betray him. She was pretty in her own right, but hardly beautiful. He guessed her age to be somewhere around forty. Her hair had faded in spots from a light auburn to a mousy brown shot with steel-gray. Despite her age, she was in good enough physical condition, with strong arms and a lean, athletic form. He hoped that she would help him when the time came.

He wanted to talk to her. He'd wanted to talk to her a hundred times before, but Mathers did not permit his slaves that liberty. The one time a fellow thrall had attempted to speak, Mathers had torn into the man with the long whip holstered opposite his scimitar. He'd beaten the man bloody, and no one had lifted a hand to help him. Not even Bobby. He'd never forgiven himself for that moment of cowardice, but he planned to make amends before the night was over. He could not take back the damage done to the man, but maybe he could help the man escape his bonds. First, however, he had to break free himself, if he could find a way.

While Bobby drifted in his own thoughts, Mathers led them to an apartment building near the military complex at Alameda. The place was as bad as Stygia itself, loaded down with Hierarchy types. Bobby saw several other groups of wraiths, led by their masters and held in the chains of servitude. A pale fog rolled across the ground, growing deeper and thicker, until the asphalt and sidewalks were almost completely obscured.

Mathers appeared more displeased than usual, and Bobby knew why: There were too many groups around this one building, and all of them would be trying for the same souls. The building Mathers' and the other groups of wraiths surrounded had seen its best days a long time ago, and now there was nothing worth seeing, save the living forms inside its cavernous, decaying shell. Like the little boy he'd seen earlier, they all looked as if they were already dead. If his earlier guesswork was right, the tennants' lack of vitality meant that they were soon to die. It was the only answer that made any sense. Those who were ready to die looked dead already to the wraiths in the Shadowlands.

Down the street, Bobby saw several people walking, dressed in various costumes and apparently on their way to a Halloween party. They all looked healthy, practically throbbed with the energies that separated them from the dead. God, he envied them their lives.

Mathers slapped Bobby on the shoulder, glaring behind his mask. "Are you deaf? We're moving on, there are too many Reapers here. We're going closer to your part of town, but don't get any stupid ideas." Bobby tensed at the reference to Chinatown as his part of town, as if he owned all of the district and could command the wraiths that dwelled behind the distant jade barrier. Hell, until he'd died, Bobby had never even believed in a life after death. How could he possibly get any "stupid ideas?" Without prior knowledge of the towering jade wall and the Heretics beyond, Bobby couldn't have planned anything, and in truth, doubted that those beyond the wall would have aided him in any case.

He'd spent many of his twenty-odd years of life in Chinatown, looked down upon as someone less valuable than his neighbors simply because his father had been Caucasian. Racism appeared in many evil forms, and Bobby had experienced more than his share while growing up in Chinatown. He'd been tolerated, not accepted. There was a substantial difference. In life he'd had shamefully blond hair, and his skin was too fair to pass for a native of China. Not that he'd ever seen China, except in photographs, but he imagined his life would have been more harsh across the ocean from where he'd been born and raised. Here, he was at least tolerated. There, they would likely have killed him and his mother both.

Of course, his mother would have never resorted to prostitution for a living in China, where she had a large and influential family. Here all she had was herself and the bastard son that she loved as her own but hated at the same time, for the social stigmata he caused her to suffer. In the land of her birth, Bobby's mother would not have been forced to sell herself by bad economic times, or to pay substantial fees to a man who fancied himself a warlord and demanded payment in cash for "protection." The security the man had offered his mother was the same sort of protection that Mathers offered — freedom from assault by any save himself — and all it cost was unending servitude.

They walked, slowly and deliberately, looking for another building that would suffice for the gathering of souls. The only sign Bobby saw, that distinguished the first building from its neighbors was the darkness that stained its inhabitants, the lack of vigor in their auras. Mathers seemed anxious to find another building filled with what Bobby had come to think of as the "near-dead." Mathers could search. Bobby, in the meantime, would ponder his best potential methods of escape. If only he had a weapon, he would have a fighting chance; without some means of defending himself against the lash and sword at his master's side, he had little hope of managing to break free.

At their backs, the San Francisco Bay lay in the distance, and even from here the moans from the waters' depths were loud and clear. The Bay of Moans was the proper name in wraith society, that much Mathers was willing to impart to them as they walked. The Bay was a special place—all of San Francisco was a special place— wanted by the Hierarchy and the Heretics alike.

Mathers' continued explaining what made the city so important to the Hierarchy. "San Francisco is home to more Renegades and Heretics than anyone likes, but they're like cockroaches—as soon as you think they've all been exterminated, they come crawling from the woodwork again." Bobby couldn't blame them; given a choice between running free to solve his own murder and serving bastards like Mathers, there was no real argument as to which he'd prefer.

The group moved slowly towards the great jade wall, and Bobby marveled at the size of it, stunned that he had never realized such a thing existed when he was alive. "It's like a small-scale version of the Great Wall of China," he thought, remembering just in time that speaking aloud resulted in severe punishment. There were patterns carved into the wall, but the fog over the city prevented him from seeing what the patterns were. The damnedest thing of all was that he was certain, knew in his heart, that what lay beyond that wall had to look entirely different from what was there in the lands of the living. He pictured the ornamental temples and castles he'd seen only in paintings and photographs, and had heard about from his mother. He imagined the ornate structures that should have existed only in China, and knew in his heart that they lay here as well, in the Shadowlands of Chinatown.

As they turned away from the wall, moving north past his home in life, Bobby saw a figure cloaked in green move away from the barrier. His glimpse of the person was very brief, but the clothing looked Oriental in design. He tried to follow the figure with his eye, but Mathers was moving too quickly, dragging the chain of thralls behind him. Despite his efforts, Bobby couldn't see the figure clearly. He knew only that it was moving closer, keeping pace with him and slowly catching up. He was afraid of the silent shape closing in on him; Bobby was last in the long line of slaves and had no one behind him, only open space between his back and the pursuing silhouette. Bobby wanted to cry out and warn Mathers, tell him that they were being followed and that they could be in danger. The dark interior voice that normally drove him towards violence told him to keep his mouth shut and wait to see what the figure wanted.

Up ahead, leading the chain of slaves, Mathers pointed out the interesting aspects of the Shadowlands' landscape. Here a house that was used as a Haunt, a safe-haven for the dead. There, a spot where someone he had known in life was murdered. For Mathers, the whole damned thing was like a field trip, or a walk down memory lane. Bobby grew more and more convinced that Mathers was insane, beyond redemption and beyond help. He knew he had to get Mathers, had to escape the thrice-damned chains that held him in service to the older, more powerful wraith and the lurking form behind him gradually presented himself in Bobby's mind as a possible form of an escape from the insanity.

Just as he was toying with the idea of a blind rush at his master — that little voice had changed its mind again, and now felt that destroying Mathers was the most important thing — he felt something slip into his hand. He wanted to scream, but managed with some effort to avoid the outburst. He moved his hand carefully to where he could see what was there, and smiled quickly before masking his pleasure.

The knife was long and wicked, carved entirely from ivory, with a blade that looked razor-keen. He was certain that it would hurt Mathers, even if it would not separate the chain that linked his left leg to the right leg of the woman who walked before him. He turned to see who had given him the blade, but all he saw was a flicker of green that faded into the mists.

The question now was where to hide the blade until the right time came, and he had no answers. Finally, he decided the only safe place was down the small of his back, between the jeans he wore and the red fabric of his tee shirt. In front of him, the woman who had twice warned him looked directly in his eyes, and smiled. He saw her soul, and she saw his, and they both liked what they saw.

After almost an hour of constant walking they stopped before another apartment building. The wooden structure was still standing, still in good repair, but looking at it closely, Bobby could see the burnt ruin lying just beneath the surface. Very soon now, the building would go up in flames, and all the people inside would flee into the night or die. Most of them looked dead already, but a few still appeared healthy.

"This is it. This is where we wait. Yes?" Mathers almost seemed like he wanted a response, applause or praise for his having found a place for the group to do his dirty work. None was forthcoming; everyone knew better. "So, make yourselves comfortable. It shouldn't be too long now."

As if to prove Mathers' point, a figure broke from the swirling fog and gray shadows and moved towards the building. The young man who approached held a bottle stuffed at its opening with a shredded length of rag. In his other hand, he held a lighter. The look of death was on him, and Bobby knew he wouldn't last the night.

As the group watched, the boy lit the rag in the bottle. He moved closer to the building and pulled back his arm for a pitch. It was Hell Night, and Mathers' had found just what he was after: A fool who thought that burning buildings to the ground was a great way to have fun. Perhaps it was the youth's initiation into a gang, or perhaps he was just stupid enough not to realize that people would die because of his actions. Either way, he served Mathers' needs and was about to provide Stygia with yet more inhabitants for its over-populated streets.

Mathers moved closer to the boy, and though it was barely noticeable, Bobby's master changed slightly, grew more vivid in color, and seemed somehow more real than he had a second ago. The young man threw the bottle, and the wraiths all watched as the flaming streamer whirled end over end towards an open window on the second floor. The bottle just barely missed its mark, and cracked, releasing the spewing tongues of flame from within. They watched the liquid fire run down from the window's edge until it hit the ground. The entire wall was aflame in less than a minute.

Mathers reached out his hand, and tapped the youth on his shoulder. The boy practically leaped out of his own shoes, stunned by what seemed to be a brush with death itself. As the arsonist turned to look behind him, Mathers placed a hand on each of the boy's shoulders, and screamed with a howl worthy of recognition in the most chilling of horror films. The fear which the scream invoked sent the boy lurching into the wall of flames.

Bobby would have been hard pressed to say which was louder, the boy's screams, or the foul laughter that ripped from Mathers' steel encased facade. Mathers bent over, laughing so hard that he simply could not stand, and the young man who had willingly set the house ablaze screamed and thrashed in the fires of his own creation.

The group looked on, mesmerized by the sight. Bobby decided unconsciously that the time had come to gain his freedom. He charged uncontrollably at Mathers, the length of chain between his feet clattering and scraping, his teeth bared in a feral grin, and pulled the blade from the back of his pants. The tip of the knife sliced through Bobby's flesh, but he did not even notice; his only thought was of his hatred for

the wraith who had tortured him and made him
a coward. The voice in the back of his head had
won at last, and he stormed towards his master
with a battle-cry on his tongue and a fire in his
heart that rivaled the flaming building before
him. Bobby felt a sharp drag on his left ankle,
but it eased almost instantly.

Mathers noticed his approach, and the
laughter stopped immediately. Mathers moved
with a dizzying speed and pulled the scimitar
from its sheath, preparing to counter the coming
assault. "I knew you'd be trouble, boy, knew it
from the first time I saw you." Mathers' voice
was not upset, it was gloating, a voice of triumph
and happiness. Bobby hurled himself towards his
master, the weight of the manacles on his ankles
barely slowing him down. The others in his
group looked on, sighing with anticipation. The
woman who was the closest thing Bobby had to
a friend, ran beside him, giving him just enough
slack to complete his charge. Had she simply
stood still, he would have been tripped by the
chain that bound them together. The woman
pulled impatiently at the chain on her own left
ankle, and the portly old man before her in the
line of slaves moved a few steps forward as well,
giving Bobby still more freedom to move.

Servant and master met in combat, and

Bobby felt the scimitar's blade slide past his defense and pierce his shoulder. The pain was just as real as it would have been were he still alive, but no blood flowed from the three-inch gash that opened across his upper arm and shoulder. His own blade missed its mark completely.

Mathers drew back with both arms, lifted his blade above his head, and prepared to deal a killing blow. A part of Bobby wondered if true death was even a possibility any longer. As the blade was reaching its apex, Bobby kicked out, forced by the chain that limited his movements to lift both legs off the ground, and drove the heel of his right foot into Mathers' stomach. Mathers exhaled a sharp gust of air and staggered backwards, dropping his sword in the process. Behind him, the wraiths enslaved by Mathers let out cries of both joy and terror. Some had hope for escape. Others simply feared what Mathers would do: If the punishment for speaking was so very severe, what could the price of betrayal be?

Mathers reached for the bullwhip at his hip, and Bobby closed in for the kill. The whip was a serious threat, capable of peeling away his flesh with each strike, but it required some distance before it could be used to cause harm. The knife in Bobby's hand needed only a few inches to cause pain. Bobby became aware of his friend again, as she pulled the other wraiths along like dogs on their leashes, giving him enough room to move and attack.

Mathers hissed beneath his mask. Bobby shoved the blade deep into his master's chest and ripped upwards, carving a hole in Mathers' torso. The mouth behind the mask screamed shrilly in pain, and Bobby grinned again as he drove the blade in a second time. No blood flowed from the wounds, but a cold red mass could be seen beneath the shredded cloth and flesh. Mathers tried to run, and Bobby brought a foot down on his knee, hearing the satisfactory sound of bones breaking and cartilage snapping in his enemy's right leg. Mathers fell to the ground, stunned by the pain, far beyond the ability to scream.

Bobby stabbed him again, and again, and again, feeling the fury in his soul ignite. A year's frustrated anger boiled through his body, burned through the emptiness that had almost consumed him and reignited feelings that he had all but forgotten. For just a moment, he could almost believe he was alive.

And then it was over, Mathers lay before him, his ruined arms held over his face, trying to ward the next blow that would fall. Behind his mask, the eyes that looked out were terrified beyond measure. Bobby felt his anger draining away and was saddened to feel it go; it had been so long since he'd really felt anything.

He reached forward, grabbed the mask that hid his tormentor's face, and pulled. The mask would not move. Mathers chuckled weakly, and the woman behind him spoke for the first time since he had known her. Her voice was lovely, "It won't come off. He has to give it to you." After a year of silence, Bobby couldn't help but cringe, instinctively, at the sound. A year of silence had left its scars on him and he had to force away the thought of what Mathers' whip would do to her. Mathers lay at his feet, incapable of causing damage, but the conditions of the last year had created an instinctive tremor at the thought of breaking the enforced code of silence.

Then Bobby smiled, and his grin was a thing of hatred. He dared the unthinkable and spoke aloud, "It'll come off, whether he wants it to or not. Just you wait and see." He'd forgotten the sound of his own voice, and it sounded harsh in his ears.

With no preamble, he reached out to Mathers, and grabbed the mask again. With his free hand he brought the knife close to Mathers' jaw line. "Do you surrender the mask, or do I carve it off of your face?" Mathers eyes grew hard with glittering hatred, and he made no response. Bobby smiled, and started carving. The screams went on for a long, long time.

While Bobby freed his prize, his friend removed one of her own: The keys to the manacles that bound them all. No sooner was the mask removed, revealing a meaty red mass with eyes and teeth as the only contrasting colors, than Mathers collapsed, sighing weakly and fading from existence. Perhaps he was dead again, and hopefully forever. Perhaps he was simply back in the hell of Stygia without weapons or mask, stuck as badly as his slaves had been. Either way, Bobby never wanted to see him again.

The woman next to him bent down and touched Bobby's leg, and he saw the manacle on his right leg snap free, falling away from him like a bad dream. She unlocked his left leg, and he exhaled in elation, free to move without the bonds that had held him for so long. Overwhelmed by emotions, looking down at his legs, and then down at hers, both unbound for the first time, he grabbed her tightly and pulled her close in a fierce hug. She joined him in the embrace, and both of them cried.

The next in the line of freed slaves took the keys from her fingers and started on his own locks, passing them down the line when he was finished. Most of them scattered into the night, shocked and stunned at their sudden freedom, and a few ran laughing through the heavy fog. Very few of them dared speak as yet, still fearing a wrath that would not come. Three others stayed around, happy to meet their saviors, happy to stay with them. Bobby and the woman separated, both feeling strange and almost content. They knew that the feelings of joy would escape much too quickly.

"I'm Bobby."

"I'm Sarah Fields." She had a beautiful smile. Everything about her was beautiful, even more so now that she no longer wore the chains of slavery. Without the manacles she seemed more real, a person instead of a moving shape that worked beside him. "That was a brave thing you did." She paused a moment, and he saw the moisture in her eyes that matched the stinging of tears that threatened to fall from his own. "But also very stupid. He's bound to come back; he'll come after us."

"I had to do it." Bobby sought the words that would make her understand why he had attacked Mathers. No words came to him; his feelings were beyond his ability to explain. "I couldn't take it anymore. I just couldn't stand to see him or be near him any longer, y'know?"

"Yeah, I do."

They both looked around, meeting the others that still waited for them. Holly Glass had always been near the other end of the line, barely noticeable in the gloomy atmosphere of Stygia. She was all of twelve years old, and had been in Mathers' servitude for almost twenty years. The idea that she had literally served as Mathers' slave for longer than she had lived filled Bobby with an arctic chill. Her eyes reflected more suffering than Bobby could hope to ever understand.

Andrew Black was the man who had long served on the opposite side of Sarah in the chain of slaves for the last seven years. He was large, with a heavy gray beard and a receding hairline. Andrew had died during the big quake back in '88, and had been a parapsychologist in life.

Michael Walker was a thin man, around the same age as Bobby himself. His hair was long and stringy, and his smile was infectious. Bobby found it hard to believe that anyone could smile after almost thirty years as a slave to Mathers. Like Holly Glass, he was from the other end of the long chain of slaves, and had hardly even noticed that there was an end to the line of manacled figures. He'd died of an overdose, convinced that he could handle the risks of shooting heroin. He'd learned his lesson a little too late.

"Where do we go now?" Holly was scared, and not afraid to admit it. "Where will we stay?"

Bobby looked around hopelessly. Then his eyes caught the serpentine length of jade wall in the distance. "If we can climb that, the Hierarchy will leave us alone. You saw how Mathers looked at the wall; you heard him talking about the Heretics on the other side. It's a sure bet he won't follow us there."

Sarah nodded, but looked doubtful. "What if it's even worse there?"

Bobby reached down and lifted Mathers' scimitar from the ground. "Then we leave and we fight anyone who tries to stop us."

The group walked towards the wall. Michael carried the chains that had bound them together, certain that they would prove useful in some way. Sarah carried the scimitar. It was hers now; she had earned it in Bobby's eyes. Holly simply held Sarah's hand, glad for even the cold comfort of a dead woman's touch. Andrew walked with his hands in his pockets, talking to Bobby in tones that told of his time as a teacher. Bobby carried his ivory knife, and the mask he had liberated from Mathers.

All of them studied the jade wall as they went, looking at the silent monument and pondering what mysteries lay beyond the carvings that adorned it. The designs were so large, so monolithic, that even from a distance, they could not be fully comprehended. The heavy fog that hid the upper half of the wall did not assist in clarifying the mysterious etchings. No one there knew what lay beyond the wall, in the Shadowlands of Chinatown. Of course everyone had their own ideas. Would the land there be better than Stygia? Would it be worse? Having spent their time among the Dead as slaves, they hardly knew anything about the Hierarchy and the Heretics. Certainly the Hierarchy was not pleased that the Heretics existed, but did that make the wraiths beyond the stone barrier evil? Bobby supposed that evil was relative; what was vile to Mathers did not necessarily agree with what Bobby thought of as wrong or corrupt.

Somebody had handed Bobby a dagger when he needed it most, and he suspected that the same somebody had come somehow from the other side of the barrier he and his new friends were approaching. If that person was typical of the denizens of the Shadowlands of Chinatown, Bobby believed he could find happiness there.

They were at the wall in less than half an hour, and looking at it from up close, they saw that there were plenty of hand holds. The climb would be harsh, the risk of falling would be very real, but they did not care. Anything was better than what they had endured, anything at all. Bobby led the way, finding a depression deep enough for his hand to fit in, and pulled himself up. His other hand found another place to grab, and he started the climb, eager to see what lay beyond the jade wall.

END

THE WAY IT GOES

Thomas Kane

uddenly, I found myself outside Walter's Restaurant once more. It was morning again in San Francisco, just like the first time, and the colorless full moon still hung behind thin clouds. My target was sitting with Von Roon and three of his men in a corner booth, and the five of them were eating Number Two Breakfast Specials. The target had her back to me, so all I saw of her were soft golden curls and the pale blue vinyl of the restaurant furniture. I felt the weight of the pistol in my back pocket.

It's no big deal, killing people. It happens every day.

Besides, nobody asked me to think about

what I was doing. DNA Incorporated doesn't pay people to think, and neither does

Mr. Praeger. I was nothing but Praeger's property — indentured servitude is a way of life in the modern corporation. If you don't accept that, you flip burgers all your life.

It's not as if I was going to make some kind of stand for high principle. *Thou shalt not kill* — what kind of garbage is that? I was living in the real world. If you fight reality, you end up like the target in there.

And so, I brushed the damp from my wiry mustache, and wiped the lenses of my glasses, which had fogged in the morning air. My hands were pale and the tendons stood out. When I looked at my skinny arms protruding from the dark gray sleeves of my imported trench coat, I knew that I was killer, but I would get myself smeared in any kind of a real fight.

Every now and then I wondered whether I'd made the wrong decisions — whether I really had to end up as a guy who made a living by shooting people from behind. But when I looked at my arms, I knew I had the body of a coward. I remember exactly why I ended up the way I did. I never had a choice. Or, if I did have a choice, I didn't know it at the time.

I positioned myself for the shot. The waitress

kept messing up my line of sight, but my position gave me the best view I could get of the target's head.

The target's name was Julie Rochon.

It didn't matter that I knew Julie's name. It's was her own fault that this was happening. Julie worked in Strategic Planning, and she'd seen all kinds of the company's most secret garbage. She should have known Praeger wouldn't let her quit. Nevertheless, there she was, trying to skip out on her job at DNA and pick up a new job with another firm. She was meeting with *Von Roon*, of all people. Von Roon recruits executives for the Ries-Dillon Consortium. And as far as Praeger is concerned, Ries-Dillon isn't just the competition, it's the anti-Christ.

Julie had been bitching for months. I wasn't surprised that she actually tried to quit — she was the kind of woman who seemed to think she had some kind of right to make herself happy. Julie was an idiot, and she deserved exactly what she was getting.

I reached into my jacket and gripped the pistol. The gun Mr. Praeger had given me was a hodgepodge weapon, cobbled together from the parts of half a dozen automatic pistols. It was the size of a toy. A mass of sticky cloth tape gave bulk to the handle. Even if I had owned a

silencer, the gun's barrel wouldn't have held one.
This was the kind of weapon that nobody could
ever trace back to DNA Inc.

I cut my eyes in each direction, pulled out
the pistol, gripped it in both of my gloved hands,
pivoted back a step and fired. Even as I squeezed
the trigger, I knew I'd botched the shot. Maybe
the jury-rigged gun had a crooked barrel. Or
maybe it was some kind of subconscious thing…
because I knew Julie's name. Either way, the
gunshot sang in my ears.

The bullet punched through plate glass. My
shot missed Julie. The round hit the skinny,
middle-aged waitress, who stood all the way on
the other side of the restaurant from where I
aimed. The waitress collapsed in a heap,
knocking dishes off a table, spurting blood all
over her white apron.

The waitress fell, and time seemed to stop. I
stared at her as she flung back her head, her face
all squeezed into a rictus of agony. People live a
million different ways, but everybody dies the
same. Cheap psychologists talk about "accepting
death" but I've never really seen why it matters.
When you die, it doesn't matter if you're brave
and noble. You're still going to die like everyone
all over the world, whimpering, helpless and
alone, with your own urine streaming down your

legs. And then there's nothing.

Before I could even level my gun again, Von Roon shoved Julie down behind the booth. Chaos broke out in the restaurant. Some people headed for the waitress' body and others ran away from it. A table toppled over, and three or four plates full of breakfast dashed across the floor. I didn't have even a remote chance of getting another shot off. Von Roon's three men were fanning out, and one of them was on his knees, poking buttons on his slim cellular telephone.

I didn't notice anyone with a weapon, but I could see this vivid image of Von Roon's men returning fire, and I could practically feel gunshots rip through my body. I didn't want to die. I'd seen people die, and I knew that there was no such thing as a good death. There was no such thing as honor and no such thing as redemption. Once you die, nothing you have or did or thought matters anymore. Death just grinds you down to nothingness. So I didn't wait to see what would happen next. I ran.

I took off pell-mell up the street, stuffing the gun in my pants-pocket, my lungs screaming for air, expecting to hear sirens at any moment, if not to feel a bullet. There were a couple of shade trees just up the street. I dove into them, looking for cover. As I crashed through the moist leaves, a blue-gray pigeon burst out and flew away, squealing, into the morning stink.

I leaned up against the moist earthy bark of the tree, panting. *Why did I ever get into the business of killing people for a living?* That's just a stupid question. I knew the reasons why. For three years, I had worked my tail off at DNA and got nowhere. Then Mr. Praeger invited me to his office, the one on the thirtieth floor. Praeger looked down from his big leather throne, smiled like a frog, and asked me if I was serious about working for DNA. Then he told me about an Executive Manager who was a problem for him, and asked me if I could help him "deal with the man." What was I supposed to do, say no to Praeger?

The real question is why I even bothered to run away after missing Julie. I had just failed a mission. When you fail Praeger, you don't get a second chance. The moment I shot the waitress, I had killed myself.

That thought hit me like a thunderbolt. Then my memory stream got foggy.

Everything that had happened since I went to Walter's seemed familiar to me. I had lived through the scene at Walter's Restaurant a million times, as if my life was a movie playing over and over again. I wandered back onto the pavement. My foot came down over a little blister in the sidewalk. Cracks radiated out from the blister in all directions. Every time I re-lived this scene, I always looked down to see the rifts below my feet, like a Grand Canyon in the bumpy black pavement.

My stream of memory ends with me gazing at the crack. As I stare into its recesses, I lapse into nightmares. I sink through the ground into a nauseous, whirling world of madness. If the shooting scene was a movie, the part where I hide in the trees would be where the film starts melting in the projector.

I can't describe the nightmares. There's nothing to talk about — just long strings of fevered dementia. I don't know how long this lasted. At last, I forced the madness from my mind. I saw the city again. The streets of San Francisco still did not seem quite real, but at least I managed to keep them from dissolving into dreams. I wandered the streets as I wandered my memories, looking for a way to get around fate.

The next thing I heared was a ringing telephone.

The phone drews me like a magnet. It was the telephone in my own apartment. Suddenly,

I realized what happened after the shooting. After I had gotten away from Walter's Restaurant, I had gone back to my own place. I collapsed onto my sofa in the damp trench coat, and lay there feeling like I was going to be sick. When I think about it, it seems really stupid to screw up a murder and then just go home. On the other hand, I don't suppose that I had any better ideas.

I picked up the phone. "Yeah."

"Hello. I wish to speak with Mr. Stephen Myers, if you please." The voice on the other end was cultured and mellifluous. I recognized the tone at once. It was Mr. Donald Mozyr, who was supposed to be my boss, although everybody knew that Praeger ran the show.

"Hello Mr. Mozyr." I squeezed up my face, trying to soften my voice and steady it, while I wondered what was about to happen to me. "It's me, speaking. What can I do for you, sir?"

"Ah, Mr. Myers. You aren't busy, are you?"

I swallowed. "No, sir, not at all. I had today off…"

"Oh, splendid. If it wouldn't be a terrible inconvenience, I was hoping you'd come down to the office for a few hours. It seems there was something Mr. Praeger wanted to speak with you about." Mozyr's voice sounded like a cheerful, beckoning songbird.

"Sure." My hand shook a little, and I accidentally rapped my mouth with the phone. "Is something, you know, wrong?"

"Oh, no, nothing like that." Mozyr laughed in a lovely, reassuring bass tone. "Mr. Praeger simply wishes to go over some matters with you — nothing very serious I'm sure. But I do wish you'd hurry. Mr. Praeger does seem eager to get started."

"Be right there." I fumbled for my cigarettes — I needed a smoke badly. There was an irony. I needed to smoke because I needed to do something meaningless and get my death.

I had no idea how to escape. I paced back and forth in my apartment. I knew thas call to the office was a set-up, but Mozyr said it was OK, and besides, what choice did I have? If I didn't go, they'd come for me. My fingers trembled like jackhammers as I reached for the cigarettes. I couldn't get the pack out of my pocket. I couldn't have handled a match anyway.

Death awaited me at the office. I knew that. I also knew that, whether going to the office was a good idea or not, I wouldn't be able to force myself to do it.

I shoved some things into my pockets, emptied my bank account at the nearest ATM, and bought a ticket for the Greyhound bus to San Diego. I thought maybe I'd cross the border into Mexico on foot, at night, and disappear forever. The bus was late, and I paced around the terminal. I glanced from the battered soda machine to the tired-looking passengers to the gang of men in sweat-stained blue coveralls, scrambling to load and unload busses.

The bus finally came. I took a seat in the back corner, by a dusty window. A clan of half a dozen Mexicans trickled in after me, filling all the seats in my area. The driver climbed on board in a few minutes, but he promptly returned to the station, and spent an interminable amount of time in there. I fidgeted in torment. However, as the bus finally trundled onto the interstate, I relaxed enough to watch the people in the nearby seats.

The Mexicans had a full-fledged family. A thin man in denim seemed to be the father. He had the responsibility of standing up and unzipping the luggage in the overhead baggage compartment whenever the baby whimpered for a toy. A golden-skinned woman in a flower-print dress sat next to him, apparently the mother. An elderly man, his tanned skin all wrinkles, sat in the seat in front of them and occasionally turned to offer a sage word.

After perhaps half an hour, the mother put the plump baby into the aisle, patted him on the back, and sent him toddling toward the remaining two members of the family. These were two young women, apparently young aunts or elder daughters. The one by the aisle scooped the infant up and set him on her lap, cooing at him.

The young women chatted as the bus drove on. They had lively faces and their dark eyes flashed as they spoke. The flow of their conversation rose and fell in incomprehensible Spanish. Occasionally, one of them chuckled, and then they both broke into gales of hilarity. Nothing seemed phony or malicious about their laughter.

The more I watched these people, the more I realized that I had nothing whatsoever in common with them. This went far beyond the fact that I didn't know a word of Spanish. The father looked vigorous; the girls seemed warm and cheerful, and they all were wholesome and content. It was easy to envy them. However, whether their lives were good or bad, they seemed utterly alien to me. I could no more have fit into that family than Mr. Praeger could go in his suit and tie to a playground, and join in the games like one of the children.

I felt an emptiness that I had never felt before. An emptiness that had always existed on the fringes of my being. I had never allowed myself to let it affect me and I hated this perfect family for delivering me my pain. Praeger hadn't had me shot yet, but inside I knew that I had already died a long and pathetic death.

By the time we get to Los Angeles, I knew that Mexico would give me no redemption. I was an empty man — a killer. I would have nothing to live for no matter where I went. And so, I bought a new ticket. I waited for five hours in the urine-smelling concrete warrens of the Los Angeles bus terminal, and then I took the bus back to San Francisco. We pulled across the Golden Gate bridge early the next morning. Up the arching bridge we went, with the suspension cables soaring to the sky on either side. Steam rose from the Bay, slowly diffusing into the air.

I returned to my apartment almost 24 hours after the moment I shot the waitress. Once I locked the door, I scooped the pistol out of my pocket with both hands, trying to keep it from clattering to the floor. Then I stared at the dull gray thing. Possibilities ran through my mind. I could have bought a real gun, pushed the sofa up against the door and defended myself. I'd shot people before, and I could have shot whomever

Praeger sent to waste me.

But that was not going to save me. It would not save me from the welling emptiness in the pit of my stomach. And what if had killed one of Praeger's men? He'd have sent somebody else to do the job, someone who knew what he was doing. Either that, or he'd wait. Eventually, I'd have come out, and then he'd have wasted me. Or, he might have just tipped off the police, and I'd have gone to the gas chamber. You can kill all the people you want, but nobody has invented a way to keep someone else from killing you.

I jiggled the clip out of the gun's handle. Little brass bullets rattled in their track. I pushed the clip back in and massaged it until it clicked into place. Then I put the pistol up to my eye, looking down the barrel to the shadow inside. I even caressed the seam that ran down the middle of the trigger. A tear rolled down my cheek and my head reeled. Time ticked away in a rhythmic, pulsing staccato of thumps. The thumping was the beat of my cold and heart.

It all came down to this. Everything in my life had really just led up to this point. I was going to die in my own hole, and that was going to be the end of everything for me. I never had much and now I was going to have nothing.

Still, those thoughts didn't explain the terror I felt inside. When I looked into my gun, my insides felt sour, from the base of my throat to the hollows of my bowels. There was something primal about this fear. It was the fear that every living thing feels in the face of death, and it was more potent than anything I had ever felt before.

Whenever I've made a decision, I've always tried to do the smartest thing. I've been rational. However, even though I knew it would be best to shoot myself, I realized that there was more to it than that. Hard realities were not the only things that shaped me. I didn't know if love existed, or hope, or honor or morality, but I was face to face with pure, animal horror. If I'd known that sooner, I might have been a different man, but it was too late.

When you die, it's too late for anything.

I hurled the pistol across the room. Then I waited. Sooner or later, Praeger's men would come and kill myself for me. If my shot had missed entirely, maybe Mr. Praeger would have let me live, punished me, but let me live. However, I'd killed a bystander. That meant police and a real investigation. Mr. Praeger was going to arrange for me to commit suicide and then let the cops pin it all on a dead man.

Sure enough, I heared a single, reverberating knock on the door.

I had no idea what came after the knock. That memory always trails off into a typhoon of horror. I do recall pain tearing through my chest, bubbling up into my head, choking out everything. I do not think anyone survives such pain. There isn't really much doubt in my mind about what happened. Praeger's men came in and drilled a bullet through my body.

Even before the bullet came, I plunged into delirium. I sank through the floor into the dream-world, screaming at the top of my lungs. My body faded before my eyes, and my whole consciousness dissolved into a crimson nightmare.

This wasn't supposed to happen to me, it was supposed to happen to Julie. I thought of her and the world faded around me. As I plunged into dreams again, memories of her rose around me. This was from before she went to Von Roon. It was from before Praeger sent me to kill her. This was the moment when I first met Julie.

I tasted liquor in my throat. Muffled strains of music rumbled from the walls, confused by the babble of conversations. The lights were dim, and the springs of a hotel bed creaked beneath the weight of two people. Julie sat on the bed next to me, her red dress a little rumpled, her face flushed with alcohol.

I was on my back, a little dizzy, and she was sitting up. I eased my arm around her hips, far less smoothly than I might have hoped. Then I propped myself up a little on one elbow, my other arm still wrapped around Julie. "Great party."

Julie just nodded. She wasn't really smiling. She looked down at me, her blue eyes steady, and as focused as they could get at that stage of drinking. I tickled her stomach through her dress, but she moved her body and kept looking at me.

"Hey Steve, are you…satisfied?"

"Huh?" I tried to slide my hand a little lower, but she shifts away. "What d'you mean?"

"Satisfied." She sighed with the sincerity of the drunk. "With your job…with your life. I mean, I know I'm not. I keep trying to imagine my life as being different. Do you want things to be different? I mean, are you happy?"

I just grunt. What kind of dumb question was that? I slid my hand upward, brushing her bosom with my knuckles.

Julie kept looking at me.

"We all sell our souls." I pulled in closer to her, working my hand closer. "That's just how it goes."

"OK, Steve." Julie wraps her arms around herself. "But is it worth it?"

I had no answer for that. I breathed heavily in her ear, dismissing what she had said. She pulled back, as if she wanted to say something more, but I ignored her. I reached up for her breast. When I touched her, it was as if something had snapped between us. She jerked away.

Julie stood up, leaving me still lying on the bed, with my arm around nothing. She pulled open the door of the hotel room and headed back toward the rest of the party, her arm protecting her breasts. And as she left the room, she looked back at me, and wrinkled up her face, as if she was looking at a snake.

I just lay on my back, half drunk and miserable. Julie was the only woman I'd come close to having in years. That was the first thing on my mind — I had blown it. But that was not the only reason I felt so miserable. Julie's questions dug into my mind like burrowing worms.

It was only a few days after that Mr. Praeger told me he wanted Julie dead. And I accepted the job.

■

Now, as I live through the scene again, I think about Julie's questions. Was it worth it? I don't dare try to answer that.

Then the nightmares begin again.

When I regain consciousness, I feel more lucid than I've felt for... for a long time. The things at Walter's, and the things in my apartment — those were just memories. What's happening now is new. I haven't remembered it before. I don't think I'm living old events any more. The things I see are real.

My gaze falls on the telephone again. Then it falls on the gun, which still lies in the corner, by my VCR. My apartment is almost the way I remember it. However, strips of yellow tape crisscross the window and run around the room. A circle of tape runs around the gun. A brownish stain marks the floor. Someone has drawn chalk marks all around the stain.

I had only one more question and my mind searched for an answer. What happened to Julie? She was the person who didn't cave in to Praeger. She was the person who made me wonder if I could defy him too. She was also the person I had tried to kill, and in trying to kill her, I had brought on my own doom. Julie was the only chance I ever had to make my life different. Now, I desperately wanted to know her fate.

I track Julie until I find her. Although Julie does not seem to see me, I cling to her unnoticed, like a piece of lint on her black satin blouse. Julie is in Praeger's office — the upper-story office where I used to meet with him. She sits upright before his broad mahogany desk, her hands clasped in the lap of her skirt, her exquisite lips pressed together. Praeger has his back turned, and he makes Julie wait, which is what he always does. Julie's cheeks look soft and creamy, with all the signs of weeping cleansed away, but I can see where tears have melted her mascara. Every muscle in her body looks taut.

Neither Julie nor Praeger seems aware of me. Being in the office is like being in a dream. The office is real, the people are real, but I am not. And so, I watch.

Slowly, magnificently, Praeger swivels in his seat, turning to face Julie. Praeger sits in a huge office chair, upholstered in alligator hide, with a high back that rises behind him like a dragon's folded wings. He stares down at Julie through his glasses, his face as plump as a baby's. "Ah, Ms. Rochon. I hear we had a... frightening experience."

Julie just smiles a polite little smile. I can see her quiver.

"It is so fortunate that we were not harmed." Praeger speaks with a European accent that lends his voice a piquant air of arrogance. "In the future we will be more careful...no?"

"Oh — yes sir." Julie nods and looks up at Praeger, batting her curled eyelashes as if looking at a lover. If there was ever a trace of defiance or independence in Julie, it is gone now, scrubbed away without a trace.

"Hmm — very good." Praeger chuckles, moving his Adam's apple but not his lips. "And so, Ms. Rochon, do we need a bit of time to be getting over the shock? A brief vacation?"

Julie shakes her head. "No, sir. I'm ready for work."

"Ah..." Praeger's voice boomed. "Then it's back to work, back to work. You're industrious, Ms Rochon. I like that. What do you think about a promotion, Ms. Rochon?"

Julie gasps. Her mouth forms a little O. I guess I'd be shocked too, if Praeger sent someone to shoot me and then offered me a promotion.

"Yes, yes. For some time I consider you for this job — ideal. You step up, become Export Consultant for joint ventures in the Amazon Basin. Of course we increase your salary, what, maybe ten, fifteen percent."

"I'll do my best, sir — I really will." Julie beams, and her voice chokes a little. Relief transfigures her face. Her ecstasy looks positively sexual.

"Of course, this is a highly sensitive project." Praeger folds his hands and stares Julie in the eyes. "If you accept, you will be placed under our Executive Security Program. We will have people keeping an eye on you, to make sure no more scary things have to happen. Do you understand?"

"I understand." Julie takes a deep breath and lets it out. Tears sparkle in her eyes. "I really am grateful, sir. I know I've made some very, very foolish choices. But you've been so wonderful..."

Praeger shrugs and turns up his palms, an expression of good humor on his roly-poly face. "Ah, yes, but that is what I am here for, no?"

Julie laughs. Then she turns her head to the side and gazes at Praeger out of the corner of her eye, with a fond, admiring smile.

I see now that Praeger is a genius. He hasn't merely intimidated Julie. He's crushed her, broken her down to nothing, and then built her up again. Julie is more than a loyal DNA employee now. She's a worshiper. To Julie, Praeger has become a combination of lover, father and god.

It is possible that when Praeger gave the order for me to waste Julie, he never meant for me to succeed. This is exactly what he had planned. Praeger got what he wanted. Julie got what she wanted as well. As for me, well, I had to play my part to make Julie believe that the threat to her life was real, to make her feel properly shocked and terrified and desperate. I gave substance to the ritual, like a goat with his guts pulled out on a heathen altar. I was a sacrifice. In fact, Praeger was probably ready to get rid of me anyway — I knew too much, and had been doing dirty work too long. I did what I was told, and I got the shaft. It's that simple.

After a few moments, Julie looks up at Praeger as if he's her best and closest friend. "The man who shot at me . . ."

"Yes. What about him?" Praeger was talking faster, and after years of working for him, I could tell he was losing interest in the conversation.

"I saw his face." Julie continued breathlessly. "I know him...his name's Steve Myers...he works in this building."

"Oh — yes." Praeger threw up his hands. "We forget about Mr. Myers now. Steve Myers is gone. We never see him again. So don't worry — get to work." Praeger laughs again, curls his mouth into a U-shaped smile, and then turns away in his chair.

My teeth grate together. I want to make Praeger — and Julie — remember who I was. I'm standing right in front of them, but they don't see me. Julie walks right through me as she heads for the door. I feel her body heat, but she doesn't even flinch, much less look at me.

I chase after Julie to the exit. I want to ask her the same question she asked me. Is she satisfied? Will she stay satisfied? Ten years from now, when she ends up the way I did, will she think working for Mr. Praeger is worth it?"

I call her name. "Ju-lie..." My voice rings in the cavernous office but Julie does not turn and the door closes in my face. I reach out to open it, but although I can feel the cool brass knob, and the tacky spots where Julie gripped it with moist fingers, I cannot make the door open. My fingers do not even wiggle the knob.

Then I hear a hollow command. "Come through the door."

I step right into the door, and the polished wood doesn't stop me from going through. Even the metal knob seems no more substantial than shadow to me.

Outside, I see three figures, looming in the broad corridor of the thirtieth floor. Julie walks away, paying no more attention to them than she does to us. An elderly secretary with her hair up in a gray bun ignores us all as well. However, we appear quite real to each other.

As the three approach, I can see them more clearly. They all wear suits and ties. The one on the left looks young. He's a little twit, with round glasses and a shock of blond hair that stands straight up. When his eyes meet mine, he grins. "You're ours, Larva."

The guy on the right has a smug, pudgy face. He puts me in mind of a well-fed worm. Worm nods a mocking greeting. "Smile...you're among friends."

However, neither Twit nor Worm comes too close to me. The one in the center walks right up and places a heavy hand on my shoulder. He is older than the other two, with heavy square spectacles and a strand of hair that artfully covers his balding scalp. "We've been following your progress for some time, Mr. Myers."

"Yeah." I curl my lip and look up at him. Suddenly I recognize the man. His name was Halperin. Halperin worked for DNA Inc. about five years ago, before his heart attack . . .his *fatal* heart attack.

"You are eligible to enter the society of the dead. My friends and I have made it possible for you to exist in that society, Mr. Myers." Halperin appraises me, his lower lip extended in a glum expression. "We are doing you a favor by bringing you to full spiritual consciousness. In return for this, you entail certain obligations to us. I trust you understand the significance of such obligations."

"We own you lock, stock and barrel." Twit breaks out in an obnoxious little chortle. "You know how it works."

I nod. I realize that this was how I had lived my life. My skull aches with that realization, and a numbness fills my brain. People like Praeger rule our lives and our deaths. I had always thought death was meaningless, but death is worse than that. Death is when people like Praeger triumph.

Then Halperin reaches toward my eyes with ashen fingers. Before I can flinch, his fingers close, and he peels a foggy membrane from my face. For the first time, I look with clear vision upon the world of dead souls. This was a world I already understood. I had lived it for years. And now, as far as I knew, I was going to live it forever.

END

Lexicon

The Underworld contains many strange phenomena, and the unfortunate denizens have adapted or invented a variety of words to describe the bizarre features of their new "lives."

Angst: The power of the Shadow.

Arcanum, The: A dangerous group of occult investigators and hunters. *Caveat anima!*

Artifact: An object that has been altered to give it special powers.

Byways: Paths through the Tempest.

Caul: An ectoplasmic covering that shields a wraith during her larval period. In some ways, it protects her, but it also warps her perceptions until it is removed.

Charon: The founder of the Hierarchy. Charon has been missing for decades.

Circle: Any group of wraiths.

Citadel: An individual stronghold within a Necropolis.

Cohort: A Circle of Hierarchy wraiths. The traditional starting number of members is 10, but attrition and Transcendence take their toll.

Corpus: The spirit body of a wraith.

Cult: Any of hundreds of Heretic sects espousing a particular path to Transcendence.

Deathlord: One of the seven leaders of the Hierarchy.

Domain: A large territory held by a wraith or group of allied wraiths.

Doomsday: When Oblivion shall overcome all of reality, and the end of time will come — or, alternatively, when the dead will walk the Earth.

Drone: A wraith who has lost its sentience and identity.

Enfant: A recently deceased wraith. An Enfant is partially amnesiac, and a Caul covers his face, altering his perceptions of whatever he encounters.

Far Shores, The: Distant realms in the Tempest, often corresponding to mortal beliefs about the afterlife.

Fetters: The ties that bind a wraith to her old life and the living world.

Gang: A Circle of Renegade wraiths.

Guild: In times past, an organization that taught a particular Arcanos to its members. The guilds were disbanded by Charon.

Harrowing, The: The nightmare ride through the Tempest that periodically torments his existence and occasionally overcomes him.

Harvest: To gather the newly deceased, either as Reaper and mentor or as slave trader.

Haunt: A place in the Shadowlands where death has a presence and wraiths are more at home.

Hierarchy, The: The largest organization of wraiths in the Underworld. The Hierarchy was originally formed by Charon to assist wraiths in attaining Transcendence. Over the centuries, however, it has become corrupt and twisted.

Heretics: Those who believe that yet *another* , better afterlife awaits wraiths who Transcend their current wretched state.

Hell: Any of countless realms claiming to be the original, real, honest-to-goodness, *actual* Hell — there are so many that they are known collectively as the Thousand Hells, or simply "the Thousand."

Host: A person possessed during Puppetry.

Juice: Pathos.

Legions: The army, police and enforcement arm of the Hierarchy.

Lemure: A young wraith, only recently deceased.

Maelstrom: Terrifying storms that occasionally envelop the Shadowlands; they are to the Tempest what Jupiter's Red Spot is to an earthly hurricane.

Malfean: An elder spectre or beast of the Void.

Mask: A Stygian artifact worn by many wraiths in order to conceal the true self.

Necropolis: A city of the dead. Necropoli reflect the cities of the living and occupy the same "geographical" location.

Nephandi: Mages who have turned to Oblivion.

Nihils: Pits in the Shadowlands that lead into the Underworld, usually dumping the wraith straight into the Tempest.

Oblivion: The negation of all things. Like total entropy, Oblivion, in its purest form, is an ordered state. The Void is its physical manifestation (or lack thereof).

Pathos: Emotion; the "food" of the spirit world.

Plasm: Any ectoplasmic substance; the spiritual stuff that makes up wraiths and their belongings alike.

Projectors: Living travelers in the Shadowlands.

Quick, The: Another term for the living.

Reaper: The wraith who first removes the Caul from an Enfant.

Relic: An ectoplasmic object brought by a wraith from the living lands.

Renegades: Wraiths who have banded together to overthrow the Hierarchy. Their individual motivations vary.

Restless, The: Another term for wraiths in general.

Shadow, The: The darker half of a wraith's personality. It must be mastered before the wraith can Transcend; conversely, it may eventually gain mastery over the wraith, forcing her to embrace Oblivion.

Shadowlands: The aspect of the Earth inhabited by wraiths. From here, wraiths can (with some difficulty) interact with the living or meet with Awakened creatures. The Shadowlands form an outer "shell" over the rest of the Underworld.

Spectre: A wraith whose Shadow has become dominant.

Stormrunning: Traveling in the Tempest.

Stygia: The largest realm in the Underworld. It is the home of the Hierarchy.

Tempest, The: The eternally raging storm of the Underworld — it hinders passage between the inner realms and the Shadowlands, and collects the nightmares and memories of those who pass through it.

Terminals: Small, rundown realms in the middle of the Tempest that serve as way stations for those traveling to Stygia. Terminals are grim, Kafkaesque places where Ferrymen rest and unruly passengers are sometimes abandoned.

Thrall: A wraith in subjugation to another of its kind.

Transcend: To leave the Underworld completely and move on to whatever awaits beyond.

Underworld, The: The land of the dead. It includes the Shadowlands, the Tempest, the Void, and all the realms therein.

Void, The: The nothingness at the heart of the Tempest. See also *Oblivion*.

Wraith: A spirit who has died but remains attached to the living world. Wraiths are also known as ghosts or "the Restless."